SHERELYN DUHART

Matters of the Heart Along the Cedar Lake Journey

Duhart Press LLC

This book was professionally typeset on Reedsy.
Find out more at reedsy.com

This book is dedicated to my family, friends, and associates who kept telling me they are waiting on this book.

To the women who have experienced domestic violence, childhood abuse verbal and physical, infidelity, molestation, low self-esteem, loneliness, illnesses and any other problems.
Trust in God and walk in faith. Remember John 3:16 For God so loved the world that He gave his only begotten Son, that whosoever believeth in Him shall not perish but have everlasting life.

The Miracle of Friendship

There is a Miracle called Friendship
that dwells within the heart
and you don't know how it happens
or when it even starts.

But the happiness it brings you
always gives a special lift
and you realize that
Friendship
Is God's most precious gift.

by Anonymous

Contents

One

Meet the Girls

I am looking out the window on a nice hot summer day that looks like a postcard. Our yard is filled with rosa laevigata, marigolds, and day lilies. As a matter of fact the subdivision has the best-looking flowers I've ever seen. Cedar Lake, Georgia is my place of residence it sits about forty miles outside of Atlanta, Georgia. We have had great times in this small city with a population of ten thousand. When we were growing up everyone was more neighborly. I can't help but think about my sister and her friends, and everything they did together.

It all began over forty years ago, my sister and her friends have kept an account of events in their diaries and journals but I must tell it the way I see it and of course from my sister 's diary that I found recently. I've always read it throughout the years. First I will start off with this trip the subdivision took its residents on.

The trip to Disney world

Everyone is gathered in the clubhouse of the subdivision. Its loud and crowded. The room is filled with excitement. Disney world just opened. The children and the girls are having a great time already.

"Ouch!" yelled Tanya.

"Help!" Sally screamed.

Diane ran to the aid of her friends who had ran into some chairs and fell flat on their faces. She made it to her friends in record time making use of her long legs. " Did you hurt yourselves?"

They helped each other off the floor. "We're fine and thanks for checking on us, you're such an angel. "Tanya said.

" We appreciate you, thank you so much." Sally said.

"Thanks, but what I'm suppose to help my neighbor. And we've played together several times. Who knows we may hang out more." She said as she moved her long, thick, brown bangs out of her face. She stands about four inches taller than Tanya and Sally.

"And I'm no angel, it just seems like I'm perfect and an angel. I'm far from that. Now back to the two of you, are you sure you're okay?"

Tanya's father Mr. Anthony Patterson came over to check on his princess. "Honey bunch are you okay?"

"Dad I'm fine. You can relax."

Her mother arrived about thirty seconds later.

" What happened? Are you hurt? Do you need to go to the hospital?" Mrs. Patterson asked. Tanya and her mother look exactly alike. Both have the same black semi coarse hair and caramel skin tone. You can tell her mom is twenty years older, but she looks good.

"Mom, like I told dad, I'm fine. I think we're more shocked than hurt."

"Yes, Mrs. Patterson we're okay." Sally said.

Sally thought to herself its so nice that Tanya's parents came and checked on her. Look at my mom she turned her back to me and is pretending nothing happened. How is it that everyone else is concerned or is looking and my mother is acting like I don't exist. I feel like crying.

Even though she wanted to cry you'll find out she's an overcomer regardless of what happens in her life. Tanya is kind of laid back and very private. She doesn't tell all her business. Diane is the oldest of all the girls.

* * *

Mrs. Perry began talking. "Greetings and hello everyone. I'm excited about our first annual trip." Everyone began listening and the excitement was at an all-time high. Everyone was admiring her cute simple look, a crisp white blouse with blue jeans, and white tennis shoes. Her brown hair was in a ponytail. Mrs. Perry is Ruth's mom.

"The chartered bus will leave in fifteen minutes. My daughter Ruth, and my husband Pastor Perry are passing out all the information you need for the trip. And of course, there are some extra goodies."

Ruth began passing out the goody bags. She is Ms. Personality in the group, you'll see the girls look up to her. She must live up to the image of being a preacher's kid.

"Here's a bag for you." Ruth said with a big smile that lights up her smooth brown skinned face and her big brown eyes light up also. Her long ponytails moved as she moved.

"Thank you young lady , you're such a cutie!" a resident of Cedar Lake said.

"Thank you, ma'am!" Smiling and blushing she did as she continued to pass out the bags. "Excuse me Mrs. Perez here is your bag."

"Thank you, you're so precious and pleasant!"

"Thanks, where is Sally?"

"She's over there somewhere, when you see her tell her to make her way to me as soon as possible so we can get on the bus in a few minutes."

"I will, thanks!"

They worked the room rather fast.

Pastor Perry, Ruth's father who stands six feet tall and has a nice caramel tone. He begin speaking to her. "My little baby doll, how many bags do you have left? I have one. I might need one of yours!"

"Daddy I have only one left!"

"Let's glance around the room and see if every adult has a bag." Mr. Perry

3

said.

They began glancing.

"Father, from what I can tell it looks like every household is taken care of."

"You know darling I think you're right; your mother knows what she's doing."

"She does!"

Mrs. Perry began speaking through a microphone. "Listen up everyone, it's time to start our journey! Lets' form a line starting at the door of the bus. I'm asking my husband to pray over the trip. "

Pastor walked towards his wife smiling and stood next to her. She handed him the microphone. "Let us pray. Father we thank you for this trip. We thank you for the opportunity for us to have fun, fellowship and to spend time with our families. We ask that you protect us as we journey to Florida from Georgia and to have your angels watch over us every step of the way. Thank you for keeping us safe. We love you Lord. It is in Jesus name we pray! Amen!"

"Amen!" everyone said, or most people said.

"Let's get on the bus, line up at the door like my wife instructed us!" Mr. Perry said.

The residents of the Cedar Lake subdivision moved rather quickly and was seated on the bus in less than thirty minutes. It's about 9 pm the bus is departing on time. The arrival time in Orlando is between seven and eight am in the morning. Everyone chatted for the next two hours and then people started dozing off one by one. That is everyone but Rachel and Patricia. Their overhead light was on and because everyone was sleeping their conversation seem to be magnified. The same goes for the light.

A woman in her early fifties seated across from them kept staring and rolling her eyes at them wishing they would go to sleep. She thought their parents would tell them, but of course they're knocked out.

Patricia, is one of the girls my sister is friends with in this story. She always gets into predicaments, some she doesn't choose and some she does. Rachel on the other hand is the book worm of the group. Both girls are very pretty, their skin tones are pale white and they're tall for their age.

They started whispering. "Why is she staring at us?"

"I don't know. I wish she would stop." She said as she put her long black hair in a ponytail."

"I'm going to ignore her.I'm changing the subject, I need to get a tan."

"I need a tan also. I'm kind of pale. I hope we can get a tan. Your skin tone is so pretty you have a natural tan."

"Thanks."

The lady across the aisle began to speak. "Can't you two whisper, you're keeping my husband and I up with your loud talking and that bright light?"

Patricia answered in a very sarcastic and disrespectful way. "We're not loud."

"Watch your tone and volume, you're going to get us in trouble."

The lady looked furious. "Little girl who do you think you're talking to?"

At that moment Patricia's mother woke up. Her seat is behind theirs. "Young ladies, go to sleep, turn that light off, no more talking!"

"Yes, ma'am We will good night!" They both obeyed.

The lady spoke under her breath. "Thank God her mother woke up. I was about to handle this smart mouth girl."

For the rest of the bus trip it was quiet as a mouse. You could almost hear a pin drop except for some occasional snoring. Rachel's father snored the loudest. He was tired from traveling. He made it home only a couple of hours before the bus left. Mrs. Walker nudged him all night so he wouldn't wake up the passengers.

Seven am the next morning Breakfast at Denny's Restaurant in Orlando, Florida

The Denny's is open 24 hours

It didn't take long for the bus to be empty. Everybody was hungry and needed to stretch and get some fresh air.

Marion one of the friends and her family were the first family to be seated. Her parents, Mr. and Mrs. Rucker had to feed those starving brothers, Derrick and James. They started asking questions an hour before they arrived.

Somehow, they placed their orders in less than five minutes.

Derrick, Marion's oldest brother began speaking. "I'm so glad we ordered our food rather fast. I'm starving!"

"Yes, big brother. I'm starving too." James said.

Mr.Bernard Rucker began staring at his wife. "Honey how are you? You've been a little quiet and distant since last night?"

"I'm fine. I had to stay up last night to do last minute packing. You don't realize how tired you are until you are being still. I think that's what's going on." Mrs. Rucker explained and yawned as she explained.

"Babe, I know that feeling too well. Maybe a couple of days you and I can stay in the hotel and just relax or maybe get a late start."

"Bernard that sounds good honey."

Derrick began speaking, of course he'd been listening to his parents. "Mom, I know sleeping on the bus didn't help. You'll have a bed tonight."

"Yes, my son a big difference."

The waitress made it back with golden pancakes, crisp bacon, cooked grits, fresh squeezed orange juice, scrambled eggs, strong black coffee, and Jimmy Dean sausage. "Here it is, I hope you enjoy it."

Marion's eyes were big. "This is a lot of food!"

"No, it's not," James said.

"Yes it is James." She smiled as she began to pray over her food. James and Derrick had started eating already.

"Just eat!" Derrick said as he chomped on some pancakes.

It was rather quiet now that the Rucker's have their breakfast. You can tell they love and care for each other. Marion is rather reserved and doesn't know her worth.

Cling! Clang! Loud noises were coming from Ellen's table. She looked at the employee. "You scared me out of my wits I almost had an accident in my pants."

"Young lady I didn't mean to startle you. I guess I need to slow down. Did I get anything on you? "asked the employee with a strange look on her face. She was acting strange.

6

"No, I'm fine." She said.

"I think you scared her with all the silver ware falling on the floor." Mr. Snow said.

Mrs. Snow nodded in agreement.

"Again. my apologies."

Mrs. Snow nodded at the young lady as she continued to cleanup. "Everything is fine, no worries, have a great rest of your shift."

"Thanks!" She said, and as she smiled and walked away.

"She sure was nervous and jumpy."

Ellen said."Yes, something wasn't right."

"Let's enjoy our breakfast." Mrs. Snow said.

The Snow's did enjoy their breakfast. As the story goes on you will see Ellen is one of the determined and strong girls in the bunch.

Everyone finished their breakfast and returned to the bus so the group can go to the hotel. Everyone is ready to go to the park especially the children.

Five hours later at Disney World

Diane and Brenda are crying crocodile tears.

Mr. Johnson began speaking, "You can cry all you want, both of you are too short and too young to ride that roller coaster. Straighten up your faces."

"Come on, let's check out this Its a Small World exhibit everyone is talking about." Mrs. Johnson said.

At that moment the other girls came running up to them. All the parents were close by.

"Come on everyone, let's check this ride out, and after that all of us can hang out for the whole trip." Patricia said.

"It'll be fun!" Rachel said.

Diane's eyes lit up. "Here we come!"

"Here we come!" Brenda said with a big smile. How quickly they forgot about the roller coaster ride.

This is the pivotal moment the friendship begins.

The girls hung out during the whole trip and had a ball. Now that I have given you a little background on the girls. I want to tell you about how they agreed to be lifetime friends.

Two

Blood is Shed

One sunny day right before the Cadette girl scout meeting, the girls were sitting at the picnic table in the park, discussing the events of the summer.

"Girls, I have so much fun when I'm with you!" Sally said.

"We play and laugh together, and we look out for each other. It all started at Disney world." Diane said.

"Yes we do look out for each other. Thanks, Rachel, for not telling my mother I was over your house when she was looking for me the other day," Ruth said. "You know I can't get in trouble. I can't embarrass my parents."

" You're welcome. I would get in trouble if my mom knew you weren't supposed to be over to the house."

"Ellen, thanks for helping me out when the girls down the street pushed me off the slide two weeks ago," Tanya said.

"Tanya, that's what I'm supposed to do. We're friends, we take care of each other, "Ellen said.

"That's right!" Sally said.

"Girls, I hope you're my friends forever," Marion said." It's kind of hard for me to make friends."

"Me too!" Tanya said.

"We should make a promise that we'll always be friends and always look out for each other," said Tanya.

"What should we do?" asked Ruth.

"Let's shed blood. I saw them do it on TV the other day. The shedding of blood means we're all in agreement to be friends for the rest of our lives." Patricia said as she reached into her shirt pocket. "I have a safety pin; we can use that."

"Let's do it!" said Rachel.

"Excuse me, isn't that going to hurt?" Tanya asked.

"Maybe, but not worth crying over!" Patricia answered.

"I'm scared of needles," Rachel said.

"Oh, come on. It's a sacrifice, and it's a safety pin." Sally said.

The girls passed the safety pin, and each girl pricked their finger. Blood was shed.

"I'm glad my blood dropped on the ground and not on my clothes." Ruth said as she stared at the droplets on the ground. "Blood on my clothes—I would get in trouble. My mother would notice it when she does laundry. And I'm scared of blood."

"I'm glad it didn't hurt." Tanya said as she examined her finger, which had already stopped bleeding.

Diane smiled and looked at everyone. "I can't go to the Cadette meeting at the clubhouse, I have blood on my shoes. I can't let it dry. I'm running home to change shoes; tell our leader I'll be there in ten minutes. This blood shedding was worth it, we're friends for life. Remember it's a secret. Gotta go, see you at the meeting." She ran home to change.

"I'm going to write this down in my diary. I think all of us should write our stories in our diaries. Some friends did something similar in one of the books I read this summer. What we did, it's not crazy."Rachel said as she pulled her long black hair away from her face.

"I 'll definitely, put this in mine." stated Ellen.

"I got a diary for my birthday earlier this year. This event will be included." Patricia said.

"I guess we all should get a diary," Marion said.

"Yes, we should!" The girls said in unison.

"Remember we can't tell anyone; we're sworn to secrecy." Rachel said.

"My friends, I'm so glad I was here, I would have cried if I missed this. I know you notice sometimes I'm not around. "Sally said.

Ruth in her perfect way said. "We wouldn't have done such a precious event without you Sally. This is almost like a vow. And we know sometimes you're not here, that doesn't change our friendship with you."

"Thanks everyone!"Sally said as she smiled.

The girls began to leave the park. My sister and her friends are excited about this oath or vow. According to my sister's diary they're on cloud nine. The story continues.

Three

Patricia and her Family

Two years later

The girls had spent a lot of times together. You always saw them together, almost inseparable. I must tell you about Patricia.

Once a month, on a Saturday, her family has a big get together. Aunts, uncles, cousins, and grandparents would all come over to their house at The Woods. Today on this beautiful sunny day, they're serving barbecue ribs, baked beans, potato salad, cole slaw, grilled hamburgers, hot dogs, and Brunswick stew. The music played loud enough for the neighbors to hear.

"Where are you going?" Mrs. Jones, her mom asked.

"The young folks are watching TV and playing games in the basement. At least it sounds like it. I'm headed that way," Uncle Richard said.

"Young people keep us young," Mrs. Jones said.

"Yes, they do. I'll be back." Uncle Richard headed downstairs to the basement.

The boys were playing pool. Reginald looked up as he saw their uncle enter the room. "Hey Uncle Richard."

Y'all look like you're having fun." Uncle Richard said as he kept walking about fifteen feet to sit with the girls while they watched TV.

George folded his arms together. "Hurry up Reginald."

12

"I'm not finished. Wait your turn." said Reginald.

Patricia frowned at her cousins. "Be quiet. We can't hear the TV. Hello, Uncle Richard."

"Hello darling. Hey boys don't be too loud." He sat in between the girls on the dark brown leather couch.

"Yeah, you're too loud," said Misty.

"Boys, I heard your parents call you. Misty, will you go upstairs and get me something to drink?"

The boys ran upstairs.

Misty said to herself and looked at her uncle. *Why in the world do I have to go get him a drink? He knows we're watching this movie. But no. I must be disturbed. Pat should go.* "Okay Uncle Richard."

Now it's just she and I. I got everyone to go upstairs. "This movie is scary. Aren't you scared? Don't you jump when something happens. You can sit in my lap if you get scared."

"Thanks Uncle. I think I'll be okay. I like scary movies. I'm a big girl."

"You know I'm here for you." Uncle Richard put his arms on the top of the sofa close enough to touch her neck. "You're growing into a lovely young lady."

She watched the movie and didn't look at her uncle. "You're right." She said . *I'm just answering him, I don't know what he said, this movie is good.*

Fifteen minutes later. None of the other children had come back to the basement.

Uncle Richard was moving closer to her, she didn't notice because he's always been a toucher.

This is my opportunity! Uncle Richard thought to himself.

He touched his niece in the wrong place.

There's a puzzled look on her face, "Stop! Uncle Richard what are you doing? Get your hands off me."

"Calm down. This is between you and I."

"No Uncle Richard, you're not supposed to touch me like that."

"Shhh! Be quiet!"

Tears rolled down her face.

He put his hands over her mouth, ripped her panties off, fondled her and then made his way with her. He forced himself on his niece. She started crying crocodile tears and was in much pain, as she laid on the sofa. Uncle Richard made his way with her for more than fifteen minutes. He allowed his body to make his way with hers. There was no way out . He had her pinned down on the sofa. Tears fell down her face like a waterfall.

"You better not tell anyone, or I'll kill you," Uncle Richard said. "Stay down here wipe your tears.

I can't believe my uncle did this to me. Lord what did I do to deserve this? I had no idea my uncle was like this. I thought he was just touchy. Oh Lord I'm scared. I'm hurting. All the special attention makes sense now. He threatened me. I need to tell my mom, but she probably won't believe me. I need help.

* * *

Uncle Richard went upstairs first making sure his clothes were intact. "I thought some of you were coming downstairs. We had been watching a movie. I think it's almost over. Patricia should be coming up."

"That movie must be entertaining," Mrs. Jones said as she bent down in the kitchen cabinets putting dishes up.

Patricia came upstairs and zipped by her mother to her bedroom. The family was eating and just having a great time. "I can't face anyone. I feel so nasty."

Mrs. Jones went to the door of the basement. "Honey come upstairs and hang with everyone."

Uncle Richard looked straight into his sister's eyes. "She just went upstairs as you were bending down. When I was downstairs, she said she wanted to take a shower and go to bed after the movie is over." *I hope she believes me. I truly don't want her to know what I did.*

"She must have tiptoed by. I didn't hear her."

"I think so she yawned a lot during the movie, and I believe she's taking a nap or going to take a nap."

" I'm so hurt. I'm so disappointed in my uncle. I'm so ashamed. What did I do to get treated like this? I'm going to cry myself to sleep. Lord, I'm hurting, please stop the pain."

Four

Conflict Everywhere

<u>Game night</u>

Sally tightened her ponytail and looked at Diane with such a sad countenance. "I know y'all are going to hang out afterwards. It hurts so bad that I can't go with you. My mom is so strict. I must go straight home, to do chores. Sometimes I feel like Cinderella. I do my sister's chores. My mom says, I have to do them because I'm the oldest."

"What! We need you to celebrate with us," Diane stated.

"Aww! We hate you can't go!" Ruth said.

"I hate it too! I guess you haven't noticed the games are the only social event I can come to. I must be at home as soon as the game is over. I clean up and take care of my siblings. I wake up at seven am every Saturday morning. There is more to it. I can't tell you the whole story. I need you to pray for me. I'm tired and don't know what to do. I can't disrespect my mother and grandmother, so I do what they tell me to do. Please eat a hamburger for me. Enjoy yourself," Sally said.

"I'll pray for you! Some parents are stricter than others. That's not unusual." Ruth said.

"She says I remind her of my father and that I act and look just like him. She hates me because of that. My siblings look like her. It doesn't help that

16

I was daddy's girl. He treated me very special. I miss my father so much. I obey all her rules to keep peace in the household. And doesn't the Bible say, Children obey your parents so that your days may be long? I want my days to be long, because I have big dreams .and one of them is getting out of that house as soon as I can. Talking about this is bringing tears to my eyes. I gotta go been talking too much, but I needed to get some of my situation off my back. Goodbye."

"Oh we'll pray for you. I had no idea all of this has been going on. And you do look like your daddy. I'll pray for your mother too." Rachel said.

"Friends, I gotta go. See you later." Sally said as she started running while waving goodbye and headed towards her mother who should be in the car waiting for her.

* * *

Sally gets in the car with her mom. Her mother didn't look happy. She slapped her.

"Ouch!" she screamed, "Mom that hurts."

"You should've been to this car fifteen minutes ago. What did I tell you about coming to the car late? I don't care what it takes, but you better be here on time. You ought to be thankful I let you go to the game. You ugly little child, looking like your ugly daddy."

"Yes ma'am."

"When you get home, I want you to clean the entire house. Don't go to bed until you finish. That'll teach you to obey me. My time is valuable."

Crocodile tears rolled down her face the whole journey home. She did her chores that night.

* * *

<u>The following Monday in the Cafeteria</u>

Sally yawned and began speaking. "How was Friday night after the game? "

"Sally we had a burger with your name on it!" Ellen said.

17

Tanya began speaking. "It was really good."

"But on a serious note we missed you! But we understand! "Ruth said.

"Thanks, my friends." Sally said.

Joyce seated a couple seats from the girls looked at Hazel. "Ruth and her friends get on my nerves. I ought to throw my hot dog at them."

Joyce threw her hot dog. "I hope it hit them in the head."

"Ouch," Tanya said. "Something hit me in the head."

Andre who was sitting right behind Joyce threw his hot dog at her. "Whew, it hit the top of her head. That's what I'm talking about. Food fight! Food Fight!"

Andrew stood up. "He threw another hot dog, it landed in someone's hair.

Tanya surprisingly threw her hot dog at Joyce. "Bingo, right in her left eye. I may be quiet and reserved but I'm fighting back today!"

Patricia stood on her seat. "Yes, fight back. I'm going to throw some fries at Hazel and Joyce. I know they hate our guts. The French fries landed right on Hazel's chest and Joyce's hair. "Ha that's what they get for always starting something."

Ellen ran around to the edge of her table." I'm going to aim at Lucille, their friend. I can get her big nose. She tries to give me the blues, this is my opportunity to get her back."

She threw her hot dog with the bun, loaded with mustard and ketchup. "Right on time, payback is rough."

Everyone in the cafeteria was throwing food. It was becoming very chaotic. Everyone's clothes had mustard and ketchup all over them. People had food in their hair. The food fight lasted ten minutes before the teachers, principals, and counselors came to stop it.

The principal spoke through a megaphone. "Stop this nonsense this minute. No one is to leave this cafeteria until it's spotless. The boys will clean the windows and the floors. The girls will clean all the tables. The cleaning supplies are being disbursed as I speak. Get to cleaning you have less than fifteen minutes to clean this place up. The teachers and I will be hovering over you to make sure it's right. A letter will be sent to all of your parents explaining why you're late for your class."

Patricia mumbled to Ellen as she cleaned the table. "How did this happen? One minute we're eating, and then we're throwing food, now we're cleaning up."

Ellen whispered as she cleaned the table next to her. "It all started when one of those girls at the table next to us threw food at Tanya. One thing led to another."

She began to clean some of the chairs in the area. "I don't think I'll get in too much trouble. My mother and father say they did stuff like this. Of course, they'll say that doesn't make it right. They'll say we have to ignore people like Hazel and Joyce."

"I think my parents will say something similar. At least I hope so."

The principal walked around with the megaphone in his hand observing them as the cafeteria was on its way to normalcy. "You're almost finished. The way it's looking I might ask your teachers not to count you tardy. And I might forego the letter to your parents. This better not happen again. You have five minutes to complete your task. Everyone look in your area and if it looks like you don't mind eating off the floors, tables, windows, and seats then your job is complete. The teachers are inspecting your areas and will dismiss you if your area is presentable."

Students began to leave the cafeteria as their area was inspected.

They were excused and headed toward their classes.

Sally began to laugh. "We got in trouble, but you have to admit it was fun."

Tanya chuckled. "Yes, it was. Too bad we can't do it again."

Rachel giggled and begin to go to her class. "Today will be a day we'll never forget. See you later my friends."

"Later!" The girls replied.

"Junior High is turning out to be a lot of fun, I wondering what's going on with Diane our friend at high school." Marion asked.

"I'm quite sure, we'll find out sooner or later." Patricia said.

Five

Slow Down Ellen

Ellen and Sean are at the town square seated on a bench near the water fountain in the middle of the square.

"The moon is shining bright. I see the Big Dipper and the Little Dipper."

"The sky is beautiful." Sean said as he put his arm around her shoulder.

"The fountain fits perfect in our town square."

"We're hitting it off pretty good. I think we make a great couple. I want us to be exclusive."

"I think I can handle being only your girl. I enjoy your company."

He kissed her in the mouth.What a surprise. *No, he didn't just kiss me.*

Sean smiling. "You're a good kisser."

Ellen blushed. "So are you!" Sean grabbed her hand.

They stayed there for about thirty minutes, kissing and watching other couples go by.

Sean drove her home in his red 1972 Toyota Celica. He walked her to the door and got a kiss again. *All this kissing, Lord I must be careful. It could lead to something else. Help!*

"Let's go to my house, my parents sleep upstairs on the third floor. I'm on the first. They won't hear us. We can finish what we started." Sean said.

"No I better go in the house., so I can make my curfew."

"Forget a curfew, we're going to my house to finish this off."

The car started back up. Ellen jumped out of the car and ran inside the house.

Sean was so mad he turned red. He drove off like a maniac.

***

As soon as she stepped in the house, her older brother Eddie confronted her before she could make it out of the living room.

"About time you made it home. I don't like that Sean guy you're hanging out with. I told dad he's bad news."

"Ah, Eddie, stop acting like an overprotective older brother. You shouldn't have told dad."

"Be careful sis, he's bad news. Just be careful. He has a reputation of loving girls and leaving them. You should be safe just don't have sex with him. I told Dad, I'll handle this Sean guy."

"Eddie, I can handle Sean. I'll let you know if I need some help."

"You're a girl and I'm a guy. I know how guys are. He better not treat you wrong."

"Calm down, Eddie."

"Later sis, this conversation is over." He walked out of the room.

She shook her head and said to herself. *My brother is so overprotective. He needs to relax.*

All that kissing she might need to slow down. And in public wow. And the story continues.

Six

I'm Glad I Waited

<u>What's going on with Ellen?</u>

Ellen called Patricia.

Patricia answered the phone while chewing a mouth full of food. "Hello!"

"Hey Patricia!"

"Hey, what's going on?"

"Girl I had a wonderful time with Sean last night. It was indescribable."

"Tell me about it!"

"Patricia, Sean and I almost made love, girl."

"My friend, what did you do to almost have sex, that sounds like something I may do?"

" I got away. He yelled at me as I ran away."

"I'm glad you had a way of escape."

"Me too."

"I have to go. I told Sean I would call him this evening."

"Slow down and be careful , please."

"Don't worry I have this under control."

She rushed off the phone, and called Sean, there was no answer.

Three hours later. *I hope Sean answers the phone.* She dials the number again, still no answer. *Where is he?*

Twenty-four hours later

Sean just wanted me for sex, he hasn't called me back, and we talk every day. I guess he's mad because he didn't conquer. He'll be alright.

One Week Later

Ellen called Patricia, who was sitting on her bed doing her homework. "Hello!" Patricia said.

"Hey Patricia, I haven't heard from Sean all week. He hasn't been at our favorite spots and he hasn't called." Ellen explained.

Patricia spoke with concern. " I'm sorry to hear that."

Tears rolled down her eyes. "I asked a couple of his friends if they've seen him. They have. I guess he's dodging me. Before that night, we would talk for hours at a time on the phone."

"Sean has some nerves. He's just mad that he didn't conquer you. I'm glad you didn't have sex with him, you get to see what he's all about. I know you're hurting."

Ellen sobbed harder and was crying very loudly. "I feel so betrayed. I feel used."

" I understand how you feel. I've been betrayed by guys too. It's humiliating, and you feel nasty. It makes you feel as though you're not respected and especially not loved. Guys take advantage of you sometimes. We need to take a stand and not allow it to happen. It's easier said than done it takes courage and boldness. We aren't anyone's doormat!"

It's not Sean's fault totally I played a major part. I should have obeyed the word of God and not let him touch me at all. I'm glad we didn't go all the way."

"Don't beat yourself up. Just repent. God forgives you. I had sex with this one guy, it took me awhile to get over him. It was at least a month."

"That's good you got over him."

"It seemed like forever but thank God I made it through. At least I think I'm over him."

Patricia this is our secret."

"It's our secret."

Ellen's brother Eddie knocks on her door.

"Who is it?"

"It's me, sis, can I come in?"

"No, not right now."

"We're waiting on you, so we can eat dinner as a family."

"Is Dad home?"

"Yes, believe it or not."

"Eddie, I need to pass on dinner. I feel sick."

"Do you need me to get you anything?"

"Everything's fine. My stomach is hurting, it feels queasy. I think I'm going to rest."

"Feel better sis!"

"Thanks bro! Excuse my rudeness Patricia. That was my brother, the family wants me to come to dinner. I told them I don't feel good. I'd better get off the phone Patricia, thanks for your encouraging words. Remember its our secret."

"Yes it is, goodbye!" Patricia said.

***

The following week, it's Wednesday morning

They are walking down the hallway, Sean is heading their way.

Her face lit up. "Hey Sean, Is everything okay? I've been calling you."

Sean didn't stop, he picked up his pace as he passed by them and didn't smile. "Hey, everything's fine."

They stared at each other. "Did he give me the cold shoulder, he acted like we don't know each other. Wow! I guess he confirmed he doesn't want to be bothered with me."

She hugged her. "Don't worry friend this too shall pass. Pray for Sean."

"It'll be hard at first. Guys can be a jerk at times. Sean didn't get he wanted and now he treats me horrible."

" Please don't beat yourself up."

"Don't worry my friend, you and I will be fine."

"Be encouraged my sister."

"Thanks, you too."

Seven

Favor Ain't Fair

⚛❧

<u>Diane is in high school</u>

Saturday afternoon around 8 pm in her bedroom relaxing and reading a good book.

Fred called her.

"Hey, this is the one and only. Did I catch you at a bad time?"

"No, its perfect timing. I was reading, Mr. one and only."

"I won't hold you long. Young lady, the homecoming dance is in a month, I was wondering if you would be my date."

" It would be my pleasure to be your date."

"Thanks my friend. I have to brush up on my dancing skills."

I have butterflies in my stomach. "Stop joking I've seen you dance. You have rhythm."

"If you say so. We'll have a good time regardless. We'll talk later."

She hung up the phone and started dancing around her room and looking in the mirror. She's talking out loud to herself. "I'm going to the dance with Fred, a gentleman, a football player, and he's smart. I'm glad he's finally coming around. I've known him since elementary school and a forever crush on him."

* * *

Monday afternoon at school, she found out through her homeroom teacher that she had been nominated to be on the Homecoming Court. She was excited and rushed home to tell her friends. She asked them to meet her in front of Sally's house.

Sally was washing dishes. She stopped.

Rachel was reading a book. She stopped.

The girls ran to meet her. They were outside within minutes.

"I miss you my friends. I wish you were in high school with me. We haven't seen each other since school started."

Ellen hugged her. "We miss you too!"

"You and I have been playing phone tag," Ruth said.

"Yes, we have. We've been so busy.

How are things going for you all?"

"I'm doing fine. The drill team is going great. My Algebra is hard. I think I can make it through," Ellen said.

"We're fine! How are you?" asked Patricia.

Rachel leaned towards Diane. "How does it feel to be in the actual high school building?"

"It's exciting. Something new every day. One thing is, I've been nominated to be part of the Homecoming Court. And guess who my date is!"

Patricia screamed with excitement. "The Fred you've gone to school with us all these years? He's a hunk!"

"How do you know?" She asked.

"I know things!" Patricia said with a big smile on her face.

Tanya clapped her hands. "Congrats!"

Rachel jumped up and down with excitement. "I want to go with you to pick out a dress." "What color are you thinking about?" Ruth said.

"I do too! "Tanya said.

Ellen had a serious look on her face as she began speaking. "We can't go with her. We'll be in the way and will probably make it harder for her to pick out her dress."

Ruth began speaking." She's right we'll be in her way, and it'll take longer."

Rachel had a look of disappointment on her face. "I guess you're right. I'm so happy for you!"

"We all are happy for you!" Sally said. "My friends I must go! Congrats my friend!"

She hugged everyone and went back home.

"Later Sally! As a matter of fact, I must go. I just wanted to see you all and spread the good news! I'll keep you updated!"

"Bye." Ellen said.

"We'll see you later!" Patricia said.

* * *

The next morning

Kimberly a classmate, walked up to Diane and stopped. "Who told you, you could be on the homecoming court. You're a freshman. How in the world did you get nominated? You're not that pretty."

Terri leaned over and got in her face. "A freshman, for a queen, unheard of. I hope you lose."

Ignorance is all around me. These girls are something special. I don't know them. A lot of nerves.

"We'll leave for now. But we're not through with you." Kimberly said and walked off heading down the hall. Terri walked beside her.

"Lord I don't have time for mess and jealously. Favor isn't fair! They'll be alright."

* * *

Between fifth and sixth period

Fred met his sweetheart near the stairway on the third floor. Their friendship has transitioned.

He kissed her on the cheek. "Hello! How is your day going?"

She blushed. "It's better, now that I see you."

28

He grabbed her hand. They began walking to their classes. They passed by other classmates, some smiled, some had a look of hatred on their face.

One classmate said, "Who does she think she is? Fred is my man ."

She turned her head quickly towards him. "Did you hear that?"

"Some people tell lies and they exaggerate, ignore that."

She said you're her man."

"I don't know that chic. Let's go to the movies Saturday."

I see you changing the subject."

"I did, you can't focus on foolishness."

"You're right. What's showing at the movies?"

"Don't know, but a movie would be a good date. Let's talk later!'"

"That'll be fine!"

"Great!" He said as he kissed her on her ruby red lips. "I must go."

"See you later! Thanks for walking me to my class." She started opening the door to her classroom.

"I'll see you later!"

* * *

The school day ended. Fred met her at her sixth period classroom door. They're riding home together. They walked to the parking lot to his car.

He opened the door for her. "Thanks for the ride in your classic ride. Your mustang is nice, clean, and sharp."

"Thanks, it's a '69 classic." He got in. He turned the radio on. The song "When Will I See You Again, " was playing.

"I like that song. When will I see you again?"

"Yeah, it's pretty cool. I like the instrumentation in it. It's nice and I guess it fits us."

"Yes, it does, this will be one of our songs."

My friend, I want to be real with you. I have liked you from the time the subdivision went to Disney World. Back then I was too shy and too young to let you know."

" I have wanted to be more than friends for a long time too. I was waiting on you."

"That's interesting we both have been waiting on the right time and here we are.You always had a smile on your face, and your beautiful brown hair in a long ponytail with those cute bangs."

"Yes, you and your walk, your intelligence has made me admire you. And you play football. To top it all you've been a gentleman! Here we are!"

Suddenly, they became shy.

All of a sudden both of them started singing because they were at a lost for words.

It was a beautiful drive home with the orange gold sunset hovering over the buildings. They caught every red light which happen to be on the long route. A couple of songs played as they traveled home.

* * *

He stopped the car in front of her house

He looked at her without flinching. "There's something I want to ask you."

While staring into his eyes she had to clear her throat. She said to herself. *He has beautiful brown eyes.* "What is it?"

He grabbed her hand. "Will you be my girl?"

"Yes, I will. It will be my pleasure."

"Whew, I feel better now . I had no idea you liked me. You through me for a loop, I couldn't respond a few minutes ago. If I had known that we would have been dating sooner."

"I was in shock and didn't know what to say"

He gave her a peck on the cheek. They got out of the car.

She didn't give him a chance to open the door for her. He grabbed her hand and they walked down the sidewalk hand in hand taking their time.

"Glancing and staring into her eyes made him want to kiss her, but he knows it's too soon.

Mr. Johnson opened the front door. " Come in the house, you'll see her tomorrow."

"Yes, sir. I can't give you a ride tomorrow evening. I have football practice."

"That's fine. See you later, boyfriend."

"Later, girlfriend!"

Her father shook his head and headed towards the kitchen.

* * *

<u>In her bedroom</u>

You better believe she's excited she started dancing in her bedroom. She pretended she was slow dancing with Fred. *He's my type of man.*

Brenda entered the room and immediately became confused. "What's gotten into you?"

"He's my new boyfriend!"

"I like him for you."

"I like him too."

"I'm so happy for you, sister."

"Thanks, Brenda."

"You're welcome. You can continue all that dancing you were doing." Brenda said jokingly.

* * *

<u>Homecoming Night</u>

At half time, the Homecoming Court rode onto the football field on a beautiful float shaped like a heart." You Are the Sunshine of My Life" by Stevie Wonder played over the loudspeaker.

The principal entered the field and began announcing, "Ladies and gentlemen, let's give a round of applause for our Homecoming Court. Our queen is Diane Johnson."

The crowd cheered loudly. Everyone who lived in The Woods had whistles and blew them continuously. The band played a song dedicated to the court.

She thought to herself. Oh, what a night, I'm homecoming queen. Thank you, Lord.

Ruth shouted, "Our girl is homecoming queen. Never heard of that before.

Thank God." "Yes our friend is the queen, congratulations." Patricia said.

Tanya and Marion jumped up and down continuously. "Yeah, God is good! She's a freshman and homecoming queen."

The girls started dancing. "Way to go !"

"I'm glad I got to see this historical moment." Sally said.

and then thought, *I'll be leaving soon. My mean mother will be here.*

Ellen looked amazed. "Her dress is so beautiful. She looks like a million dollars."

The principal began speaking." Excuse me everyone, I need to announce the king. Our homecoming king is Fred Williams. He's one of our football players. Congratulations to our King and Queen." He came running out of the locker room with his tuxedo on.

The crowd began cheering and dancing to the music.

"Ladies and gentlemen, I present to you our king and queen." He whispered in the principal's ear. "Well ladies and gentlemen Fred is here for a few minutes he has to put that football uniform back on. Again, I present our queen and king. Give them a loud thunderous clap and shouts of support."

The crowd is loud and excited. The band is playing loudly. It's just a great time.

* * *

Cedar Lake won the game twenty to seven. So excited he showered quickly and changed back into his tuxedo. The court had to take pictures.

* * *

Homecoming Dance

Fred waited on Diane at the entrance of the gym.

She walked rapidly towards him . "You look suave in that black tuxedo with purple accessories."

"Thanks honey, you look ravishing in your purple dress. Let's dance, the DJ is playing "Could it be I'm falling in Love," by the Spinners, I love that song."

"Me too let's dance until we can't dance anymore!"

He smiled. "Sounds like a plan!"

They danced through several songs, mostly slow ones. They were inseparable.

About ten feet away Sean was at the drink table. Milton a player from Hall walked up to him.

"Great game! I bet you can't beat us the next time we play you," Milton bragged.

Sean replied, "All that bragging you're doing, if your team is capable it should've happened tonight. You're just a bunch of talk; back it up on the field."

"The referees cheated. That's why we lost."

"Man stop the lies and get out of my face."

"You calling me a liar? "Milton pushed Sean into the drink table. The table turned over.

Sean popped Milton on his left jawbone.

Milton hit Sean in the mouth. Sean's mouth started bleeding. They grabbed at each other, they knocked tables and chairs over. They were making a big mess.

Fred turned to Diane, "Excuse me."

She reached to grab his coattail but missed it. "Fred no! I can't believe this is happening. It's ruining my night."

The guys were rolling on the floor near her. "Fred and Sean please stop."

The guys were fighting intensely.

A bystander asked. "Can someone stop them?"

"You guys have torn my dress! It's falling off me! You need to stop fighting! Tonight isn't the night." She ran into the ladies' room.

Mrs. Talley ran behind her. Mrs. Talley said to herself. *What a way to end a perfect night for our homecoming queen.* "Darling let me help you. I keep some safety pins. We can pin your dress up."

Mrs. Talley, do you believe out of everything that could happen today my dress has been torn? I want to go home! Please tell him, I'm ready. If he and Sean wouldn't have been fighting, this wouldn't have happened."

Mrs. Talley hugged her. "I understand. Try to focus on the good memories. This too shall pass."

"I know but it hurts. I'm embarrassed, and my dress is torn to pieces."

"Honey, it's going to be okay. I'm going to get him."

Tears rolled down her face like a waterfall. "Thanks Ms. Talley. I appreciate you! You're amazing."

Mrs. Tally hugged her again. "That's what I'm here for. Let me go get him so you can go home."

It was necessary to make sure nothing personal was showing and she attempted to get herself together emotionally. She came out of the lady's room. The fight had ended. The male chaperones stopped the fight.

The Ride home

Tears flowed like hard steady raindrops. "You and Sean messed up a perfect evening with your fighting. Look at my dress. Its messed up I can't even put it in the closet and have great memories. I'm so devastated."

"Sweetheart I'm so sorry. I don't know how I can make it up to you?"

There's no way you can make it up. I know I have to forgive you, but I'm not going to do that right now or anytime soon."

"I deserve that."He said.

The drive was quiet the rest of the ride home.

They made it to the house. She jumped out of the car. "Don't worry about walking me to the door. I need to be by myself."

"Honey, I'm so sorry."

" I'll talk to you tomorrow."

Watching his baby walk down the sidewalk in her sexy cool way really made him regret what he had done.

* * *

Saturday came, she didn't take his calls all day Saturday and all day Sunday. She stayed in her room sulking all weekend.

* * *

Monday morning- fifteen minutes before school

Fred ran to catch up with his baby as she walked through the front door of the school. He grabbed her by the arm.

"Good morning. I hope you've forgiven me. I'm truly sorry. I didn't mean to ruin our special night."

"Good morning, honey. I forgive you. I thought about you and your fellow players. I can't believe you all were fighting. I think I understand. The night was still good. I have pictures of me in my dress and with you. Everything is fine."

'What a relief. I thought you were going to break up with me. I know how you ladies are about special occasions and your dresses. I'll walk you to your class." He reaches for her books to carry them.

"I wasn't going to break up with you. We can put that behind us now and move forward."

"For sure! Can I give you a ride home this evening?"

I would love that, but I have a ride."

"Just tell your friend you have another ride." "I can't do that. I didn't know you're so persistent."

"Girl, I want to be with you!"

"I want to be with you, my dear. I can't ride home with you, I drove. You can come by the house after school."

"I'll see you then." He kissed her on the check.

"Later baby!"

A smile was plastered all over her face.

* * *

Monday evening after school, everyone was standing in front of Sally's house. Diane was walking up her driveway.

The girls walked fast to catch up with her. "Hello Queen!" The girls yelled.

I know they want to ask me about Friday night and what happened with her on

Friday.

The girls started talking as soon as they reached her.

" I know you might not want to be bothered right now. I wanted to tell you; you looked beautiful Friday night." Ruth said.

"Thanks."

"Is everything okay?" Ellen asked in her direct assertive way.

"Everything is fine." She replied.

Patricia looking rather confused began to speak. "I think you're not telling us something. He didn't walk you to the door. You know we were looking out the window waiting for you to come home. The Fred I know is a gentleman what's going on?"

"We're nosy, what's going on?" Rachel asked.

"My dear friends, we're fine. We had a disagreement. I forgave him. Now if you don't mind, I'm going in the house. I'm very tired. You'll know more details later."

"Get some rest my friend. We'll talk later." Tanya said.

She went into the house.

Marion began speaking. "Our buddy is having the time of her life at Cedar Lake High." She thought to herself. *I wish I could be as confident as she is.*

"She sure is!" Ellen said.

"Maybe our school year will become more exciting. I'm dreading tomorrow, I might have to dissect an animal." Ruth said.

"You'll be fine. It'll be a piece of cake." Rachel said.

"Yes, maybe something interesting will happen soon for one of us other than biology class." Patricia said.

"I hope so!" Marion said.

"I have to leave. I'll see you tomorrow! "Patricia said.

They all embraced and said good-bye.

Eight

Jail Bird

Game Time A New School Year

Less than a minute left in the game.

The score is 20-20. They need to hold Hall back.

The cheerleaders are performing the teddy bear stunt. "Elevate your mind! Get yourself together! Elevate your mind! Get yourself together!"

"We're number one! We're number one!" They tumbled, did splits, and danced while the band played, and the fans chanted, "C-L-H-S, C-L-H-S CEDAR LAKE TIGERS!"

The girls are in position. Jeanine a senior who has been on the squad since the tenth grade started screaming at Sally and Ellen. "Newbies, I need for you to keep the line straight. I can see you're out of line in my peripheral view. Get it together before the people notice!'"

They lined up correctly without the crowd noticing. Sally began to speak under her breath." She's such a grouch; I'm glad the cheer is over let's make sure we're tight and right. I hope we win."

Ellen began speaking. "Yes, she is. She must be on her cycle."

Roseanne, a seasoned cheerleader whispered. "Don't worry about her newbies. That's just her way. She's nice, just look past that hardness. Stay focused, we need to cheer our team."

Ellen replied. "Thanks for the heads up. Yes, we need a miracle!"

"Thanks Roseanne. Come on Tigers!" Sally said.

Jeanine looked back. "The line looks great get ready for another cheer we need to motivate the crowd, so we can inspire our team."

Hall is on the second yard line and its first down! There's only ten seconds left in the game." the announcer said.

"She was worried about a line we should have been cheering." Ellen said.

The cheerleaders began to cheer: "You can do it! Let's go Tigers. You can do it! Defense Tigers! Defense Tigers!"

The announcer began speaking. "Touchdown Hall with five seconds in the game to go. It's not enough time for Cedar Lake to do anything. Well audience it's a wrap by the time they kick the ball to the Tigers the game will be over. Hall wins this one. Congratulations Hall Warriors."

Sally looked at Ellen. "The guys tried. I guess we can't win them all."

Ellen said. "They did put up a fight. We'll tell them they did great, when we see them at Burger King."

* * *

Showdown at Burger King after the game

It was so crowded. Students were in the parking lot. The cheerleaders, pep squad, and the players from both teams were there. Fred, Sean, the girls, and other players are walking towards the front door of the Burger King.

Joseph Marshall the quarterback for Hall was seated on the hood of an convertible. Suddenly he stood up. "Hey Sean and Fred, we ate you up tonight. You thought you were going to be undefeated. What you got to say about that?"

Everyone kept walking.

The famous Kimberly is in the same convertible with Joseph. "Diane yeah, what you gotta say? We beat the blank out of you!"

Terri, Kimberly's sidekick is in the car next to them. "Rachel and Patricia, Now, you don't have anything to say. We shut up the Tigers mouths tonight."

Diane glanced at them. "Patricia and Rachel, guess who that is, its Kimberly and Terri, the ones I beat up."

Rachel looked over there. "They're becoming a nuisance."

"Yes, they are. A thorn in the flesh." Patricia said.

"Why are you're ignoring us?" a Hall football player asked as he ran toward Fred. He pushed him.

"Man, you'd better leave me alone." Fred replied, he turned away from him and attempted to walk into the restaurant.

The guy pushed him into to the glass door. Fred turned around and popped him upside the head.

Kimberly and Terri ran over to the entrance of the Burger King, and started grabbing Patricia and Rachel's hair, trying to pull it out. In a matter of seconds fights broke out in the parking lot.

The manager comes outside screaming and holding his hands up in the air. "Stop it. You're destroying my restaurant. I'm going to call the police. This has gotten out of control."

He runs back inside. He dials 911.

"911 what's your emergency?" asked the operator.

"There are a bunch of high school students fighting and tearing up my restaurant. It's a mess. My employees are scared half to death. They're all over the parking lot."

"My address is three twenty University Avenue."

"We'll have some squad cars over there shortly. A couple of them are in the area."

" Thanks. Please hurry. Good-bye!"

It was extremely loud with screams. The guys were hitting each other so hard you could hear the blows. One guy hit someone so hard his nose started bleeding. They were tearing clothes off each other. It's a big chaotic scene. Sirens and flashing blue lights showed up within minutes. The students didn't hear or see them.

Officers pulled out their handcuffs and grabbed Fred. "You're under arrest young man for disturbing the peace and damaging this man's business."

Fred looked at the officer. "I didn't do anything. I was defending myself. I couldn't stand there and let him beat me up."

The officer didn't respond to him. He put him in the police van.

Marion saw a cop headed her direction. She started running. "Please don't take me to jail. My parents will kill me if I go to jail."

The police ignored her but continued to escort her to the van. He began putting her in the van.

The police left with four vans full of students. The ride to the station seemed long.

Tears rolled down Rachel's face. "How am I going to tell my parents? I'm in jail for fighting. How am I going to explain this one? Lord help me."

Ellen held her head down. "I don't know what we're going to do. I think we have to tell the truth." *We're in serious trouble, my poor friends, Tanya looks nervous. Marion is crying so hard she's sniffling. Lord help us.*

Patricia covered her face to hide her tears. "I have no clue how I'll explain this one. My mother might say you should have walked away. How can you walk away when they grabbed us from behind?"

Rachel shook her head in disgust. "We need to come up with something. Sally will be glad she doesn't come to Burger King after the game. At least she's not going to jail."

"Yeah, one advantage for her." Ellen said.

* * *

Jailhouse Rock

Everyone has been put in a holding cell at the Cedar Lake jailhouse. The room is small, musty, and crowded.

They are distraught.

Tanya is seated next to Patricia while in the holding cell. She leans onto Patricia's shoulder. "I wish I would stop crying."

Patricia began speaking. "We should cry, we've never been in jail before."

Rachel chimed in. "This one will definitely be in my journal diary whatever you call it."

"Mines too." Diane responded.

Ruth said. "It all happened so fast."

"Correct, I could've sworn we went to get something to eat. Can you believe it?" Tanya said.

Ellen said. "It's a reality. One I thought I would never experience. Me a jailbird, never! "

"Not one of my dreams." Rachel said.

"Mines either! It's rather embarrassing." Ruth said.

"I know this sounds crazy, but I'm going to try to get a nap in before our parents come. I'm so sleepy and tired." Diane said as she yawned.

"How can you sleep in this place? I'm going to keep my eyes wide open?" Ellen said.

"My eyelids feel like they're drooping." Diane said.

"When you're tired, you're tired. You just don't care where you are." Rachel said.

By then her eyes were closed. She was sitting straight up sleeping hard that fast.

"Look at our friend she's sound asleep. I guess she knows we're here and we're not going to let anyone bother her." Ellen said.

"Yes, we'll handle anyone!" Marion said in agreement.

The girls became quiet after she went to sleep. They watched other people that were in the holding cell. All kind of people were in there. People dressed in raggedy faded jeans, professional dressed ladies, ladies of the evening, and old ladies. Anybody you can think of.

* * *

Approximately one hour later

Tanya jumped in her mothers' arms. "I'm so glad to see you. Being in jail, what a horrifying experience."

Mrs. Patterson hugged her daughter tightly. "I know it was. I'm somewhat confused about how all this came about. We'll talk about that in the car."

Marion walked over to her father; tears are stilling rolling down her face. "Dad, I'm so glad to see you." They hug each other.

Mr. Rucker responded. "Good to see you're okay. I hope you have a sound explanation for all of this."

Pat looked in the crowd for her family. "Uncle Richard!" Where's my mom?"

"Your mom sent me; she figured a man needed to come. I'm the one since your father is out of town." Uncle Richard said.

I guess I can't be picky. I'm thankful I'm out of that holding cell. "Thanks Uncle Richard." She said reluctantly. *Lord help me I don't want his hands on me.*

Pastor Perry was hugging Ruth and headed towards the door. "Everyone it's one a.m., let's get out of here, our daughters and their classmates have been in jail long enough."

The crowd agreed. "Yes! We've seen enough of this place."

* * *

Truth or consequences

Everyone got in their cars.

Mrs. Patterson seated in the passenger seat up front, turns to her daughter in the back seat. "Honey, tell me the whole truth about how these fights started."

"I really can't tell you. The only thing I know is we were about to walk into Burger King. I had my hand on the door handle. Someone pulled my hair. The next thing I know I was on the ground fighting for my life."

"Did you know who you were fighting?"

"Mom, the only thing, I know is that they go to Hall High. I believe their names are Kimberly and Terri, they love to cause trouble."

Mr. Patterson stopped at the red light. "Where do they live? They must be very unruly."

"Yes, they are daddy. They live in a subdivision down the street from us. The Warrior students were fighting the Tigers. It's a big rivalry. Kimberly and Terri are always picking on my friends. I usually don't be involved because I'm quiet and laid back, I guess I was right there to be picked on this time."

Mr. Patterson moaned. "Yes, you are my dear. I guess that's why I'm surprised. Those teams have been rivals for a long time. Sounds like one fight led to another."

"The football players have fought the guys from Hall before. Mom and Dad there was no way I could've avoided it. I couldn't run. I was caught right in the middle. At least I didn't pick the fight?"

Mr. Patterson nodded his head in agreement. "I know sometimes you must protect yourself. I'm just thankful the officers didn't charge you."

"Yeah, me too," She answered.

They arrived at their house and parked in the garage.

Mrs. Patterson started getting out of the car. "You aren't going back to Burger King. I forbid you."

He opened the side door to the house that leads to the kitchen. "Your mom is right. I forbid you to. You can go to a McDonald's to eat."

"I know I have to obey you. You don't understand. Burger King is the spot."

Mrs. Patterson put her hand on her right hip. "We understand, we were your age once."

"I don't think that'll solve the problem. Kimberly and Terri are vicious. I hope going to jail has calmed them down. I guess going to another restaurant makes a lot of sense."

Mr. Patterson motioned them to come upstairs. "Let's go to bed, I'm tired. We'll continue this conversation tomorrow."

"I know you're tired. Goodnight." Mrs. Patterson said as they went upstairs.

Tanya yawned. "Goodnight mom and dad." *I'm glad we're going to bed. I'm tired of answering questions.*

Eleven am Saturday morning

Mr. Patterson called Pastor Perry.

Phone rings.

He got up from the kitchen table to answer the phone. "Hello."

"Good morning. This is Mr. Patterson, Tanya's father."

"Hey, parenting is tough isn't it? Did you get any sleep?"

"We went to bed before three a.m. I wanted to know the truth before we went to bed. Pastor after talking to Tanya, the wife and I decided the girls shouldn't go back to Burger King anymore, especially that one. I want to make sure all of us agree. It makes a difference if we stand together."

"Thus far we're on the same page. I told Ruth the same thing. She wasn't happy initially. She began to understand before she went to bed. Even if she didn't it's my responsibility to protect my daughter."

Mr. Patterson put his cup of coffee down on the kitchen table. "You're so right. We should call the other parents too. McDonald's sounds good no more Burger King."

Mr. Perry put some cheerios in his mouth. " I'll call the Johnsons, Walkers, and the Snows. You call the others. Let's do that today."

"Sounds like a plan. I'll call them today."

* * *

Mr. Perry called Mr. Snow. The phone rang.

"Hello," Mr. Snow said as he ran to answer the phone.

"Hello!" this is Pastor Perry, "How are you this evening?"

"I'm great considering our incident last night. These teenage or adolescent years are something."

"Our girls seem to be targets lately by some girls in the subdivision down the street. The parents agree that they need to stay away from Burger King for a while."

"That makes sense, from my understanding that's the hangout."

"We're telling them to go to McDonald's."

"I'll tell my daughter. I need to talk to her about some other stuff. I'll include this. I'm glad everyone is on the same page. Thanks Pastor Perry, let me know the updates."

"You're welcome. I'll keep you posted. Good-bye!"

"Good-bye! See you on Sunday."

Nine

The Bullying has to Stop

Ten minutes are left on their lunch break. The girls are gathered at Rachel's locker.

Ellen is running and almost out of breath. "Rachel what's up?"

"My friends I need to know if you will be my models for some tops, I'm making for a fashion show in a couple of months. I need your commitment before I enter the contest."

"Do we have to rehearse?" Patricia asked.

"There are two rehearsals. I'm paying for everything." Rachel replied.

"Count me in." Patricia said.

"Me too!" Marion said.

"Thanks. I'll give you more details soon. I appreciate you, you always come through. I guess we'd better go, don't want to be late for class. Later my friends."

"See you later!" everyone said

Everyone's class was toward the east side of the school. Rachel had to go west to her class. She was minding her own business.

Adrienne, a fellow classmate mumbled to her friends Hope, London, Holly, and Chelsea. "Here she comes. Rachel is her name; she's one of those girls.

Kimberly and Terri told us about those girls."

Hope sticks her foot out in her pathway. Rachel tripped and fell on the concrete walkway.

Adrienne began hitting her in the back. "This will teach you to leave my friends Kimberly and Terri alone."

Hope started pulling hair. "You won't be cute anymore once I pull all of your hair out."

She started screaming as loud as she could. "Stop it! Let me up!" No one came to her rescue. This hallway is in a dead-end corner, not that much traffic even though the gym is near, everyone uses the door on the opposite side of the gym.

London and Chelsea kicked her all over her body.

"Let's stop now; we're going to be late for class. We'll get some more of her this evening. We can ride her bus this evening to do more damage." Adrienne said. "Let's go before someone comes."

She couldn't move, laying helplessly on the concrete sidewalk.

Bobby opened the side door to the gym, which is directly across from her class. Larry just happened to be right behind him. "Larry look over there in the hallway it looks like someone is dead, looks like Rachel I hope not. That would be awful. I can tell by her long black hair. Come on let's go check it out."

"What happened?" Larry asked as he ran to see what's going on.

Bobby touches her. " Are you okay? Can you move?"

"Let's get her up Bobby?"

"Guys I'm alright. Just help me up. I hurt a little."

"Who did this to you?" Bobby asked.

"I think they're friends with Kimberly and Terri. I've seen them together on several occasions. I believe one of them is pregnant. Her stomach is really big and round."

"That's strange. Girls, you all are strange. Can you walk?" Bobby asked.

"Don't you need to go to the nurse's office?" Larry asked.

"These thick jeans saved me. I hope I still have hair."

"Girl, you still have plenty of beautiful hair. You want us to help you to your class. You're going to make a report of this correct?" Bobby asked.

"Yes, I'll make a report. Thanks guys." *I really don't want to file a report. There might be repercussions.*

She walked slowly into her classroom. The guys watched her for a second to confirm she can walk.

* * *

The End of the School Day

The girls headed towards the bus.

"I'm not riding the bus today. My mother and I are going to run a couple of errands." Ruth said.

"Ok!" they said in unison. They continued to head towards the bus.

Rachel glanced at their bus and saw who was getting on it. "Ruth, ask your mother can I go with you this evening. It's an emergency. I'll tell you about it when I get in the car."

She motioned her to come. "Is everything alright? Of course, you can ride. Come on let's tell my mom."

Rachel looked rather shaken up. "I'm coming." She turned to her other friends

"I 'm not riding the bus. I have an emergency. I'll tell you about it tomorrow."

They entered the car

"Mom, Rachel needs a ride home. She said it's an emergency."

"Sure, what's going on?" Ruth's mom asked as she started the car.

"Some girls beat me up today. I don't know their names. I do know one of them is pregnant. I just saw them get on our bus. One thing I do know is they don't live in the Woods. I don't feel like fighting this evening. Bobby and Larry found me lying in the hallway."

"What?" Ruth screamed.

"Thank God you're okay. Please report them. I'll call your parents once we get to our first stop." Ruth's mom said.

" It happened right after we talked at lunch."

"Oh my, you're the only one that has a class over on that end. They're so wrong."

"They're vicious. They kicked me and pulled my hair."

"People can be so cruel. You deserve to be treated special today. How about a Wendy's hamburger and fries?" Ruth's mom said.

"Thanks Mrs. Perry. I appreciate it."

"There's a payphone at this Exxon gas station I'm stopping at. You all stay in the car. The service attendant will put gas in the car. I'm going to call your parents. I'll be back."

She makes the call, but no one answers.

Mrs. Perry walks back to the car. "No one answered the phone. We probably should try to get home sooner."

"Mrs. Perry, I forgot to tell you they have a networking event this evening. They told me they wouldn't make it home until nine pm."

"I don't want them to worry about you." Mrs. Perry said.

"They know I'm pretty responsible."

"As a parent I'll make sure your parents know you were with me. We can go into Wendy's after I try to call again. You girls go ahead and place your orders; here is twenty dollars. Order me a number two with a coke."

* * *

The girls went into Wendy's. Mrs. Perry made the call, no answer, and she came into Wendy's soon after that.

Inside Wendy's, everyone's seated

Mrs. Perry ate on her sandwich. "Now tell me about this fight."

"The only thing I know is they hang around these girls named Kimberly and Terri. While they were beating my they kept saying I think I'm cute. It's the third week of school, I don't know these girls, especially a pregnant girl."

"These girls are trouble. Stay away from them. I had a similar problem when I was your age. Make sure you tell your mom and the proper authorities at school. That's what I did. It made a difference, they left me alone."

"They did."

"I had to let them know, they weren't going to run over me."

"I guess I can't be scared."

"Don't be scared, you have to report these bullies!"

"Thanks Mrs. Perry."

* * *

Rachel made it home safe. By the time her parents made it home she was sound asleep.

She woke up at midnight to go to the bathroom.

The Next Day at School-Its Lunchtime

Tanya drank a sip of milk. "Rachel, what's going on? You were acting strange when we were heading towards the bus yesterday. The next thing we knew you were catching a ride with Ruth."

Sally took a bite of her cookie. "What happened?"

"I don't know what's going on. I had a fight with some girls yesterday. I know they hang around Kimberly and Terri. After lunch one of them tripped me, I fell, and they kept hitting me, kicking me, and pulling my hair. They left me lying there. Bobby and Larry helped me up. Yesterday after school, they got on our bus. I didn't feel like getting hit any more. Did you notice some new people on the bus?"

"I did. They sat on the back seat of the bus. And they got off at our stop and then started walking towards the next subdivision. They looked suspicious. I had no idea all that had happened." Ellen said.

"Was it four of them?"

"Yes, it was." Ellen responded.

Patricia began to get up. "We can walk you to your class. I hate that you're on other the side of the school. We can get you there early and then we can go to our classes."

"There's safety in numbers." Marion said.

"My friends, that's so thoughtful and sweet. It's not necessary."

"I think you'd better let your pride down and let us walk you to your class." Ruth said.

"I'm not being proud. I just don't think it's necessary."

"Are you sure?" Marion asked.

"Yes!"

The bell rings for everyone to head to their fourth period class.

"Bye!" Rachel said.

"Bye!" everyone said.

"Be safe!" Ruth said.

Everyone headed to their class.

Rachel thought to herself. *Whew! I passed the place the fight happened yesterday. I don't see a sign of them. I'm going down the steps to my class. Oh no, there they're coming towards me.*

Adrienne and Chelsea pushed her up against the locker. They pushed her so hard it made a loud noise. I'm surprised no one came running to see what's going on.

"We got her in the perfect position to beat her up." Adrienne said. "I'll get my share in after you do some damage."

She started thinking about what she should do. I sure hate to kick this pregnant woman, but since she's stupid enough to fight me. I'm stupid enough to kick her to get her off me. Lord give me strength.

Rachel kicked Chelsea so hard she fell and then ran to her class. She ran so fast she almost knocked a couple of classmates down.

"What are you running from?" Mr. Clay asked. "Is someone chasing you?"

"I need some intervention Mr. Clay. I need to tell you now before class start."

By this time Adrienne and Chelsea were standing outside the class watching and waiting.

"Mr. Clay if you can look in the hallway without being obvious. Those two girls have been fighting me since yesterday. One is pregnant, her name is Chelsea. And the other is Adrienne. Yesterday it was four of them. They tripped me, and I fell. They kicked me, pulled my hair. They followed me home, they rode my bus yesterday. Today, they had me up against the locker."

"Don't worry. I'll handle this during fifth period. I'll see to it that Adrienne and Chelsea are reprimanded."

"Thanks Mr. Clay."

"You're welcome. It's taken care of. Stay focused on what you need to do."

"I appreciate you Mr. Clay."

Mr. Clay was true to his word. Adrienne and Chelsea were suspended for a week.

Later that evening

Rachel called Ruth. The phone rings.

The phone was sitting on the cherry finished nightstand in her bedroom and she answered it rather fast. "Hello!"

"I'm calling to tell you Mr. Clay took care of those girls. He made sure they're suspended."

"That's a relief."

"You tell me, I'm relieved."

"I know you are, are you coming to the game tomorrow?"

"Yes, I'll be there. See you there."

"Yes, it'll be big fun."

Ten

That's not my Baby

Patricia and one of her classmates, Bryan are at the Holiday Inn, in downtown Cedar Lake. They've known each other since elementary school. They walked into their room at the hotel. Her parents are out of town.

Bryan turns the TV on. "Are you hungry?"

"I am. What about some pizza?"

"Great I can order it and they'll deliver it. You like supreme."

"Sounds good. I'm going to watch this movie."

"I'll order the pizza." Bryan walks over to the phone and starts ordering the pizza.

A few minutes later

"The pizza will be here in thirty minutes. I guess we can relax and watch TV."

"This movie is good. I don't know the name of it."

Bryan decides to lie down in the bed to watch TV. Patricia is seated at the edge of the bed.

Bryan thought to *himself I don't why she's sitting down there. We didn't come here to sit. I know she's not that naive. I'll let her slide but after the pizza comes*

52

and we eat, it'll be let's get it on time. "This movie is pretty good, after I eat my pizza, I'm going to take my shower, what about you?"

"I'll probably take my shower too!"

They continued to watch TV. The pizza came. Of course, it was good.

Approximately one hour later

"Come take a shower with me." Bryan said.

"No, I'm not ready for that."

"What do you mean?"

"A shower shows everything."

"You don't want me to see you in the light! I'll let you have that one. You know we've been knowing each other for ever."

I know. You take your shower, then I'll take mine."

Thirty minutes later

They were in the bed watching TV soon after she had taken her shower.

The kissing had begun. Patricia was enjoying it and not stopping him. It went from one thing to another. She had sex with Bryan like it was nothing.

"Bryan it feels so good!"

"Thanks baby!" Bryan said as he kept making love to her.

She was moaning and groaning. They made love all night long.

They fell asleep at two am.

This is something else. They forgot the word of God says, it is good for a man not to touch a woman. They both act like they never read the word before.

Following week at school

Bryan is cordial but, all the long night conversations they had, were long gone. He acted like she didn't exist anymore. There are only three or four words exchanged between them when they see each other. What a drastic change? Patricia is hurt and now she wants to repent for hanging out with Bryan and having sex.

Lunchtime in the school cafeteria

Patricia walked up to Bryan. "Hey Bryan, how are you doing today?"

Bryan smiled in a surprised way. "Hello how are you doing?"

"I'm fine. I've called you twice and both times we've talked for less than a minute. You promised you would call back, but you haven't. What's going on?"

"Nothing my dear. I apologize. I've been a little busy. I promise I'll make it up to you!"

"You've been acting strange since that night."

"No, I haven't. It's just your imagination. Babe, I do have to meet a couple of people I'll call you tonight."

Bryan didn't wait for her to answer. Her face looked like she was extremely disappointed. *This is the guy I had sex with, I betcha I'll learn to obey God's word from now on. That'll never happen again.*

* * *

Patricia stayed close to the phone.

She kept looking at the phone while doing her homework, 8 pm, 9 pm, 10 pm no call. *Patricia thought to herself. I knew he was lying. I shouldn't have had sex with him. I knew better. Lord forgive me for having sex with Bryan. I feel so bad. Lord I'm so sorry. God please forgive me.*

Praying to God gave her peace and it helped her fall asleep.

The next day at school

I believe he's hiding from me. No sign of him at all. Is he dodging me? I'm so hurt. Don't know what I'm going to do. Lord help me.

Days went by. No word from Bryan.

* * *

Sixty Days later

Patricia raised up from her sleep like something scared her. I haven't had my period in three months. I know I'm irregular. I hope I'm not pregnant. I must get a test today after school. Oh Lord, I can't be pregnant!

8 hours later

Oh Lord let me run in this bathroom and start this pregnancy test. I'll wait five minutes to make sure it's ready.

Five minutes passed.

"Jesus I'm pregnant! I hope no one heard me! Oh Lord help me!"

Patricia begins weeping uncontrollably, it continued all through the night.

The next morning

Patricia called Bryan from her mother's phone line.

"Hello!" said Bryan.

"Bryan I'm pregnant with your baby!"

"This is no way to greet people in the morning time no hello or good morning." Bryan said.

"I did it because the last few times we talked I say one sentence and you're off the phone. And you haven't called. You got my cookies and just left me alone. I'm pregnant with your baby."

"You're mistaken that's not my baby! That's some other dude's baby." Bryan said.

"No, you're mistaken you're the only guy I've slept with. You know you're the first." *But it doesn't feel like he's the first. Thanks to my nasty uncle.*

"You've got me mixed up with someone else. I have to go." Bryan said as he hung up the phone.

Patricia just looked at the phone in disbelief. "The nerve of him to just hang up the phone." I can't have this baby I'm still in high school. How I wish I could take that night at the hotel back. How can he treat me like this? I'm so hurt." Tears rolled down her eyes.

The Following Week

She did the unthinkable thing this Monday morning. The baby is gone. The baby is not alive. Oh My!

Lord help me. I can't stop crying. I keep crying day and night. My eyes are red. I wear sunglasses. Bryan is nowhere in sight. It's like he's a ghost.

Eleven

Diane's Senior Year

* * *

Diane runs into the kitchen to talk to her parents. "Mom, Dad, I got accepted to Purdue University! I really want to go to Purdue. It's close to your sister's house, and the engineering degree they have to offer is what I really want."

"Are you sure?" asked her Mom.

Her Dad smiled and reached out to hug her. "I believe Purdue's tuition is somewhat cheaper than MIT. I want you to be happy. Your college fund and your scholarships should take care of everything."

Her mother reached out to hug her. "We're so proud of you."

"Thanks, Mom. Thanks, Dad. I'm going to call my friends and tell them the latest news."

"My baby girl is growing up!" her father said.

"Goodnight!" She hugged both of them and ran to her bedroom to call Ruth.

She dialed the number. The phone rung.

"Hello!" Ruth answered.

"I've been accepted to Purdue University." she said.

"Congratulations. I'll miss you."

"Thanks, my graduation is approaching fast! I'm elated. I couldn't wait until tomorrow. I'll call Sally. I know she's home. Love you!"

"Love you, too! Good -bye!"

She dialed Sally's number. Mrs. Perez answered the phone. "Hello!"

"Hi, Mrs. Perez, this is Diane. May I speak with Sally? I won't keep her long. I just want to tell her I was accepted to Purdue University."

"Congratulations! Hold on. Diane is on the phone."

Sally who was already sweating from cleaning up, she rushed to pick up the phone, barely missing a fall. "What's going on?"

"Girl, I was accepted to Purdue University!"

"Congratulations! You deserve it!"

"Thanks, I'm going to miss you."

"I'll miss you too. We knew the time was coming but it came so fast."

'Yes, it has, too fast. I'm not going to hold you. I just wanted to tell you. We'll talk later!"

"Later!"

She could not contain herself so she called Fred.

"Hey baby, how was practice?"

"It was very productive. I'm tired."

"I'm not going to hold you, sweetie. I was accepted to Purdue University. This is the school I have always wanted to attend."

"I know. Congratulations honey. I'm so proud of you. I don't know what college I'll go to. Ohio State was number one in football last year. They're looking at me. I might get a full scholarship. We wouldn't be too far from each other. I wouldn't mind being an Ohio Buckeye."

"I think the universities are six hours from each other."

" I do want us to be a couple after we leave high school. One day I hope to marry you. I think we have a lot in common. We both want to travel, we both like people, we're ambitious. Our backgrounds are similar."

"I feel the same way, babe. We have similar aspirations. I think we'll make a perfect couple."

"We'll get married after we finish college, or maybe our senior year. I've got nothing but love for you."

"That's wonderful. Let's get through high school. Are you excited about the prom?"

"Of course, I'll be in my baby's arms!"

Honey, you know how to say the right thing. I love you for that."

"I love you too!"

"Talk to you later!"

"Later!"

My sister and her friends have grown up fast. It's almost time for all of them to separate. Diane, my sister is the first to go. I'm going to miss my sister. We're close even, I know it doesn't seem like it because or her friends. But we are.

* * *

Prom Night

The theme for the prom "Stay connected: Love Will Keep Us Together."

" I love this song by Rod Stewart. What's the name of it?"

"Honey, it's 'Tonight's the Night."

"Perfect song!"

" Let's dance. I can't believe we're going to be separated. You'll have come to our dances especially homecoming at Ohio State. I'll come to yours; I hope they aren't on the same weekend. What am I talking about? If we have a football game, I won't be able to come to yours."

"I guess we'll be making some sacrifices."

"That's what you do when you love and care for someone."

"You got that right!"

They continued to dance. The DJ played "I Just Want to Be Your Everything."

by Andy Gibb.

They were slow dancing. They danced for about thirty minutes.

Fred looked into her bright brown beautiful eyes. "Let's get some punch." They walked off the dance floor together holding hands.

He reached for the silver ladle to scoop the punch in the matching cups.

"Thanks honey, it never fails you're the perfect gentleman."

"To be a gentleman to you is what I desire to always be to you, my queen."

They sat down at a table to finish their drink. They sat through a couple of songs while watching their classmates have a great time.

"The prom committee gets an a plus on superb decorating, awesome music, great tasting food that is laid out to fit kings and queens. This night will be a memory I"ll replay over and over."

"Its obvious they were insistent on paying attention to every intricate detail for tonight to be perfect for us."

" Its truly a display of perfection. That's our song. We have to dance."

"Let's go we must dance the night away."

She began speaking as she continued to dance. "Listen to those lyrics its truly our song and it talks about the qualities and events of our storybook romance, that's truly a miracle."

"Yes, like you said we'll have great memories. Let's dance the night away."

About an hour later after dancing through at least five songs and drinking more punch to cool off.

He grabbed her soft arm and headed towards the exit. "Let's go."

The prom is truly jumping and hot right now. You're trying to leave while the party is hot!"

"It will be over in less than thirty minutes."

They waved at a few classmates. They leave the prom in his Mustang. He had plans for the rest of the night. In his slick subtle controlling way he manged to drive off with his girl in his spotless powerful Mustang.

"I'm going to drive us to Atlanta to have dinner at this hotel. It's about an hour away."

"Don't drive me to Atlanta. Dinner at midnight? I want to go home. I don't know what's gotten into you. My parents didn't say I can go to Atlanta tonight. Take me home!"

Looking very disgusted and mad, he turned the car around and headed toward their homes. The fifteen-minute drive was filled with silence. It seemed like the longest uncomfortable ride they had ever taken.

When they arrived, she jumped out of the car. She walked up the sidewalk tears rolling down her face.

He got out the car and runs to catch her. " Slow down. I'm sorry."

"Good night."

He's standing on the sidewalk. *Boy did I mess up tonight.*

She went into the house without looking at him.

Looking so lost and confused, he stood on the sidewalk thinking. Should I knock on the door? No, I'd better go home. Her parents will want to know what's going on. She's not going to see me and she's very mad at me. Yes, I have messed up.

Full of despair and regrets, he walked slowly to his car hoping she would come back outside. She didn't. He drove off wishing he could erase the last thirty minutes of his stupid decisions.

While tears moved down her smooth brown skin, she watched him drive off. Not many seconds later she dashed up stairs just like a quiet mouse. The goal was not to disturb anyone. She sobbed on her pillow.

Diane woke Brenda up. *As much as she's trying to be quiet, I hear her sobbing.* "I need to check on my sister."

Brenda got out of her bed to check on her sister.

Brenda opens the door to her sister's bedroom. "Are you okay?" Brenda came in the room.

"I'm okay."

"You don't sound okay. I can hear you through the walls."

Diane sits up. "I'm just disappointed in Fred. He started driving me to Atlanta to a hotel to supposedly have dinner at midnight. I told him to take me home. He apologized. I'm just hurt and disappointed."

"Sounds strange. Who drives to a hotel in Atlanta to have dinner at midnight? He's making me mad. "He's acting like a jerk. Did you break up?"

"No."

I grabbed her hand. " I hope you all can get through this."

Diane yawned. "I hope so. I guess we'd better go to bed. Maybe I can sleep this off. Bren, I don't want to talk to him for the rest of the weekend. I don't want to talk to anyone. Tell them I'm busy studying for my finals, which is true."

I leaned over and kissed my sister. "Are you sure?"

"I'll wait to tell them about my escapade with him. But I'm not ready."

"Now go to bed and rest. This too shall pass. I love you, sis." I headed towards the door.

"Thanks, sis. I love you too."

* * *

The next day

Its noon time on a hot, beautiful day. He called her all weekend. I'm glad we have a separate phone—those calls would have gotten on our parents' nerves. I checked on my sister, she did spend the day studying. She stayed in her room all day.

* * *

She hasn't come out of her room all weekend.

"Diane, how are you?" her sister asked.

"I'm okay. I got a lot accomplished."

" Your persistent and determined boyfriend has dialed our number seven times today. Please call him back. I'm tired of talking to him. All your friends have called more than once. Remember you have seven friends, and each one has called at least twice. Our phone sounds like a call center. Ring, ring, ring, ring,"

"Don't answer the phone. I don't want to talk to anyone until tomorrow."

"If anyone calls, I'll tell them you're not available."

"Thanks Brenda."

Brenda walks out of her sisters room shaking her head.

* * *

On Monday morning we avoided our friends by going in the side entrance.
I didn't see my sister until after lunch.

"Brenda here he comes. I've dodged him all day."

"Oh no, what she we do?"

"Nothing he's real close."

Fred hugged them. Diane was hesitant to give out any hugs. "Hello girls."

"Hello."

"Honey, we need to talk. Don't run from me. You can't run forever."

The girls showed up, just in time.

Everyone said hello to each other.

"Diane!" Marion yelled.

"Why have you been avoiding us?" asked Ruth.

He observed conversations everyone is talking at the same time. *Wow as I glance at her friends its obvious I'm not the only one in trouble or being ignored by my baby. She's ignoring everyone.* "Honey, I have to go, I'll get with you this evening. Later young ladies." He walked away.

Patricia stared at him as he left. "What's going on?"

"I called you three times this weekend," explained Marion.

"We need to talk to you," Ellen said. "We'll come by your house this evening."

"Not this evening. Maybe tomorrow."

"Why not?" asked Sally.

"Not a good time. Trust me," replied Diane.

"Oh!" Patricia said.

"No time for your girls?" Rachel asked.

"I'll get with you later this week. Brenda let's go," She said.

* * *

63

After school, Diane went home and put on some shorts, trying to relax before Fred arrived.

When the doorbell rang, I opened the door and seated him in the den.

She came down after five long minutes dressed in jeans and a t-shirt wearing house shoes. When she entered the room, anger displayed all over her face, she plopped down on the sofa. "Hello."

They stood and gave each other hugs. Her hug was a very loose hug. The tension is in the air, they're seated on opposite ends of the sofa.

"I know you're mad at me and you have every right to be."

Looking out the corner of her eyes. "I am. I'm disappointed in you."

"I wasn't thinking. The prom is special to a female. My sister had to explain to me what women think about proms, weddings, and special occasions. I just know I messed up. Sweetheart, do you forgive me?"

"To attempt to take my virginity any night without permission isn't the right night. Yes, you messed up; it put a damper on the night. Its a night we ladies dream about." "What do I need to do to make it right?"

"I'm so disappointed in you. Of course, I want to have sex with you, but within the confounds of marriage. I know waiting until you're married is not common these days. I want to do it the way God wants me to. I thought you did too."

He slid very cautiously and very slowly towards her. Movement or eye contact wasn't on her mind.

"I do want to wait, I just got carried away. Baby, the last thing I want to do is disrespect you."

She turned around and looked him in the eye. You need to pray, those dreams and desires come to me. I pray, and they go away. It has happened more than once. At times I wanted to say let's try it. I prefer to be obedient to God."

He stared at her with disbelief. "Really?"

"Yes, believe it my dear."

"Thanks for being real and sharing your innermost thoughts, struggles, and desires. Do you forgive me?"

"Yes, I forgive you"

"I'm glad. I love you."

"I love you."

"Why don't you stay over and watch Poseidon Adventure with me? I finished all my exams today."

"Me too. You want to order some pizza?"

"I like supreme!"

"You think Brenda and your parents want some?"

"They might. I know Mom said she would show some houses this evening. Not sure where Dad is."

"Two large pizzas should be enough. Is Pizza Hut okay?"

"Yep!"

"Call Brenda down."

"Brenda, come watch a movie and have pizza with us! We're ordering it right now, you like meat lovers and supreme right?"

It's so thoughtful of them to include me. "Yes, I do. I'll be down in a few minutes."

"Fred is on the phone ordering the pizza now."

* * *

Mom and Dad pulled in the driveway just as the pizza man was leaving.

Mr. Johnson entered the house talking loudly. "Hey! I can smell the pepperoni and sausage on the pizza, its enticing. I know you have enough pizza for us. We're dog tired. What's that you're watching on TV?"

"Poseidon Adventure, Dad. Come watch it with us. It's enough pizza for everyone."

They joined us in the den.

Mrs. Johnson grabbed a napkin and a slice of pizza. "Thanks for ordering pizza, I appreciate not having to cook." Mrs. Johnson said.

He responded with a big wad of pizza in his mouth. "You're welcome."

Mr. Johnson grabbed a slice and started putting it in his mouth." Thank you, Lord, for this food, let it be nourishment to our bodies in Jesus name." He takes a bite. "Mm mmmm good!"

65

"Dad is it good?"

Dad grabbed another slice of pizza. "Yes, honey. But I need to say this, the two of you are getting ready to embark on a new season of life. Fred, you're such a gentleman. I wish you much success."

"Thanks, Mr. Johnson. You've been a positive influence in my life. I appreciate you. Even if I wasn't dating your daughter, I would say the same thing."

She looked at Fred and then her father. "Enough of all that mushy stuff."

"No, you have a wise father that I respect. He walks in integrity. We've had conversations about you. To be honest I admire him. He's like a role model."

"You still pouring it on."

Mr. Johnson smiled. "Don't stop him. I appreciate all your kind words."

"Thanks sir."

Brenda began speaking. "I'm going to miss my sister."

"I'm going to miss you too!"

"Ugh let's change the subject. It's getting a little mushy!" Mrs. Johnson said.

Mr. Johnson said. "My darling daughter you'll be missed."

The night turned out to be filled with great conversation and plenty of laughter. Memories were created.

* * *

Two weeks later

<u>Graduation Night</u>

After her graduation, our family invited Fred and a bunch of their friends to a party at the club house for a late dinner to celebrate. Mom greeted Fred and his parents as they arrived.

"Thanks for inviting us, that's so considerate of you. Here's a gift for Diane." Mrs. Williams handed Mom a wrapped box.

"Well, thanks. And the party wouldn't be complete if you weren't here. Diane will appreciate this."

"Come on in, have a seat," Dad said. "Does anyone want anything to drink? We'll have a toast for all the graduates as soon as the other guys get here."

"They should be here in a minute." Fred said.

Sean, Patrick, and Bob walked in with their graduation hats on their head. "We made it. Its official! "

"Yes, we did!" Fred yelled as he welcomed his friends in.

Diane walked down the hallway of the clubhouse, wearing a beautiful purple sun dress The dress looked good on her brown skin tone. Her thick brown hair was in one pony tail. "Hello, we did it we're graduates!"

"Yes, we did," said Bob.

Dad enters the room. "Congratulations graduates! Let's eat. We need to pray over our food. Dear Father, who sits high and looks low, we thank you for all the graduates. I ask that you continue to watch over them as they begin a new phase of their lives. Lead and guide them every day. Let them be a success in their new endeavors. We want to thank you for this food we are about to receive. Let it be nourishment to our bodies. In Jesus' name, Amen."

"Get as much as you want," Mom said. "There are grilled hamburgers, chicken, steak, hot dogs, baked potatoes, salad, and corn on the cob, baked beans, and slaw. Just make yourself at home."

Bob rubbed his stomach. "I'm so hungry, I could eat a house."

Fred licked his lips. "Me too!"

Everyone grabbed and gathered their food. That didn't take long. I believe everyone was starving.

Patricia put a piece of steak in her mouth. "The food must be good. There is silence, the only thing you can hear is chewing and the silverware hitting their plates."

Diane finished drinking a sip of tea. "Yes, mom and dad you put your foot in this food. Thanks for the party for me and my friends. I love you!"

"We love you! You're welcome." Her parents said.

Fred stood up. "I hate to break the quietness, I know the food is good, but I need to do something and I need everyone's attention." He turned to her and handed her a box.

"It's a small white box. What are you up to?" Her eyes get big.

Anxious and ready he grabbed her smooth soft hand. "Diane, will you

67

marry me?"

"Fred, yes I'll marry you."

He kissed her on the cheek.

She blushed and smiled like a little girl. "Babe you caught me by surprise."

Fred chuckled as he stared at his fiance. "That was my goal!"

She began to stare into his eyes. "Well, you succeeded!"

Everyone was overjoyed. "Oh!"

"Ahhh!" Ruth smiled.

"My baby girl will be getting married soon. I'm happy for her, but this might be a little too soon." Mom said.

"Mr. and Mrs. Johnson, I know she's the girl for me. I don't want to lose her. I'm letting everyone know. She's my girl and I love her."

Her father said, "I've observed you over the years and have admired your maturity. I believe you'll do right by her. Any other guy I would say, it's too soon to talk about marriage."

"Thanks for your kind words. I don't want to live my life with the regret of missing out on my blessing. I see what God is doing in my life."

"Dad, we're not going to rush the wedding."

Mr. Johnson nodded. "We'll trust God's timing."

Fred said, "I don't know how we're going to do it. I believe we can make it. We can get married in a year or so. I do know I want to spend the rest of my life with you. Here's another gift." He handed her an envelope.

She ripped it open and started reading the paper inside. "You're going to Purdue! You're going to play football for Purdue. Oh, what a night! I'm so happy." She reaches out to hug her man.

Mr. Johnson got up and shook his hand and would not let go of it. "Well, well, well!" That's divine. You can watch out for my baby girl!"

Mrs. Johnson chimed in. "Only thing I have to say is God is good!"

"Congratulations, you two," said Patricia.

"Congratulations," said Marion.

"Thanks everyone!" They said in unison.

"I appreciate you honey. Thanks for everything you do. I thank God for you. We can make it because we know that with God all things are possible."

He grabbed her slender small waist. "You're so right. "We have to trust in God."

"We do!" She smiled at him. "We'll talk some more later. Everyone eat up my parents cooked enough food for an army."

Twelve

Making Sweet Sweet Memories

Tuesday evening the first week of their senior year

Hey friends it's our senior year. I'm sure ready for it. Diane is experiencing a new life in college, wow, I can't wait."

"Me neither. I'm so excited for them. It's like a dream come true. They're at the same school. They know they want to spend the rest of their lives together. That's amazing." Tanya said.

Marion began speaking. "It's a miracle it's very rare. I guess we must pray for them."

"We do need to pray for them." Ruth responded.

Patricia sarcastically began to speak. "That's automatic, we always pray for our friends. It's doesn't have to be spoken."

"What is wrong with you?"

"It's nothing don't concern yourself." She responded.

Sally's eyes lit up with intentions of changing the subject. "Don't meant to interrupt, you know what we should do? I think as soon as we graduate, we should go on a trip."

Rachel smiled. "That's a great idea. Let's invite Diane—she should be back in Cedar Lake by then."

"How about the beach?" Patricia asked.

70

Tanya nodded her head in agreement. "Excellent idea!"

"Which beach?" asked Ellen.

"Rachel, why don't you organize it? You're great with planning," Marion said.

"I'll be glad to plan it. I think we should go to Tampa. Everyone goes to Orlando and Daytona. Most of us have been to Disney World correct?"

"You're right," Sally declared.

"I want to be in Florida the first week after graduation." Patricia said.

"Me too!" Tanya said.

"I'll start planning it my friends. I might need your help, especially your input as I gather information." Rachel said.

"Of course." The girls said in unison.

"I have to go! I'll see you tomorrow," Patricia waved good-bye.

"I need to leave to! Good-bye!" Sally said.

"Goodbye! "Rachel said. "I guess it's time to go!"

"Good-bye!" The girls said.

* * *

Two months later

Diane came home for Thanksgiving. She was glad to be among her friends and family.

On Thanksgiving Day, she called the girls to meet outside in front of our house.

Sally ran to meet her friend. "Diane!" They ran to each other and hugged.

"I missed being around you my friend. You inspire me."

"Sally, my friend the feeling is mutual."

The other girls came running. They smothered her in hugs.

"I miss you!" Tanya said.

Patricia hugged her. "Welcome home, friend!"

Ellen got her hug in. "You look like a brick house. You haven't gained any weight."

Ruth smiles. "It feels like we're missing a link in our circle since you've been gone to Purdue."

Diane nodded in agreement. "Just think how I feel."

"We're planning a trip next year, the first weekend we're out of school. We want you to come. We're going to the beach," said Sally.

"I'll need a vacation. That will be perfect timing. Keep me posted. "

"We will."

"Let's do lunch tomorrow!" Patricia said.

"I think I might be able to get away, my reason will be Diane is home." Sally said. "I probably have to be home before two hours is up."

"Sally whatever time you can spend with us, we'll be thankful." Diane said.

"Yeah, we just want everyone there tomorrow. Let's keep it simple and go to Cracker Barrel." Ruth said.

Marion began speaking. "We have so much to talk about."

"Yes, we do!" Rachel said as she shivered. "My friends I love you and would love to stay out here and talk. It's 36 degrees. You know I'm cold-natured."

Ellen began talking, she looked as though she's walking in her sleep. "Its cold alright and do you see what I have on? I had to come see you. I'll see you all tomorrow. I'm going to bed. You know I like my beauty rest."

"Bye sleepy head Ellen and cold-natured Rachel. I'll see all of you tomorrow. If you have time today. Call me. Love you my friends!" Diane said.

"We love you too!" Rachel said as she wrapped her scarf around her face.

"Bye!" everyone said

* * *

The next day

Friday was a biting crisp cold winter; the sun was shining bright. The girls met at Cracker Barrel.

Ruth entered the restaurant with a big smile. "Good morning."

"Good morning, sister friend," answered Diane. "You sound like you're energized and ready for shopping."

"I am. Macy's has these black leather boots on sale that I want," she answered.

"They sell quality merchandise and of course the cutest clothes." said Ruth. "Look, our buddies are here."

They waved at them to come to the table.

"How long have you been here?" asked Rachel.

"About fifteen minutes," answered Ruth.

"Hello everyone, I'm glad you made it." said Diane. The girls took their seat.

Rhoda, Sean's new girl is being seated directly across from them. She saw Ellen and snickered. "Hello Ellen." She didn't answer.

Rhoda said out loud for everyone to hear. "She doesn't speak to me, now that I'm dating her ex-boyfriend. Sean dumped her after he got what he wanted."

"Yes, I heard," Rhoda's friend said.

Marion and Rachel looked at each other with a surprised expression.

Marian said. "I like Cedar Lake, but sometimes the small city can be irritating. They have a lot of nerve and loud with their insults."

Rachel said, "Don't look but they keep staring at us. I don't want to eat my breakfast with people staring at me."

"Don't worry about what they're saying. Rhoda thinks Sean is hot stuff. He changes women almost as often as he changes his underwear. She'll find out soon. My brother warned me, and I didn't listen," explained Ellen.

Marion looked at them with disgust. "We'll treat them as invisible. We're not moving."

"Enough of them. Let's talk about our trip," exclaimed Rachel. "Will it be for a week or just the weekend?"

"I think I need a week, just to be lazy," said Ellen.

"Yes, a week will be great!" said Marion with excitement in her voice.

"We can shop there too. I know they have a lot of outlet malls and designer stores in Florida." Ruth said.

"It would be great if I can find a heavy coat today. Its cold up north," Diane responded.

"It's that cold, I can't imagine. I might need to buy a coat. I'm considering Purdue," Patricia explained. "I like everything about it. We'll see how everything pans out."

"Patricia. Let me know if I can help you. I can help with your application and I heard about some scholarships at Purdue, that will fit you perfect."

"Thanks,I'll let you know, Purdue is in the top three of my choices."

"Hey y'all, we'd better order our food, so we can get out of here to catch those deals," Rachel said.

"Have you noticed we ignored our neighbors and they moved?"Sally said. Ellen chuckled. "Good riddance!"

"That's what they should've done. No one has time for foolishness!" Diane said. "You girls need to give me the details of all your beaus, potential beaus, and the flirts. I want to know every detail. You've mentioned some of them in your letters, but it's nothing like being in person."

Tanya began to speak, "Are you sure you want to hear the details?"

Diane smiled. "I can't wait!"

Patricia asked. "Tell us about Fred and you. You don't want to hear about our guys. None of us have nothing solid."

"Patricia speak for yourself. We're close but you don't know everything." Rachel said.

"How are you and your fiance doing? I hope everything is great."

"Believe it or not. Everything is going great with Fred and me. I was so nervous at first, I just knew we would break up. But by some miracle it's been sweet as pie." She said, and thought *I'm lying to my friends."*

The waitress walked up. "Hello ladies are you ready to place your orders?"

"Yes, I'm starving!" Ellen said.

Diane thought. *Whew I'm glad the waitress showed up.* "I'm ready too. I want some pancakes and sausage."

"I got that and what would you have today?" The waitress asked as she looked at Patricia.

"I'll have pancakes, bacon, and eggs." Patricia said.

Everyone placed their order and continued talking.

"I need to tell you about my man. Some drama has occurred. I'm so disgusted. Some girls are always coming up to me starting trouble with me." Marion said.

"What are they doing?" asked Rachel.

"First, they acted like they were giving me a real compliment. The next thing out of their mouth is how are you and your beau, Clyde doing? They told me some lies about him kissing another girl in the hall. They just take liberties and ask and say anything to me. I stopped responding to them."

"Wow, you have some busybodies on your hands. Hopefully they'll mind their own business." Tanya said.

"I really like Clyde. He's the first person who has shown me some respect and treated me like a queen. I don't want to mess this up."

"They can't mess up your blessing. Don't worry about them and those lies. Don't listen to that foolishness." Ruth said.

"I'm enjoying my blessing. Trying not to get distracted, if I wasn't a lady, I would fight them," responded Marion.

"You're right if we weren't ladies, we would fight them. Don't believe those girls." Diane said.

"Whatever you do, don't run to him and ask him. If it's something for you to know, you'll find out. I have a guy I like. We're taking it slow." Patricia said.

"Congratulations! I'm excited for you. You deserve to be happy." Rachel said.

"Yes, I'm happy for you!" Diane said.

"Yes, you do! We'll keep you in our prayers!" Ruth said.

"There she goes!" Patricia said. "Our preacher. Just pray don't announce we don't have to know you pray for us all the time. I just do it and don't announce it like you do!"

"I'm just saying I'm going to pray! It's nothing new Patricia."

"You're so right, nothing new! Can't do nothing but love you, but sometimes." Patricia said.

The waitress walked up and interrupted Patricia before she could finish her statement. "Here are your drinks. Your food should be out in a minute."

"May I have some water?" Rachel asked.

"Please bring me some also!" Sally said. "Thank you so much!"

"You're welcome. I'll bring everyone some water. Anything else?" the waitress asked.

"No, thank you!" Tanya said.

"I'll be right back. "the waitress said.

"Marion I'm happy for you! And the rest of you, who are you dating?" Diane asked.

Rachel chuckled. "I have friends no one special."

"Same here!" Ellen said.

"Here we are, be careful ladies these plates are hot!" the waitress said.

The girls were ready to eat. They said their grace and began to chow down and continued catching up with each other. It was a great time.

* * *

<u>Six months later</u>

The prom was at the Hilton Hotel in Cedar Lake. The young ladies rode to the prom in two limousines, that's everyone but Sally. Unfortunately, Marion has broken up with Clyde. The girl's dresses were beautiful, but Ellen had the best-looking dress on, it was royal blue with a train. She looked gorgeous. She wore her hair up which gave her an elegant look. The ballroom had a silver disco ball hanging from the ceiling. The disc jockey played "Good Times" by Chic and "What a Fool Believes" by the Doobie Brothers. Everyone at the prom went down the Soul Train line.

"Man, that was fun," Marion said.

"Yes, it was!" replied her date, Robert. "Let's get something to drink. Did I tell you, you look stunning and so beautiful?"

"No, thanks! You look rather handsome in your tuxedo." Ellen was happy with her date. Finally, someone other than a jock had asked her out.

"Thanks, Ellen."

On the other side of the room, our friends are dancing with Teddy and Tyler to McFadden and Whitehead's "Ain't No Stopping Us Now."

Ruth talked as she continued to dance. "This should be one of our theme songs for life."

"Yes," said Teddy. "The words are motivating."

"Right Teddy, we can't let anyone stop us from doing what we're called to do."

Teddy laughed and began to cut a cool dance step. "You can't tell me I can't dance."

Ruth giggled and continued to have fun with her date as she began to move back and forth doing some dance. "No, I can't! But you can't do this move!"

"Yes I can, watch me!"

"Yes, you got that one on me."

They kept dancing and so did some other classmates. Everyone danced and continued to have fun. Some people were sweating. They were creating memories.

* * *

Outside the main ballroom, they were getting their pictures taken.

Tanya snapped a picture. "Patricia, that's going to be a beautiful picture of you and Roosevelt, the red and white combination you have on makes both of you glow."

They took pictures with their personal cameras.

The photographer motioned the girls to get in position.

They got in position to take pictures. Patricia walked directly behind her. She stepped on Ellen's dress.

"You're standing on the trail of my dress.You're putting your footprints all over it. Get off it, you're ruining my dress."

Patricia looked dumbfounded. " I'm sorry I didn't know I was on your dress. Please forgive me."

Ellen pulled the back of her dress around, to see if it's torn. " You tore my dress with your high heels."

Patricia frowned up. "No, I didn't. Someone else did that."

"No one has stepped on my dress all night. You're the first."

"I'm sorry."

"Come on girls," Tanya motioned. "We're holding the photographer up."

They lined up to take the picture. The photographer made sure the long train was wrapped around to show its beauty.

Marion spoke. "I wish Sally was here. It's just not right without her."

Ellen nodded. "Yeah, me too! And no it isn't, one linking is missing."

"We couldn't force her." Patricia said.

"I want to get a few more young ladies." The photographer said.

The girls took their pictures and danced some more for about two hours.

The last song of the night was "Shake Your Groove Thing" by Peaches and Herb. The balloons dropped from the ceiling at midnight.

They cried and hugged each other. Their emotions have been high all night. They headed towards the door.

Everyone got in the limousine they came in.

The limousine driver of the first car made sure everyone is seated and comfortable. "Ladies and gentlemen, it's about twenty minutes until we get to the after party. There's some sparkling non-alcohol champagne and soft drinks in the mini refrigerator.

Patricia opened the refrigerator. "I'll serve everyone. Tell me what you want."

"Give me something sparkling," Tyler said.

"Coming right up, Rachel what do you want?"

"Give me an orange juice." Rachel answered.

"Ellen and Roosevelt what will you have?"

"Coke," Ellen and Roosevelt said in unison.

Patricia started speaking with a sweet sound. "Jonathan what do you want?"

"I'll have a sprite." Jonathan answered.

Her date received his drink." I think that's everyone."

Patricia got a drink for her. She began opening it up and for some reason she wasn't holding it straight. Jonathan nudged her and down went the drink in Ellen's lap on her beautiful dress.

Ellen became disgusted. "Patricia I'm so sick of you. First you tore a hole in my dress, now this!"

"Johnathan nudged me. It was more of a push and that's how it wasted on your dress. I'm so sorry."

Jonathan began to vouch for Patricia. "I did nudge or push her, maybe a little too hard. It's my fault not hers."

"I guess I'll let her slide, I don't understand how she keeps messing up my dress."

"I hate to admit, but sometimes I can be clumsy. Please forgive me," Patricia said. *I'm a big liar. I want that dress. My friend looks cute in it, and I'm jealous. I need help Lord. I did both incidents on purpose. I used Jonathan as an excuse.*

"I guess I forgive you." Ellen said.

She reached over to hug her. "Thanks my friend."

Ellen thought. Patricia lied. She thinks I'm stupid. I'm going to let everything slide I don't want to mess up our night, even though I know she's acting jealous. I'm a little disappointed in my friend.

Marion held her bottle of sparkling cider. "Let's toast to our future! Much success to everyone!"

"Cheers! Congratulations looks like we made it. I wish all of us the best in the world!"Jonathan said.

Patricia smiling big and wide. "Johnathan that's so sweet of you. Same to you!"

Everyone toasted and congratulated each you.

Everyone made it to the after party safely and continued to have fun. Their curfew was one am. The night ended up being a night of fun and great memories.

* * *

Graduation Night

Diane finished her first year of college with a 4.0. She came home and went backstage to take pictures during graduation.

The girls came towards her. "Come on, Marion and Tanya, we need the both of you in the picture. It's not complete without the two of you."

"Here we come," replied Marion.

"Hurry up!" said Sally. The girls got in position to take the picture. She held the camera steady. "Everyone say New beginnings!"

"New beginnings!" yelled the girls.

"It's our year!" proclaimed Ruth.

They took quite a few pictures.

"It's time to go. They're lining up," said Tanya.

"We'll see you later at the party," said Rachel.

***

They lined up and received their diplomas as "Pomp and Circumstance" played. All of the girls received scholarships and were Summa Cum Laude graduates.

After the ceremony, they all went to The Woods clubhouse. A lot of their neighbors and friends were there waiting for them. The song "Looks Like We Made It" by Barry Manilow played.

The girls of Cedar Lake walked in and hugged everyone. You couldn't hear yourself talk.

"Congratulations, Tanya," said Mrs. Perez, Sally's mother.

Tanya gloating. "Thanks."

"You're welcome!" said Mrs. Perez.

Sally tried to hug her mom. "Mom thanks for letting me come to the graduation party."

Her mom wouldn't let Sally hug her. "You can't stay long. We'll be leaving in a few minutes."

Sally looks at her mom with disgust. *She gets on my nerves.*

Patricia walked up to Sally just in time. "Sally come on we're taking a picture by the fireplace."

"That's a great place to take a picture." Sally said.

The girls lined up by the fireplace, holding their diplomas in their hands.

"Say, we did it!" Mr. Perry said.

"We did it!" They yelled.

Everyone was having a great time mingling. Pictures were taken all over the place. The food table was a beautiful display . They sat down at a table reminiscing. Everyone kept telling them congratulation. The noise level was at an all-time high. So much laughter and some tears in the room.

Sally saw her mother heading for the door. "Girls, I have to go."

"Oh, no." The girls said.

"Yes, but do you see my mother over there at the door holding her purse looking at me. That's my cue to let me know it's time to go."

Ruth nodded. "You must have something to do early in the morning."

"Why are you leaving so early," Rachel asked.

"No, we don't have anything to do. I can't explain my mother. She gets on my nerves. I try to honor her, so my days will be long. Pray for me. I gotta go before she gets mad."

Ellen finished chewing on some crackers. "Sally doesn't get a chance to have that much fun. It's kind of sad."

Tanya interjected. "I think we'd better stay out of that household. We need to pray. She gets to do some things; remember she goes to the games. Let's stop talking about Mrs. Perez and Sally."

"Something isn't right." Rachel said as she drunk some punch.

"We're just concerned." Tanya said.

"We should pray. We can't control that situation." Marion said.

"Let's enjoy today for Sally and for ourselves. I feel like dancing." Patricia said.

"Yes!" Rachel agreed.

My sister wrote in her diary: Well, my friends are official graduates of Cedar Lake High School. The party was a great success: food, fun, and fellowship. My friends are ready for college. Time for the senior trip.

Thirteen

Florida Here We Come

The girls rented a van. They loaded up and went to pick up Sally. Ruth pulled into Sally's driveway, and everyone crossed their fingers. Ruth honked the horn. Marion had left a message for Sally the previous night. Ellen and Tanya had confirmed with her the week before. The others called her within the last couple of weeks.

The door opened, and Sally stepped out.

"She's coming. I see a suitcase!" Marion said.

"I see it too," said Tanya.

"Oh my God, I can't wait to go on vacation." Rachel said. "I'm glad everyone is going. It wouldn't be the same unless everyone was here." Patricia opened the van door.

"I made it girls." She put her suitcase in back with the others and hopped in the van. "I did extra chores to make sure I could go. I've been walking on egg shells."

"We're glad to see you. I'm glad we all made it!" said Tanya.

Ruth looked at everyone. "Yes, Sally we're glad you're here with us. Everyone please buckle up."

Sally chuckled. "Not as glad as I am."

"The drive is about seven or eight hours, right?" Marion asked.

Patricia put her seat belt on and started getting comfortable. "That's not bad."

Ellen reclined her seat. "I'm glad school is over. I'll miss high school, but I'm ready to move to the next phase of my life."

"Yes we are and I'm excited, said Ruth. I guess we should pray that God will watch over us as we go on this trip. Who wants to pray?"

"Why don't you pray, since you thought about it?" said Tanya.

"Lord, we thank you for this day. We ask that you watch over us as we travel to the Tampa area. We thank you in advance for sending your angels to watch over us. In Jesus name, amen."

"Amen!" they said in unison.

"I think I'm going to sleep. I stayed up late packing last night," Rachel said.

"You're always sleeping," said Patricia.

"Girl, I've got to get my beauty rest in."

"We all do," replied Marion. "That's why we look so great."

Sally looked at her. "Now let's remain modest. You know some of our classmates think we're full of ourselves."

"You know we don't care what they think."Patricia said.

"No we don't. I think I'm going to get some of that beauty rest Rachel is getting," said Marion.

" I'll stay up with you to keep you company," said Diane.

"Cool, we can catch up."

"This is a much needed vacation," she replied.

"Yes, all that studying is no joke!" Ruth replied.

"How far is the drive?"

"According to the map it's about a seven hour drive, not too long and not too short. It gives me a chance to think." Ruth said.

"Yes, we can think and talk. It feels so good to be out of school. And just to be with my girls."

"I hear you my friend. We might have our differences, but we have each other's backs and for the most part there's no competition with each other."

"Yes, for sure! Now that you mentioned that. Ruth I've tried to make new friends outside our group. Every time I try it's a flop. I had a friend that thought it was funny that I didn't make student body president. I looked at her and said if anything you should be saying I'm am sorry you didn't make it. Maybe next time."

"What did she say?"

"Nothing, she just stood there looking weird."

"I guess you said, some friend."

"Yes, I keep her at a distance."

" Something similar happen to me. As you know I have all four years of college paid for. But before I got that scholarship I had been turned down or didn't get a few before. This classmate Michelle laughed when I didn't get a couple of scholarships. It was strange. I said to myself what's funny. This isn't a laughing matter."

"On the note of friendship what's going on between you and Patricia, we've noticed some tension?"

"I've asked Patricia about that and she said there's nothing we need to talk about. It caught me by surprise. "

"I'm glad a conversation has taken place. Everyone has said it happens every time you say you're going to pray, that's when she has something to say to you."

"I hear the two of you talking about me! I have told you it's no big deal but since the both of you are insisting on making an issue of it. Yes, Ruth I have a problem with you, stop announcing you're going to pray just do it, no announcement is necessary." Patricia stated.

" I never thought about that. It never occurred to me that can be irritating. I do apologize! I guess it sounded a like a holier than though person. I apologize Patricia. I will consider that and watch out for that."

"Thanks for considering making the change. I'm going back to sleep. I hope everyone that had something to say, heard this conversation." Patricia said.

"You're welcome!" Ruth said.

Someone was snoring loud.

"They're knocked out. They must be tired. A couple of them are snoring. I can't tell who it is."

"They must be worn out. Changing the subject, what is it like having your man at college with you?"

"We've grown closer. We've had challenges in the beginning. its a miracle we're still together.I was too embarrassed to tell you last Thanksgiving."

"What kind of challenges?"

"Females of course, they would come up to him and kiss him in the mouth. He wouldn't do anything. He looked like he liked it."

"What did you do?"

"I didn't talk to him for days; He called my room I wouldn't answer."

"He thought it was over."

"It was as far as I'm concerned, until God spoke to me and told me I had to forgive him. I returned his call."

"What did he say?"

"He apologized for days. I didn't have any more problems after that."

"He needed to. I know you had to wrap your head around the boldness of those females. I'm glad he got his act together. "

"Me too. I was on my way out."

"Forgiving people is no joke. It's a must if we're going to serve God. He gives us choices."

"I'm glad I chose to forgive and let go."

"I'm glad you did too. God is good."

Ruth turned the music on. They listened to the album Winner Takes All by the Isley Brothers. She kept rewinding to "I Wanna Be with You," "Let's Fall in Love," and "You're the Key to My Heart." It helped the time go by fast.

They talked for hours while the other girls slept through the eight-hour drive to Redington Beach, Florida.

Several Hours Later

"Where are we?" Ellen yawned, trying to wake up.

"Our exit is the next one," replied Ruth.

"I don't believe I slept the whole trip."

"Everyone did except Diane for the most part. She's only been asleep the last thirty minutes."

"Are we there yet?" Rachel asked.

"Yes," replied Ellen. "This is our exit."

"The hotel is on the beach, right?" Patricia asked.

"Yes," answered Ruth.

Tanya began speaking as she yawned. "Thank God we made it safely."

"Yes, thank God. You're a good one. I don't know if I could've driven the whole time. We appreciate you!" Marion said.

"We sure do. And look at this beautiful hotel." Rachel said.

"That it is!" Rachel said as the van pulled into the parking lot.

Inside the Hotel

The hotel lobby was decorated with plants and beautiful fountains. The front desk and walls had a classy cherry finish. They checked in and went up to their rooms.

Rachel walked down the hotel hallway glancing at the numbers on the doors. "Here's our room, Tanya and Sally. Room 1006."

Tanya opened the door. "We have an ocean front view room. Ellen; you're in here with us."

Sally entered the room and maneuvered straight to the window. "The palm trees extend past our room. The water the sand, the view is nice. "

The others peeked in. "Ooooo! Aww!" The girls said

The other girls walked two doors down after looking at their friends' room.

Marion walked at a fast pace. "I guess the rest of us are down the hall."

Their room was in the corner. They opened the door to their room.

Diane walked in. "Very inviting."

Patricia plops on the bed. "Wow, this bed feels comfortable. It feels fluffy and soft."

.

"I think I'm going to change into my bathing suit and swim for a while. Anyone care to join me?" Patricia asked. "I'll be leaving in about fifteen minutes. I'll call the others and ask them."

Ellen walked toward the patio door. " I will. I think I'll sit on the patio and enjoy the breeze and the view until then."

* * *

Everyone agreed to join Patricia. The girls made it to the ocean. The warm, blue-green water felt warm and relaxing.

Patricia put her feet in the ocean. "Oooh, the water temperature is just right, not to hot nor cold!"

Diane tipped toed in the water as if she was scared. "Yes, it does."

"It's beautiful," said Marion, as she glanced ahead. "Girl look at three o'clock. That's a fine specimen over there."

Patricia stared up and down at the guy. It's a wonder he didn't feel the stare. "For sure he's fine."

"He has a six-pack," responded Diane.

" You have a man," said Sally.

"Girl, just because I have a boyfriend doesn't mean I can't look. Just as long as I don't touch and stare."

"Don't look hard, we don't want him to see you," Marion said.

"What are you saying?" asked Diane.

"It means we don't know what he likes, so get out of the way. You're taken," She said.

"Girls, girls, we aren't here to catch a man. But he's good eye candy," Rachel said.

The guy walked by and waved. The girls stared at him as he walked by.

Tanya laid her towel down on the sand. "He's fine and he's gone. Let's sit on the beach under our umbrellas."

Patricia put more suntan lotion on. "I need my tan to get darker. Ruth, I want to be your color."

Ruth laughed. "Much success to you, my friend. Your skin tone is fine like it is. That's the way God made you. Walk in it."

"Don't start!" Patricia said.

"I must. You need to know you're fearfully and wonderfully made." Ruth answered.

Patricia began to lay down on her back with her sunglasses on. "Alright, I'll try! Let's just have fun on the beach. The sun feels good."

Diane sat under her umbrella. "Doing nothing is something I don't get to do often. Girls lets enjoy this time. We don't have to rush."

"You're so right!" Tanya said as she sat on her towel with her summer hat on.

***

After about one hour on the beach. "Let's go to the buffet on the hotel patio. My beautiful pecan skin doesn't need a tan. I think I have enough vitamin D for today." said Tanya.

" At least we don't have to worry about waiting on the food," Diane said.

"I guess we need to put our sarongs on." Sally said.

The girls walked toward the hotel, which was less than twenty-five feet away.

They played in the sand with their toes as they walked.

"The sand is soothing!" Patricia said.

"The food smells great and yes the sand is perfect," Ruth said.

Yes, I smell seafood and chicken," Sally said.

Rachel rubbed her stomach. "I'm starving."

"I gotta have some shrimp, scallops, fish, slaw, and potato salad," Marion said.

"Me too," said Ellen.

"We're almost there. I can't wait!" Diane said.

* * *

The girls got their food, said their grace, and started eating their delicious food.

Diane began speaking as she chewed on some chicken. "Hey y'all, did I ask if you still write in your diaries? I write in mine every day."

"Yes, I do," said Marion. "I write about us all the time.

"I do!" replied Tanya. "I write all the time about our friendship. Going to college is going to be scary for me. It's hard for me to make friends. For years I didn't feel like I belonged to our group. When we were in the tenth grade, I finally realized I was worthy of your friendship, but look how long it took

89

me to realize it. I have no friends other than you. Every time I tried to hang with others, I felt out of place, like an oddball."

"We had no idea!"

"None of us knew you felt like that," Ruth said.

"Unfortunately, I'm an expert at hiding the way I feel," Tanya said.

"I see." Sally took a bite of her fish.

Tanya smiled. "It's going to be interesting in college. I hope going to an all-girl's school will be a perfect fit for me. I like Spelman's curriculum. Morehouse is next door, Clark Atlanta, and Morris Brown colleges are nearby."

Diane appeared to be in deep thought. "Just listen to people they'll tell you a lot about themselves. I learned a lot at Purdue, by just listening. I was telling Ruth on the way here, how I've tried to make friends outside our circle. I've had no success."

Ruth was listening intently. "Listening makes plenty of sense. I've had similar experiences Tanya. I'm thankful for you all! God is good. Did we say our grace?"

Tanya chuckled as she ate her fries. " Thanks for sharing. I'm going to listen more."

Rachel laughed. "It's easy for you Tanya you're quiet and reserved. Our Marion is quiet too. It might be challenging for me."

"Me too!" Patricia said.

Diane smiled. "You can do it. People tell on themselves when they talk too much."

"Sounds like you're saying just because they're smiling in your face doesn't mean they're for you." Ellen stated.

"Correct, smiling faces sometimes tell lies." Diane said.

"And my friends, Tanya and I aren't that quiet." Marion said jokingly.

"It's just that we don't need to say anything." Tanya said with a smile.

Everyone laughed and continued talking.

***

On the second day of vacation, Rachel reserved a twelve-passenger pontoon boat for the girls to sail. They made their one o'clock departure, even though they were sleepy.

Rachel approached a man at the dock. "Is Mr. Jack here?"

"I'm Mr. Jack," he answered.

"I have tickets for eight people."

"Great jump on and take a seat." Mr.Jack said.

They began entering the boat.

"I guess it doesn't matter where we sit. We're talking up eight of the twelve seats," Ellen said.

"The tables are pretty long," said Sally.

"Sally, that bathing suit is cute," said Rachel. "I have two new ones and three old ones."

"I hear you, what woman wants to wear the same bathing suit every day?" Patricia said.

Ellen stared at Rachel. "Rachel thinks she's cute in her bathing suit. She's always throwing her hips. She's going to throw them out of socket."

"Why are you watching me?" asked Rachel. "We all have our own walk. I can't help the way I walk."

"No, you put extra in yours."

"Worry about yourself, look at you and leave me alone."

The waitress walked up with pen and paper in hand. Her entrance diffused that conversation. "Hello how are you doing today? May I take your drink orders?"

Diane yawned. "Excuse me. I want some coffee. I need to wake up."

"I'll have some too," said Ruth.

"I want some French fries," Patricia said.

"The breakfast combo," Tanya said.

"I'll have that too," Sally said.

"I'll have the hamburger combo." Marion said.

"Same here." Rachel said.

Thirty minutes later

"Let's say our grace and eat our food. "Sally said.

They finished eating.

The song Why Can't we be friends by War was playing on the radio.

"I love this song!" Pat said as she stood up and started dancing.

Rachel jumped up and starting dancing.

"Get it girls." Ruth said as she took a picture.

"I had to get a taste of this dancing. I love this song!" Marion said.

The song changed to the Electric Slide. The girls start screaming.

"The electric slide will do it every time; it gets everyone on the dance floor!" Ellen said.

Yes, it does, you know I'm a wall flower! Tanya said.

"Good times!" Sally said.

The girls danced to "Love Train," Dancing Machine," "September," "Get Down on It," and "Got to be Real." After all the dancing the girls ate some more.

They danced and ate for about an hour. After all that, they had to sit it down.

Twenty minutes later

Out in the ocean there were about twenty dolphins swimming and jumping in the air.

"How amazing and beautiful!" Marion said. "They look like Flipper's family."

"They're dancing in the air." Rachel said.

"Look at those two kissing." Patricia said.

"Oh my that one is looking at me out the corner of his eye." Ruth said.

"I see him!" Diane said.

"So cute, I must get a picture." Tanya said.

"Me too." the girls said in unison.

"The dolphins are putting on a performance for us." Ellen said.

"Yes, they are." Sally said.

They watched the dolphins for about thirty minutes and left.

***

On their way back to the hotel they propped their feet up. Those girls who wanted a tan, put their suntan lotion on. Ruth , Tanya and Diane don't need a tan their skin is pecan and medium brown. They have beautiful skin from head to toe.

Marion said. "I'm going to take a nap. This water is so relaxing."

"Knock yourself out, some people are sleep , some people are getting tans. Its your prerogative." Patricia said.

Marion laughed. "I guess I'll be in good company."

"Sweet dreams." Tanya said.

***

Almost back at the hotel

Ellen said, "It's so beautiful, we've had a great day! Thank you, Lord."

Sally chimed in. "So far this has been an awesome trip!"

"It's so relaxing, great fun with my friends," Tanya said.

"Yes, my friends, I'm enjoying myself," Patricia said.

"The sunset is over the hotel. We're almost there!" Marion there.

"Its beautiful. Yes, I guess we'd better pack our things up." Rachel said.

"For sure! We need to pack our stuff!" They all agreed.

***

The Third Day

On the third day, they went Jet Skiing

Hello, may I help you?" asked the gentleman in charge of the Jet Skis.

"We have paid reservations for four Jet skis," said Patricia.

"You can get your life jackets right over there. The keys are in the jet. The ones reserved for you are the four lined up on the first row."

Jet skiing was still a new sport, so Mr. Jack reviewed all the safety rules with them.

"The main rule to remember, is when in shallow water, drive the jet ski

93

slow," he said.

"Can you take a picture of us when we get on the Jet skis?" Ruth asked.

"Yes, I can." He replied.

The girls got on the Jet Skis.

Patricia began posing for the picture. "Everyone said, Friends forever!"

The rental guy continued taking their picture.

"Friends forever!" the girls said.

"I hope we'll be friends forever, sometimes I wonder." Ruth said under her breath.

The rental guy said, "I'll take another one just in case."

The rental guy said, "Have fun. You have two hours on your rental. Be safe."

"See you then." Ruth sped off with Diane on the back of the ski.

Patricia adjusted her sunglasses. "Wait up." Tanya is on the ski with her.

"They must be doing at least seventy miles per hour."

"Don't worry, we'll catch up," Patricia replied.

"I think they need to slow down. We're not experts on these things." Ellen said.

"You're right, we truly don't want any accidents," Sally said.

"Look at all that water they're splashing." Rachel said.

"It's about six feet high." Marion replied. "And I know they're going at least eighty miles per hour."

"They're a distance from us. I guess we'd better catch up with them." Rachel said. "I'll speed up a little."

"A little won't hurt."

They sped up and caught with the others in less than a minute.

"Bout time you made it!" Patricia said.

"We were a little hesitant about driving too fast." Marion said.

"It doesn't look or feel so bad when you're driving but looking at you all it looked rather scary." Rachel said.

"We're glad you made it!" Tanya said

"Now let's race back to the beach!" Ruth said.

"First jet ski that arrives is the winner!" Diane said.

"On your mark get set ready go!" Sally said as she sped off first.

The girls took off, leaving trails of water splashing in the air. Ellen and Sally were in first place. Rachel and Marion were a close second. The tortoises were gaining on them. And the last shall be first.

"Press a little harder, we're about to pass them, that's it keep pushing, keep going, yeah, we passed we're about to win. Put the pedal to the medal! That's it!" Tanya said. "We won!"

"Congrats!" The girls said in unison.

"Let's race again, I think they cheated." Rachel said.

"No, she didn't, they won, they didn't cheat." Ellen said.

"Let's race again, I'll show you!" Patricia said.

"Move over, you're too close!" Marion said.

"There's plenty of room," Tanya said.

"Let's get this race started." Patricia agreed.

"If you must race again, on your mark get set ready go!" Diane said.

"They're rather close!" Ruth said.

"Yeah, a little too close for comfort!" Sally said.

Boom! Boom!

"Oh, the jet skis have crashed!" Diane yelled!

The girls are screaming at the top of their lungs.

"Should we go out there!" Ruth asked.

"No, the water police are about 10 feet away. See them over there to the right!" Sally said.

Ellen began speaking as tears rolled down her eyes, "They're just lying on top of the water!"

"The water police jumped into the water and began putting them on the boat and driving them to shore." Diane said.

"I hope they are checking all of their vitals." Sally said.

"Me too!" said Ellen.

The water police arrived with our friends. Of course, we were trying to get to them.

"Move back give us space and air!" The officer named Mitchell said. "Hey Jerry, this one needs some oxygen!"

"Here it comes, what about the other one?" Jerry asked.

"Thank God, that one came to just a second ago." Mitchell said. He put the oxygen on Patricia.

"Jerry what is going on with the others?" Mitchell asked.

"They're great also. Yes, they're fine that's why I'm over here checking on you." Jerry said.

Mitchell walks over to the other girls. "We're going to write them tickets. I noticed their reckless boat riding. The blessing is they had their life jackets on. What are their names?"

"Why do you need their names?" Diane asked.

"I regret doing this, but I have to write all four of them tickets." Mr. Mitchell said.

"The good thing is it's a misdemeanor and not a felony!" Jerry said.

"Correct," Mitchell said as he walked over to the guilty girls.

"Sorry ladies, we must issue these tickets, Jerry said. We need your signatures."

They signed with no problem, but they did have somewhat of an attitude, there was some eye rolling and noses turned up. They probably need to be grateful they didn't go to jail.

* * *

Thirty minutes later the girls are eating their food

Everyone, please forgive me for acting like a fool today. I let competition get the best of me. It could have cost someone their life." Patricia said.

"I forgive you. I'm thankful God spared your life." Ruth said.

"Thanks. I apologize."

"Forgive me," Tanya said.

"Please forgive me!" Rachel said.

"Forgive me too!" Marion said.

" We're just so grateful everyone is okay." Diane spoke as the eldest.

96

***

Two days later at the big mall in Tampa. The parking lot and the parking garage is crowded. The girls made it into the mall, and decided to split up in two groups to save time.

"Look, the cookie store! I always get cookies when I come to the mall. I got to have some." Tanya said.

"Me too!" Everyone said.

They placed their orders.

"These white chocolate macadamia nuts are so soft and chewy, they're cooked just right," said Diane.

Patricia began to speak even though she had cookies all in her mouth. "Mines are good too! Have you noticed or is it just me? There are a lot of pregnant women in this mall. We've been here less than fifteen minutes."

Diane said. " I haven't noticed. I know I don't want to get pregnant without being married. Living together is so common. It seems like the marriage covenant means nothing."

"Patricia cleared her throat. "It does seem like an epidemic. I was about to be a part of that epidemic."

" What are you saying?" Tanya asked in a curious way.

"Bryan and I had sex once. I know it was too soon, as I reflect on our relationship, if that's what you called it. I gave up the cookies early. As soon as I did, he started acting rude and abusive. I got pregnant. I had a secret abortion. It was a horrible experience. I'm so relieved, now that I've shared this with you," Patricia said.

Tanya reassured her friend. "Don't beat yourself up. God forgives you. You know thousands of women have had abortions and made it through."

Tears roll down her face. "Thanks."

Diane hugged her friend. "Pat, no one's perfect. You can't go through life condemning yourself. Maybe we should sit down for a minute."

The girls sat on a bench near Macy's.

She continued to share her story as tears continued to roll. "It was very painful. There was so much blood. I was so scared."

They wiped her tears.

" I'm sorry," Tanya said.

"When you saw all the pregnant women, it brought up the memories of your pregnancy?" asked Ellen.

"Yes. I haven't forgiven myself. I would ask myself why I had sex with him, and why did I have an abortion?"

" I know it's easier said than done, but you have to stop beating yourself up." Rachel said as she put her hand on Patricia's shoulder and continued to console her.

Patricia continued to cry as she began to answer, "Bryan was so furious when I told him I was pregnant."

Diane's face showed how angry she is. " I'm glad you left him alone. The nerve of him to get mad. Please forgive yourself. In life, we make mistakes, but we can't hold on to it. Not forgiving ourselves holds us hostage. God wants us to be free. He has forgiven us, so why can't we forgive ourselves?"

Tanya whose been listening intently begins to speak. " All of us have made mistakes, and we'll continue to make mistakes throughout our lives. Your story will help someone in the future."

Patricia hugged Tanya. " Thanks for encouraging me."

Tanya spoke immediately. "Honey, this too shall pass. We've all have done something we regret. I always regretted losing my temper and getting mad over trivial things. I've gotten better. If you need someone to talk to, Pat, you know we're here for you."

Rachel reaches out to hug her. "You can call me anytime day or night. I'll be there for you."

Tears continued to roll down her face. "I know I sinned by having sex and having an abortion. We've been taught thou shalt not kill. The sex, the abortion, one thing led to another. I was feeling a little guilty, somewhat embarrassed. I needed to let it out. Hey, please don't mention this to the other girls. I'm not ready to tell them yet."

Tanya said, "You can count on me."

"Me too!" the others said in unison.

The other part of the gang walked up just as soon as they agreed to keep this secret.

Marion began speaking as she organized all her shopping bags. "What sales or bargains did you find?"

Ellen laughed. "We're so greedy. We sat here and ate those cookies and didn't buy one thing."

"I believe those cookies were the best I ever had." Rachel said.

"I agree." Diane said. "By the time I ate mine and drank my drink. I couldn't move."

"We started running our mouths and people watching. Time flew by." Patricia said.

Sally asked. "Do you want to shop?"

"The only thing I want to do now is look at the shoes in that store right over there." Diane said as she pointed to the store.

"The shoe store will be enough for me." Tanya said.

"Me too!" Ellen said. "I need to do some walking." I'm stuffed.

"Let's go time waits for no one." Ruth said.

They ended up shopping for almost four hours. Everyone walked out the mall with three bags or more. It was a great time, such a bonding experience for the girls who learned about Patricia's experience. The girls vowed to be loyal.

* * *

The final Day in Florida

Early the next morning, the girls loaded their luggage into the van, Sally, stood at the curb with her bags.

Ruth asked, "Sally, aren't you going to load your luggage?"

"I will. Just be patient."

"Sally, what are you waiting on?" asked Rachel.

"What are you up to or doing? Marion asked.

"You're acting strange!" Diane said.

A taxi pulled up next to the van. Sally waved at the driver to let him know she would be there in a minute. They looked at her, wondering why a taxi had pulled up.

"Cedar Lake won't see me until Thanksgiving. The University of Tampa will see me in twenty minutes. My freshman year starts on Monday. I can't go back to that house. My mother and grandmother treated me like a stepchild. I was beaten and put down for no reason at all. I think once I get settled on campus. I'm going to see a psychologist. My inheritance from my father's death will help me financially. "

Patricia looked like this is unbelievable. "You've been holding this in all these years."

"The only reason I did the few things I did, because my mother didn't want anyone to know how mean she is."

Rachel's thinking and soaking it in all in. "I guess it makes sense. I never thought of her as mean. I'm reminiscing; yes, you did just go to the games, and not all of them. You never went to the dances, the proms; you couldn't hang out at the McDonald's and Burger Kings. I thought your mother was strict, but not mean and abusive. She's always been courteous and pleasant towards me."

"Yes, she is to everyone but me. There's a vast difference in the way she treated me in comparison to Pam, June and Renee. They know she mistreated me; they were always by my side though."

Marion was puzzled and still in awe. "I wish I would've known! I'm going to miss you."

"She was strict! Think about it how many times have you been to my house."

Ellen paused and thought. "You're so right. I never thought about it. I'll call you and we meet in the cul de sac. And you never stayed long."

"Please give me a hug!" Tanya said with sadness in her voice.

"There will be no losing contact. We'll be in touch. I must go. The meter's running. I couldn't leave without an explanation. Please don't see this as a good-bye, but as a see you later."

"See you later. I'll call to get your address," said Marion.

"Later, gator, yes, this isn't a good-bye. Love you!" said Tanya.

"I'm so proud of you. You were able to resist and stand. I had no idea."

affirmed Rachel.

They said their good-byes, and then she entered the cab and yelled out the window.

"See you later. Love all of you!" The cab pulled off.

"Wow, I had no idea." Diane said as she opened the door to the van.

Marion said, "Neither did I."

"I guess if you think about it, it makes sense now," Ruth said. "Its still unbelievable."

"I'm in shock. Ms. Perez is mean and abusive. I know she's very direct and can come off mean. All this time I thought nothing of it." Rachel said.

The girls vowed to keep praying and checking on each other. They're concerned about everybody being all over the United States.

Fourteen

Cinderella has Moved

Its 10 am in the morning

"Wow, its nicer than what I thought it would be." Sally said out loud to herself.

Sally's dormitory room smelled like fresh paint. The walls were painted light beige. The furniture consisted of just a bed and a small desk, with a cherry finish. The Berber carpet was also beige. The multicolored curtains had a mix of orange, brown, and beige. Its time to start unpacking her clothes and other items. The room has bunk beds, of course she chose the bottom bed. First come first serve.

Two hours later around 12 noon

Someone was opening the door it's got to be Sally's roommate who else.

"Hello! my name is Teresa." she said as she stood five feet seven inches with curly hair and smooth pecan colored skin. "You must be my roommate."

"Yes, I am, my name is Sally, I'm from Cedar Lake, Georgia not too far from Atlanta. It's so nice to meet you Teresa!"

"I'm from Birmingham, Alabama. It's nice to meet you to!"

"I chose the bottom bed! I hope you don't mind!"

"It's okay. I probably won't be here that much. I have a boyfriend who lives off campus." Teresa said.

"Oh!"

"You sound surprised. As a matter of fact, I came to drop my luggage off. John and I are going to have lunch today. I'll return later to unpack."

Teresa had to leave. They both agreed they would talk later. She loved the room, but the elegant, classy room didn't take away the nervousness and the uncomfortable feelings she was experiencing. She needed to call her family. They would be looking for her later on today.

The phone rings

No one knows my dormitory phone number. Sally thought to herself. "Greetings!"

"This is your mom."

"Hello mom, I have great news for you. You always told me to grow up, and you said when I turned eighteen you wanted me out of the house. It's official. I have enrolled in college. I received a full scholarship. I used my inheritance to pay for everything else. I'm enrolled as a freshman at the University of Tampa."

Her mom took the phone away from her ear and looked at it. "You did what?"

"I'm a college student."

Pausing before she answered, Sally's mom finally said something, "I can't believe it. You need to come home."

"Sorry, mom. I won't be coming home."

"What do you mean?"

"Mom, you know. I don't want to get into that."

"Get into what?"

"I won't be home until the holidays."

"Who told you this was acceptable? You did this behind my back. You're not grown. Are you living on campus? Is there security on campus? I demand you to come home right now."

"Mom, I know this is a total shock to you. I had to do it. I needed my freedom. I didn't mean to do anything behind your back. You treated me like Cinderella at times."

"I need you to catch the next flight back to Cedar Lake. I feel like I've been totally disrespected."

"I didn't mean to disrespect you. I had to get out of the house, before I do something crazy. I couldn't take it anymore."

"I don't want to hear none of that. I'm your mother and you're coming home now."

"I had to leave Cedar Lake. Mom, I have to go good-bye."

Her *mom* looked *at* the phone *and* burst into tears. *My child thinks she's grown. Who told her this was okay or acceptable? I need help. Lord help me. What did I do wrong? I just don't understand.*

Sally has embarked on a new adventure. Her mother couldn't say anything, because she always said she wanted her to leave. Death and life are in the power of the tongue.

I regret how I treated my daughter. I didn't realize she was so unhappy. Now that I think about it, I treated her like I was treated. I feel awful. Oh my, I carried it from one generation to another. The physical and verbal abuse. Oh Lord forgive me. I need help. It'll be a miracle if my daughter forgives me. Help me treat her with love and patience. Help me to show her love. Tears rolled down her eyes.

* * *

That evening

Ruth called Sally.

The phone rang. She ran to answer the phone. "Hello! It must be easy to find me. My mother has called too."

Sally we had to tell your mom. She called our parents looking for you. How is it going? Do you like your dormitory room? What's the campus like?"

"The campus is very pretty. It seems easy to get around. I'm excited about my new life. I guess it's what you call a leap of faith."

"I'm so proud of you."

"Please forgive your mother so you can receive all you're supposed to have. I know forgiveness can be hard sometimes. Girl, I'm speaking from experience. Thank God, he's been helping me the past few years with unforgiveness. I was mad at my first cousin. At family functions she would talk about me so bad. I was making myself sick, being mad at her. She talked about my hair, my nose, my butt, just anything you could think of. I started getting headaches. I took pain medicine. My headaches wouldn't leave. One day I heard a sermon about forgiveness. I said out loud I forgive this cousin. I had no more headaches after I said that. I called that a miracle. The word talks about how can we expect God to forgive you, when you can't forgive the person you see?"

"You know, you're so right. Thanks for reminding me. I'm not that knowledgeable about the Bible, but I do know we're to forgive people. Girl, pray for me."

"It's done. Let's pray for each other."

"It's done. Love you my friend."

"Love you too! Talk to you later!"

The next day

Maria Perez called her daughter again.

Phone rings in her dormitory room.

"Hello."

"Hello, I'm calling to see what day you're coming home."

"Mom, for the hundredth time I'm not dropping out of college. When you call can you talk about something else except me coming back to Cedar Lake?"

"I 'm going to call you until you change your mind."

"Mom please. I'm not going to answer the phone. This is getting on my nerves. I don't have any peace. I'm getting off the phone now. Good-bye!"

105

It's 6:30 pm the next day

Sally is combing her hair.

"Your mother has called at least three times today. Four times yesterday. Are you dodging her? Did you get the messages?" Teresa asked.

"I apologize Teresa. I must admit I'm dodging her. I love my mom. Maybe one day I can share more of my story. We might need to unplug the phone. She's going to keep calling."

"I don't want to do that. My family might try to call me. But maybe I can tell them I'll call them. I'm sorry to hear that about your mom. Is there anything I can do to help?"

"Not really. If you believe in prayer, pray for me."

"As a matter of fact, I do. I will."

"Thanks Teresa."

Fifteen

A Journey to Each Girls College

Two months later

Tanya was ready to move into the dorm at Spelman College.

"You have everything in the car?" asked her mother, Jean Patterson. Your father is tying everything down in the car."

"Yes, I do." Tanya yelled as she glanced over the room to make sure she wasn't leaving anything. Then she ran down the stairs.

"Let's go, honey, you and baby girl come on. Time waits for no one." said Mr. Patterson.

"I'm coming."

They ran to the car.

"I can't believe my baby girl is moving out of the house," said Mrs. Patterson. "I'll miss you. I hope you come home on the weekends."

"I'll come every weekend."

"Cedar Lake won't be the same without you my darling." Mr. Patterson said. "I'm going to miss you very much baby girl."

"Mom and dad, you're going to make me cry!"

"You're late. I've cried already." Mrs. Patterson said.

"Aw Mom. It's going to be alright."

"We're going to hold you to that." her mother said.

<u>At the college</u>

"You're preregistered. The school said all we must do is get in line. The line shouldn't be long because it's just a matter of just picking up an envelope," Her father explained. "That's what the office told me."

"Daddy, I'm glad you and Mom were able to take off work to take me to college, even though it's only thirty minutes away."

"You're our baby girl," her mom replied.

"I wouldn't have it any other way." her father said as he grabbed his daughter and his wife.

"Mom and dad please don't make me cry."

Mrs. Patterson smiled. "You don't make us cry."

"I'll try not to!"

"Let's change the subject."

"To sum it up, we're putting it all in God's hands. We know He'll watch over you! You're going to be our future dentist, Dr. Patterson." her father said.

"Yes, he will! And yes to our dentist!" her mother agreed.

"I'm believing that too!" Tanya said.

* * *

<u>Ellen's College</u>

Ellen attended the University of California at Los Angeles. The campus is four and half miles from the beach. It's filled with trees and Spanish colonial architecture. The white stucco department buildings were all at least four stories high, built to withstand strong weather and earthquakes.

She stopped a passing male student that was walking towards her. "Can you tell me where the Lanier dormitory is? I just finished registering for my classes. I've gotten lost on this big campus. Am I heading in the right direction?"

"Yes, pretty lady. It's over there." The male student pointed. "You're almost there."

"Thanks," she responded.

"What's your name?"

"I'm Ellen!"

"I'm John. Maybe we can hang out sometimes. Can I call you?"

"Yes, I'm in Room 521. "

"Thanks, the receptionist will connect me, right?"

"Correct!"

"Great talk to you later."

"Later."

Ellen entered the dormitory room and was so shocked. The room had a strange smell and dingy white walls. The drapes needed cleaning. You can see the dust on the drapes. The carpet was clean, but she could tell it was about ten years old—or more. The light fixtures were dusty. The mirror needed to be cleaned. The dusting, cleaning, and unpacking began. She did unpack her radio to listen to music as she started this mission.

One hour later

Carrie, her roommate, entered. She looked like she might be of Asian descent. She had a curly hair cut. Her hair was a gorgeous dark brown. She had the most beautiful smile; her teeth were white as snow. She had to be five feet two inches.

Carrie began speaking. "Hello! My name is Carrie. I guess we're roommates."

Ellen is excited about meeting her roommate. "I'm Ellen, it's my pleasure meeting you. I hope you want to change this room up."

Carrie began to speak. "It's icky, and can you turn that music off. That's not my type of music."

Who does she think she is? We're roommates she's going to have to compromise. Ellen began to speak. "I'll turn it down, but I won't turn it off."

Carrie responded with authority. "I think you need to turn it off. Make sure you buy some headphones, so I won't have to hear it. You Americans and your music."

"Carrie, you're starting off on the wrong foot demanding I turn off my music and talking about Americans."

"I don't care what you think. I don't like your music."

"We may need to have a change of roommates if you're not going to compromise and if you dislike Americans." She said in a demanding voice. "I think you should ask for a room change since I made it to the room first."

"I'll do that. I can tell I don't want to be your roommate." Carrie grabbed her bags and hurried out the room.

Wow, she must hate Americans with a passion. Forget her. I'm going to clean this room and decorate it with my teal, chocolate comforter and curtains. It'll be the best-looking room on campus. Where's my Lysol?

Ellen had that dormitory room smelling and looking brand new within a couple of hours.

This room looks better and smells clean. If I get a new roommate that'll be fine. If I don't, that's fine too she thought to herself. She started unpacking her room.

* * *

Ruth is in Boston, Massachusetts

Ruth's dormitory at Harvard was a beige brick building four stories high. The room had bunk beds, bookshelves on the wall, and a desk. Ruth had a small refrigerator. The bathrooms were shared by two rooms. She lived in a coed dormitory.

Ruth headed to the cafeteria in the student union for something to eat.

The cafeteria line was long.

The lady in front of her checked out the food.

"This food presentation is perfect. The smell is so inviting."

"The food looks healthy and rich in vitamins, especially the vegetables," said Ruth.

"I'm so hungry. I hope I don't overeat," replied the lady.

"Where are you from? Is this your first semester?" asked Ruth.

"I'm from Philadelphia, and I'm a freshman." she replied.

"I'm from Cedar Lake, Georgia. It's a small city about forty-five minutes from Atlanta," said Ruth.

"My name is Candy." the freshman said as she moved her blonde hair off her face.

"My name is Ruth."

"What's your major?" asked Candy

"I plan to be a surgeon."

"I want to be a pediatrician," said Cindy.

"What do you think of Harvard now that you're here?"

"It's pretty cool," Candy responded.

"Yes, it is. I hope to see you around the campus. What dorm do you live in?"

"I live in the Kendrick dorm."

"I do too."

"We'll see each other again."

Ruth began to pay for her food by showing her student id. The cashier started speaking. 'You have to pay for your food; your ID is not acceptable?"

"What do you mean, I have completed my registration? A look of pure disgust was on her face. "I can't believe this after I paid all this tuition."

Ruth stood near the cashier. She was waiting to see what happened to Candy.

It's Candy's turn to meet the cashier to pay for her meal.

"Ma'am your ID is not acceptable."

She threw her tray at the cashier. "Keep your food!"

"That wasn't necessary." the cashier responded as she began wiping off the food.

"It was necessary, you're full of bull."

The cashier continued wiping the food. "You're crazy!" She left to clean herself up.

Candy began to leave. "No one wants that nasty food anyway."

"Let's walk to Burger King across the street!"

"I would love a whopper. That cafeteria incident isn't making sense. That just makes me so mad. The office is closed, we can't make a liar out of that cafeteria woman."

"We have to go to the register's office tomorrow. It doesn't make sense. For now, let's enjoy a burger."

"Sounds like a plan. I'll try to calm down!"

"Please do. It's got to be a mistake."

* * *

The dormitory and the campus are a hit. The girls did get their ID's fixed. Candy and Ruth went to the cafeteria the next day.

Candy began speaking. "I told you, you're full of crap. My ID is fine. You need to fix your cash register."

"I'm glad you got your ID fixed. Please keep moving and don't hold up the line." The cashier responded.

"I will but you're in denial."

Ruth went through the line. She just shook her head.

* * *

Marion's new college experience

When she arrived at Yale University, she admired the landscape on the campus, its breath taking. The trees displayed burnt orange, golden, and bright red leaves. The fall foliage against the New Haven skyline was a beautiful sight to see, which reminded her of Cedar Lake. The old European-style campus had skyscraper looking buildings. The bookstore was in the center of campus. Double-decker buses carried students from one end of campus to the other.

Her parents and her brother came with her to Yale. They made it a family affair.

Ten minutes later

Mom, Dad, look at my dorm, it's amazing. Look at Welch Hall, it looks like something in the movies. I love the look. It has a Gothic look. It looks sturdy, I like it because it's different and full of history. I believe I made the right decision."

"Yes, darling I see what you're talking about." Mr. Rucker said.

"It's different!" her mom said. "Now let's go see your room. We can help you clean the room and unpack."

"Sounds like a plan!" Derrick and James her brothers said.

"I'm glad you all are here to help! Let's check it out. I know I'm going to love it." Marion said.

Everyone headed to her room.

* * *

Patricia's Campus

Patricia is majoring in Accounting at the prestigious Columbia University, located in Upper Manhattan, in New York City with at least fifty buildings on campus. Some of the buildings look like state capitol buildings. It's a rather large campus that dates back to 1754. The campus population is more than twenty thousand. Most of the buildings have an ancient look, and the landscaping is trimmed, colorful, and beautiful.

A tall slender male student is coming her way.

Patricia began to speak to the man, her face had turned red, she was about to cry. "Where is the library? I'm so lost, I feel like I'm going in circles."

"Don't fret, calm down. Everyone gets lost. It's about two blocks away. I can show you; I know it can be overwhelming," said the young gentleman.

"Thanks, I guess you can tell I was about to cry. That's embarrassing. All these buildings threw me off. I hope it's not out of your way. I appreciate your help."

"It's not, my name is Rusty. I can carry your books too."

"Thanks. She handed her books to him. "My name is Patricia. Does it really show that I'm a freshman?"

"Yes, it does. Don't worry, it happens to the best of us."

"You're a sophomore?"

"No, I'm a junior. "

"Where are you from?"

"Bridgeport, Connecticut. And you?"

"Cedar Lake, Georgia, right outside of Atlanta."

"I know where Atlanta is. Cedar Lake should be easy to find. Maybe we can hang out. I'll call you, what's your phone number"

"777-888-9311 is my number. What are they doing over there?

Rusty began to speak. "That's the first week of school pep rally to welcome everyone back to school and to welcome the freshman like you. Let's check it out! Then I can walk you to the building you're looking for."

"Rusty it looks like the place to be. Lots of fun!"

"It is. They sell popcorn and hot dogs. It's a mini carnival right here on campus."

"Look at those dancers!"

They're pretty good!"

They attended the carnival/pep rally and had a great time. She did make it to the building she was looking for.

* * *

Rachel's campus - Temple University Philadelphia

After her first week on campus, her mother called.

"Hey, what are you doing?"

"I just got back from eating."

"How is the food?" her mother.

"It's pretty decent. I'm not starving, Mom.

The dorm is huge. The laundry room appears to have twenty washers and dryers. The campus is beautiful. There are a lot of men. My roommate seems very cool. Everything's fine, so far. Don't worry!"

"There's nothing like having a great roommate! Who knows you might meet your husband!"

"At the right time mom. I will."

"You're right, you'll meet him at the right time. I just want the best for my daughter."

"Thanks mom."

Rachel call me if you need anything. I don't want you needing money or anything."

"Don't you be concerned. I don't have a pride problem."

"Just want to remind you that's what I'm here for."

"Mom, I have to go. Thanks for calling. I appreciate you mom. You're the best!"

"I love you! Good night, my baby girl. Promise me you will call me at least once a week."

"I can do that. Let us make a phone date for every Saturday morning. How does that sound?"

"Perfect. Love you!"

"Love you too!"

"Good-bye!"

"Good-bye!

The girls settled in with ease. They all adjusted quite easily, with a few hiccups.

Sixteen

Ellen Met a Guy

One evening as Ellen left her last class; a guy watched and followed her. He walked behind her for two blocks and then decided to say something. He was a little apprehensive about approaching her but was persistent and determined. Ellen hadn't been aware that he was following her. He's muscular standing six feet wearing a white t-shirt.

"Do you need some help with your books?"

Ellen paused before she spoke. "Honestly, I think I do. These books are kind of heavy."

The young man reached for the books. "Where are you going? We seem to be going the same direction. I noticed you two blocks away."

"Oh, did you? I didn't notice you. I'm going to my dorm, the one at the end of the street, the red brick building."

"That works out fine. My dorm is right before yours. A few extra steps won't hurt me. What's your name?"

"Thanks for helping me. My name is Ellen. And yours?"

"My name is Kenneth."

"It's a pleasure meeting you."

"You're a freshman, right?" he asked.

"Yes, and you?"

"Yes. Can I call you? Seeing we both are new; we can help each other out."

"Everyone needs help at times. i think it would be nice to hear from you."
She gave him her number.

"I'll call you this week for sure," he said, with excitement in his voice.

"That'll be nice." Smiling as she responded. "Are you from California?"

"Yes, I'm from Santa Anna, it's about forty-five minutes to an hour from here."

"Where are you from Ellen?"

"I'm from Cedar Lake, Georgia right outside of Atlanta."

"Wow, you're far away from home. What made you come to the west coast? There are so many colleges on the east coast."

"It was either USC or UCLA. I've always been fascinated with both, watching their football teams and their bands. They seemed like the perfect schools. I had to come."

"I get what you're saying. They do look exciting on TV."

"I'm happy about my choice. From what I can tell it's everything I thought it would be. One bonus is the city bus runs inside this big campus, that's a plus. I didn't bring a car with me."

"Ellen if you ever need anything or a ride, I can take you. It'll be my pleasure don't worry about getting around."

"Thanks, that's so thoughtful, I'll let you know."

"You're welcome. I'm glad I met you!"

"The feeling is mutual! I'm excited about being in California, at UCLA everything."

"California is cool. I think you'll love it."

"I have to go. I look forward to seeing you soon." Ellen said as she put her hand on the door handle to her dormitory."

"You'll see me very soon. Good night."

Ellen smiled. "Good night." She entered the dormitory.

Kenneth started walking to his dormitory.

* * *

The anticipation and excitement was all over him. He was ready to get to know her. He called his brother back home.

"Hey brother. I met this chick named Ellen. She's fine; she has curves like no other. As far as I can tell, she's my kind of girl."

"Dawg, lil brother, you're about business. I say go for it."

"I plan to. I'll let you know how it turns out. What's up with you?"

"Nothing. Just working hard. I'm coming to visit you soon. I hope I get to meet this girl."

"I hope you do too."

"I can't wait. I was headed out the door. Call me with an update on Ms. Ellen."

"For sure. Later bro!"

* * *

The next day he called Ellen. "Can you talk?"

"I most definitely can. I just finished studying for the evening." She smiled.

"Will you go to the dance with me in three weeks? You know its homecoming. I know it's soon, but Homecoming comes fast."

"Yes, I think so and understand. I need to find something to wear for homecoming. You know how we women are."

Yes, I do. Thanks for saying you'll go."

"You're welcome. Kenneth it sounds like fun."

"It will be."

* * *

Over the next month or so, they became closer. They talked and saw each other every time they could squeeze it in. He tried to play it cool, but they both mentioned the relationship to their parents and friends. Kenneth's friends and family were very happy for him. The girls were excited, not all of them initially.

Shame on Patricia and Marion

One night Patricia got a phone call from Marion.

"Girl, what do you think of Ellen and her new boyfriend?"

"We'll see how long it lasts, you know she can't keep a man," replied Marion.

"She's so full of herself. She gets on my nerves. She thinks everything is about her."

"Why does she always get a man?" asked Marion.

"I don't know, but if you think about it, all the guys have treated her like dirt. I'm somewhat jealous. She makes meeting men easy. I know this isn't the way we're supposed to act toward our friend."

"I'm a little jealous. Honestly, we have no reason to be, first she's our friend, and every guy has been a jerk. I tell myself that I'm worthy of true love. I remind myself that I'm fearfully and wonderfully made. I'm beautiful, and when God made me, he didn't make any junk. I'm beginning to realize I deserved to be treated like a queen. Sometimes I get caught up, and I need to remind myself of who I am. I need to be happy for her."

"Marion, you're right. I'm beginning to learn that I'm beautiful and I deserve the best. I get jealous, and hours later I realize I shouldn't be."

"Don't worry. We both are growing in that area. We'll support our friend. We can't be jealous of her. It's not her fault we have personal issues with ourselves. Let's make a conscious effort to support her."

* * *

Patricia called Ellen. The phone rings.

"Hello!"

"Hello my friend, congrats on your new beau."

"Thanks, my friend!"

"I have to admit, I wasn't happy for you at first. I was jealous. You always seem to find a man. Well, I mean they find you. It's hard for me at times."

"What, I can't believe it! All you have going for yourself, you're beautiful. Men look at you, and try to get your attention, but you're always in another world. There were times when guys were flirting with me. And their friends were flirting with you. You acted nonchalant and as though you're not interested."

"No I don't, you're telling a story. Now you're going to have me paying attention to myself."

"I thought you knew what you're doing. I would shake my head and say to myself, that's our friend, she doesn't have a care in the world."

"Thanks my friend. I'll try to do better. I'm glad you're happy and in love. I wish you the best. I'll see you soon. I can't wait."

"Thanks, Patricia. Remember to practice paying attention to the men when they talk to you."

"I will. My other line is ringing. Talk to you later."

"Good-bye."

Is it a trick?

As soon as she hung up the phone, it rang again. "Who could this be?" Ellen asks out loud. "Hello!"

"I've been trying to call you." Kenneth said.

"I was on the phone with Patricia."

"You seem very close. I can't wait to meet your friends and family. Honey, we both have been studying so hard I decided to go to the beach this weekend and you're coming with me. I rented a condo. We have it from Friday evening to early Sunday afternoon."

"We do need to relax, where did you get the money?"

"Don't worry about that. I have means."

I felt like we need a break from the everyday routine."

"I'm not comfortable spending the night with you yet."

"I understand my dear, but it's bound to happen one day."

"Mm, don't be so sure of yourself."

"Honey, nothing is going to happen. I respect you and your values. Just relax we'll leave after our last class on tomorrow."

"I'm going to trust you on this one." She responded with hesitancy in her voice. *I hope he's not up to no good. I do enjoy being with him, I'm just not ready to be totally intimate with him. Maybe I shouldn't go, but I want to be with him.*

I hope this isn't a trick from the enemy, help me Lord!

Seventeen

The Weekend Trip

<u>Ellen traveled with Kenneth on a Friday evening</u>

Kenneth is outside her dormitory room sitting in his car with his shades on. His car is a vibrant red Corvette. The car is about seven years old but it's in mint condition. His father bought it for a graduation present.

She headed towards the car, its about twenty five feet away. She opened the passenger door to get in. "Hello sweetheart. Let's get this trip started honey. The last time I was on the beach I was with my friends we went to Tampa. It was a good time."

"And hello to you my dear lady.There's a full-size kitchen in the condo,cable,and the beach right outside the door." Kenneth said as he started the car and headed off the campus.

"That's convenient. Maybe we can eat in tonight and have breakfast tomorrow and Sunday. We can go to the grocery store near the freeway. I can cook a delectable breakfast."

"I can't wait to taste it. We'll have a great time."

"You know I was hesitant at first."

"I know."

"I'm glad you know! I just want to do right by God."

"Believe me, I truly understand where you're coming from. I read the Bible too."

* * *

It's 10:30 pm later that night

Sleep has caught up with her. He turned the TV off. He starts caressing her not caring about her feelings or beliefs. There were nonstop kisses all over her, she bagan to wake up. He's in trouble.

She began to speak as she woke up. "What are you doing ?"

"Just loving on my baby," Kenneth said as he kissed and continued to caress her, not giving her the opportunity to say anything.

" Stop please, get off of me. You're hurting me." She tried to push him off her, but to no avail. She gave up and began to enjoy every minute of it.

* * *

It's 1 am is in the bathroom

She's not loud. She prayed, sobbed, and cried softly.

"Dear Lord, I can't believe I came up here. I knew there was a strong possibility we might have sex. I'm feeling very guilty. Please forgive me Lord. I repent. This was not a wise move on my part. I should've said not. Help me be stong."

The crying and sobbing continued even after she prayed and asked God for forgiveness. Kenneth was knocked out.

She stayed in the bathroom crying for an hour.

Early Saturday morning its 5 am

She's up studying on the couch. She's trying to hide her feelings.

I can't believe I had sex with him last night. I just let him have his way. I don't think I fought him off as hard as I could. It was feeling good, so I just gave in. I hope he still loves me, now that I've given it up.

He came down the stair. "Good morning, my love. Did you have a peaceful sleep?"

"Good morning. I did. It was very relaxing" *Liar, liar. That lie came out rather fast. I need help.*

He made his way to the sofa and sat next to her. "Great, that was my goal. You've been stressing, that's one of the reasons I brought you here. I hope you enjoyed last night."

She stared at him. "To be honest I wanted to wait, but after you started caressing me, I gave in. My hindsight tells me I shouldn't have come to the beach."

" I knew you weren't ready, but the timing felt so right. When I made the reservations, I thought about us having sex, but then I said she's not ready. Shoots, you turn me on."

"The feeling is mutual. It's both of our faults. If we want to please God, we need to do the right thing."

"Forgive me, for making my way with you. I do want to spend the rest of my life with you. Do you forgive me?"

Yes, I do. I'm hope you're sincere about wanting to spend the rest of your life with me."

"I'm serious. I do want to marry you."

"I want to marry you too. Not today though."

"Maybe next year."

"Next year sounds like a plan.Its perfect."

* * *

The Next Hour on the Beach

Kenneth started singing to her. They found a cozy spot under a pier to watch the sailboats come in. Music was coming from the lounge at the edge of the pier.

"Sweetheart, what I find in you makes me want to do the right thing so you don't get away. We need to remain focused and finish school. What do you think?"

"I think we can make it work. Like you said, we do have to be focused."

"I thought about it. I want to get married this spring. That's still next year."

"I can handle that."

"Thanks babe."

Kissing happened to be on the agenda, they kissed like it was going out of style.

They ate lunch while the warm sun beamed down on them.

"Mmm good, taste this strawberry," He puts it in her mouth.

"It's fresh and sweet."

"The sandwiches you made are so tasty. I'm loving this spicy mustard."

"Thanks Ken, the potato chips are great, you can't have a sandwich without chips. I need to admit this was a great idea despite what happened last night. A getaway from the campus is what I needed. Now that I've put a little food in my stomach, I want to lay in the sun to get some color."

"I guess we both can use some color."

* * *

One hour later

Both stood up and started dusting sand off them. They're headed back to the condo after gathering the umbrella, towels, and the picnic basket.

She sighed as she began to speak. "There's one thing we haven't mentioned, our parents, especially my father. They aren't going to be happy with me getting married so soon."

"My mother and my father will probably be against it initially, but when they see we're serious they'll support us."

"My father is like a mountain, but eventually he'll cave in."

"Our parents will be fine."

They continued to have a very relaxing weekend. They had sex three more times before they left the condo. No resistance occurred at all. She enjoyed every minute of it. They managed to get some studying in.

* * *

Sunday night

<u>Lying down in the bed back at the dormitory</u>

I enjoyed every minute of the weekend. I feel somewhat guilty because I did give my life to the Lord and I know I disobeyed the word of God. It talks about it in I Corinthians 7. It's good for a man not to touch a woman. And it says if you can't contain yourself its best to get married. We do need to get married. Lord I hope he is sincere. I sure disobeyed you. Please forgive me.

Eighteen

Am I Pregnant?

Ellen is in her dormitory room sitting at her desk on a brisk Monday morning and just happened to be looking at her calendar. She's nervous; she's thumping her pencil on the calendar pad rather quickly.

Oh, my cousin with the red hair hasn't shown up. The last time she showed up was September 14th. Today is November 13th. Lord I hope I'm not pregnant. I should have had at least one cycle since Kenneth, and I went to the beach. I've skipped one month before, but not two months. I have been feeling a little nauseous. My parents are going to scream all the way to Mexico if I'm pregnant. I don't think I'll tell anyone, not even Kenneth. Lord, help me I've truly messed up.

* * *

Its 4 pm Monday. The clinic is about to close.

Ellen walked in the clinic door. She checks out the waiting room to see who may be in there.

She speaks softly under her breath."Whew no one is here. What a relief. Let me go up to this counter and get this testing started. Good evening, I need to take a pregnancy test. How much does it cost?"

"It's five dollars. Most of the cost is included in your tuition." The woman

127

behind the counter explained.

Ellen reached into her wallet and gave the woman five dollars.

"You came at a perfect time. You don't have to wait. Come on back. The nurse will be with you momentarily." said the receptionist.

Oh Lord be with me. I'm so scared. I hope and pray I'm not pregnant. Please don't let me be.

The nurse came in and gave the test to her. Talking about heart beating fast, her's was beating ninety miles a minute. The test was completed so fast and she left as quickly as possible. She didn't want to be seen. Some of her anxiety has gone, the first thing to do was take the test. Now the results will be back soon. A nervous wreck she is. The visit to the clinic was only ten minutes, she's very grateful for that,and no one saw her.

* * *

The Results are In

It's Wednesday afternoon at 4 pm

After entering into the clinic and scoping the place out, she walked up to the counter to speak with the receptionist. "Good evening, I'm Ellen Snow I came in Monday to take a pregnancy test. The nurse told me the results would be in today."

The receptionist looked up at her. "Oh yes I remember you. You always come in at the right time. Just sign in and I'll take you to the room to see the doctor."

The receptionist walked her down the hallway to the patient room.

I walked alongside the receptionist. This sure seemed like a long walk today.

"Here you are, just wait in here the doctor will be here in a minute," the receptionist said.

Lord I'm trying to relax.

Ten minutes has passed.

The doctor walked in with the stethoscope around her neck, and her writing pad in her left hand with several envelopes attached to it. "Good evening Ms. Snow. How are you doing today?"

What a dumb question. "I'm doing okay, considering. I came in to get the results of my pregnancy test. I'm full of anxiety."

She sits down and began to look at the charts on her pad. "Yes, I'm aware of that. The results are in and you're seven weeks pregnant."

"Oh no," Ellen burst into tears and began sobbing loud and hard. "My father and mother are going to kill me. How am I going to tell my boyfriend?"

"Well Ms. Snow. You'll figure out something. It's not the end of the world. Women have babies every day. There are some pamphlets up front you can read. I'm going to prescribe some prenatal vitamins. Let me check your vitals. I need you to make the necessary appointments, stop by the receptionist desk on the way out."

She looked up at the doctor. "I saw those pamphlets and I guess I'll make my appointments. One thing I'm not going to do is have an abortion. I've messed up once. I'm not about to mess up again. God has forgiven me for having sex outside of marriage. I can't stand the thought of having an abortion."

The doctor nodded. "I understand thanks for sharing. You're a young healthy girl. You're welcome to call me. I advise you to eat healthy because you're eating for two. I look forward to working with you during your pregnancy."

Ellen gets up to leave. "Thanks doctor. I guess I need to get ready. I'll be calling you asking questions about my new adventure."

"You'll be fine!" the doctor said.

She walked out the clinic trying to keep herself together emotionally.

Nineteen

Tell the Truth

Sally was the first of the girls to make it to Cedar Lake. She noticed how festive her hometown is. It looked so nice with the fall colors and the harvest look. Sally is thinking hard. *The ride home is taking a long time. Maybe I'm a little anxious, my hands are* sweating. *Oh Lord be with me; you know I'm scared.*

"We're here!" the taxi driver said.

Sally began speaking in a nervous sounding voice. "How much is it?"

"Twenty- dollars."

Sally hands him the money. The taxi driver gets her luggage out. She got out, received her belongings and begin walking down the sidewalk to the front door of her family home. "Here I go!" *The sidewalk length seemed so long.*

Sally knocked on the door.

"Who is it?" asked her mom.

"It's me!" she responded.

She opened the door. "Sally!"

She entered the foyer, puts her suitcase down to hug her mom.

They hugged each other for a long time. "I missed you mom."

"I missed you too! It's been different around here without you. Thank God you made it home safely," her mom said. "Let's sit in the living room and talk for a few minutes. I know you might be tired from traveling but I want to clear the air, so this will be a great visit for the both of us."

They take a seat on the pure white sofa in the living room.

"Before you start, I want to say Mom, please forgive me for leaving without telling you. I had to get away! It wasn't easy growing up in this house." said Sally.

"I apologize for everything you went through. You should have come home after you took your trip. You disrespected me. You embarrassed me. I was so hurt."

"I didn't come home because I needed to get away. I was tired of you hitting me for no reason. I was about to have a nervous breakdown at the age of seventeen. I did what I thought was necessary. I didn't mean to disrespect you. I would ask you what I did to get a beating you would say, I'm beating you because I want to and I'm the parent."

"I apologize, I know I was angry a lot when you were here. I do take my anger out on people. Please forgive me. When you didn't come home, I had to do a little soul searching, and try to figure out why you wouldn't come home. You made me look at myself. Your friend's parents would congratulate me on allowing you to go to college early. I would acknowledge them, but I would wonder if they knew I didn't approve. I couldn't tell anyone outside this house the truth. You're supposed to honor your parents, so your days may be long, even if your parents aren't doing what you think they should do."

"Mom, I accept your apology. I don't mean to make you feel bad. You pushed me away with the way you treated me. I couldn't participate in high school activities. High school was supposed to be fun. I missed out on a lot of activities. There would be times I would just sit in my room and cry. I did all the housework. You treated me like Cinderella. I was miserable. It was not my intentions to disrespect you or not honor you."

Tears rolled down Mrs. Perez's face. "I wish I could take those years back. I was going through something myself. Please forgive me for taking it out on you. I had displaced anger and full of depression. I couldn't tell you, because you were a child. I'm doing better."

Sally looks into her mom's eyes. "I had no idea. I was so consumed with my hurt and pain."

Mrs. Perez nods her head. "It was no excuse to treat you the way I did."

She reaches out to hug her mom. "I forgive you mom."

"Thanks, my dear, I really appreciate you." They hug for at least thirty seconds.

"They get up and started walking into the kitchen. Pam, Renee and June were sitting at the bar on the wooden bar stools. Their grandma was sitting in the next room on the den on the sofa.

Pam ran to hug her. "We thought you weren't going to ever finish talking. I missed you."

Renee and June, hugged and kept hugging their sister, it seemed to last forever. "I missed you all."

Renee didn't want to let go of her sister." You have to tell us all about college life, big sis."

"Don't worry. I'll tell you everything."

She noticed her grandmother, sitting with a mean look on her face. "Hello, Grandma."

Sally's grandmother didn't look her way and acted as though she didn't hear her. Its a must or its necessary for her to ignore her grandmother's behavior. Even though her heart is disappointed and hurt. Pressing on is a must despite this awkward moment.

"Mom, sisters, I'm going to change. When will dinner be ready?"

Mom peeked in the oven. "Dinner will be served in one hour."

"Great I'm starving."

The family had a great dinner and evening only because Sally ignored her grandma. Her grandma made faces at her the entire evening.

* * *

Ellen's house

On Saturday evening, Mr. Snow was at home because it was slow at the grocery store. The Snows were watching TV and eating pizza.

Mr. Snow began speaking in a stern voice. "Your mother tells me that you have a boyfriend and you're serious." Aren't you supposed to be focused on your schoolwork? Aren't those the rules we set before you left home?"

A look of disappointment and discouragement showed on her face as she began to respond. "Dad, it's nothing serious. He's just a friend I study with."

"Why are you lying to me? Or are you saying your mother is lying?"

"I do study with him."

"I understand you study with him. Let me ask you this. Why am I the last to know about this engagement? You know the neighbors talk."

At that moment no words or sound could she speak. Its probably best so she wouldn't be tempted to lie.

"How long have you been dating?"

"Since September."

"You've been dating him two months and you're talking about marriage. You need to break up with him. Don't waste my money."

"Aw, Dad, they might stay focused. Give her a chance," said Eddie.

"I don't want to hear any of that. Break up with him, or I'll stop paying for your college."

"Now, honey, don't be so hard on her. I just wanted you to talk to her."

"I don't want to hear any more about this Kenneth guy." Mr. Snow said. "I've nothing else to say." He leaves the room.

I love my father but sometimes he can be so controlling. I'm over a thousand miles from him on a regular and he think he can control me. No disrespect intended. I do want to obey him, but I'm just about grown. I'm want to believe he's not serious, but the father I know he's very serious.

***

Unfortunately, the girls didn't go shopping, out to eat, drink coffee, or even see a girl's flick together. They met in the culdesac twice but that's it. And those conversations lasted only fifteen minutes. It was kind of chaotic in all the households for Thanksgiving. Sally and Ellen had enough going on as you can tell.

Twenty

Kenneth the Cheater

On Sunday evening, the last day of the Thanksgiving holiday, Kenneth and Ellen walked to their favorite hamburger joint, holding hands. The waitress greeted them.

"Good evening, Peggy. Give us our usual table."

"Hey Peggy, how are you?" asked Ellen.

"I'm fine. It's been busy today. I'll get your drinks. I just cleaned your table," Peggy said.

Kenneth pulled a seat out for her to sit down. He made sure she was comfortable. Then he sat down. The restaurant is based on the Happy Day's theme. There's a jukebox playing the Happy Days theme. Pictures of the Happy Days gang lined upon the wall. There are pictures of high school girls wearing the poodle skirts with white bobby socks. The boys had on the blue jeans with white socks. The guys had on the penny loafers.

"Ken, I called you two or three days in a row, no answer. What happened? I called your dormitory room. Your roommate Charles acted like he didn't know anything. I was worried sick. I couldn't find you anywhere. What happened?"

"I went home . I was there just for one day. Then I came back to the campus."

"Your roommate said he hadn't seen you."

"He drinks and gets drunk a lot. He didn't know."

"Ken, I needed to talk to you. You said you'd be at your mother's. It's like you were invisible during the holidays."

"I'm sorry, baby. I didn't mean for you to worry."

"I've been feeling sick. My period hasn't come. I took the pregnancy test before I went home for Thanksgiving. It said I was pregnant."

"Why didn't you tell me you had missed your periods and you took all of these tests?"

Ken looked at her with disgust written all over his face.

Ellen screams at the top of her voice. "You weren't available! I didn't want to say anything until I knew for sure. I didn't want to alarm you."

"Alarm me? You're pregnant!"

"I'm sorry for not telling you sooner. It was very emotional for me. My parents don't want me to date you. They think dating is a distraction. They want us to finish school. I'm glad you wanted to marry me before you found out I was pregnant."

Ken took a deep breath.

"Of course, we had the marriage discussion before now. How many months are you?"

"I'm seven weeks per the campus doctor. Ken, I feel like crying."

Kenneth reaches out and hugs her. "Don't cry. It's not the end of the world."

Peggy walks up. "Is everything okay?"

"Yes, it's okay,We'll be all right."

"I'm glad. Here are your drinks."

"Sweetheart, don't worry, we'll figure this out." Ken held her tight.

"We have to. My father told me we can't date. He doesn't want me to get distracted. If he finds out I'm pregnant, he might have a heart attack. He told me if he found out we're still dating; he wouldn't pay my college tuition."

"Oh really. I'm glad he's in Georgia and we're in California. We have to tell him one day."

"We will. Let's concentrate on what's important now, the baby and getting married."

" We should've been more responsible. It's too late to turn back now. We need to finish school. You'll have the baby this June. I do love you, Ellen. You're having my baby."

"I'm glad, excited, nervous, anxious, all of the above. "

"Relax my dear."

They appeared to have real love. They had only known each other about three months, and she was already pregnant. Three months is not long enough to get to know someone. She hadn't met his parents yet, nor had he met hers. Time would tell what kind of love they really have.

Surprise! Surprise!

As it turned out, he had another side to him. He had another woman on the side. Her name is Sabrina, and while Ellen had no clue about the affair, Sabrina has known about her from the beginning. He got away with it because Sabrina was a student at another university, about a mile away. I must say this diary is interesting. The affair or playboy stuff needs to stop, its going to be ugly when its all out in the open.

The following Saturday afternoon, he and Sabrina met for brunch. The sun shone bright and warm. It was a day for sunglasses, watermelon, shorts, and a refreshing glass of lemonade. Kenneth and Sabrina met at a restaurant that always smelled like onions, fries, and hot apple pie. It is the students' favorite places to eat on the weekend. A lot of college students worked there.

"Hello, my lady, you sure are looking great."

"Hello, darling, so do you. What a beautiful day," replied Sabrina.

"What do you want to eat? I have a taste for a hamburger."

"I think I had better have a salad," said Sabrina. "I told the server you were on your way. She'll be back in a few minutes."

"I have a hole in my stomach. Some food needs to get in there."

"I want to know if you've broken up with her. You told me you would. I think I deserve to be treated better than this. Get rid of her," said Sabrina.

"Oh, I handled that last week, no worries. Calm down, I'll told her she has to go." He motioned for the waitress, so the subject can be changed.

The waitress walked up with the prettiest smile on her face. "Hello to my favorite regulars."

"Hello, Rhonda, how are you today?" he replied with a sigh of relief in his voice.

"Hello." Sabrina's voice was flat.

"Do you want the usual?" asked Rhonda.

They placed the order, and Rhonda went off to fill it.

"It seems like you're avoiding my question," Sabrina said. "You answered but you kept it short. You had enough time to say more before Rhonda arrived."

"Sabrina, I told you I handled that. You're beginning to nag me. I said no worries!"

"I hear you," said Sabrina.

"I'm glad, so you can stop badgering me. Can we change the subject?" asked Kenneth with a slight touch of anger in his voice.

"We can, just be a man of your word."

"Did you get your grade for your Calculus test you took on Tuesday? I know you were concerned."

"No, not yet. The professor said he would have our grades out this coming Tuesday."

"I hope you made an A."

"Thanks. How are your classes coming?"

"They're going great. I have a 3.8 average. I can keep my scholarships. I was sweating for a minute."

"I take it you passed your English and Trig classes that were giving you trouble."

"Yes, honey. I conquered both. It was rough."

"I should be able to keep my scholarship too. I think my Calculus grade should be no less than a B."

"Honey, we're on the right track."

"Yes, we are. Just handle Ellen."

Kenneth gave Sabrina a look then changed the subject.

* * *

Kenneth knew how to play the game. He called Ellen that evening as soon as he got back to his room. "Hello, darling, how has your day gone?"

"It has been great! I got everything accomplished. How was your study group?"

"We got a lot accomplished. Everyone pitched in to help with the project. We figured out how to demonstrate the product, and we created a presentation."

"Everyone is doing their part, that's the way it should be. I hope you make an A on this project." replied Ellen.

"I appreciate you. Did you check out the movie times?"

"The movie starts at nine," she answered with a smile.

***

They had a beautiful, romantic evening. The movie was thrilling. The temperature was right. The moon was beautiful and just right for the walk home. Kenneth watched her go inside the dorm after a long beautiful conversation outside of her dormitory hall. When he got back to his dorm, Sabrina was waiting on him.

* * *

"I've been calling you all evening. I've been throwing up. It started about an hour after you left me. I thought I needed to go to the emergency room. I feel a lot better after I drank some ginger ale, took some medicine, and stayed in the bathroom all this afternoon. It's got to be food poisoning." Sabrina sighed with relief.

"I'm glad you're feeling better. I apologize for being unavailable. I was in a meeting with the group to finish a project we're working on. How long you've been standing outside my dorm waiting on me?"

"I guess it does look like I'm stalking you. I got a little desperate. I just wanted my baby to comfort me. You've been working on that project all this time?" asked Sabrina.

"Are you trying to say you don't believe me? I have no reason to lie."

"You were with that girl you said you broke up with. Who works on a project on a Saturday night, with all the parties on campus? If you are lying

139

to me, your lies will find you out."

"That's so true. The truth will come out. Let me walk you to your dormitory."

They began their walk on a beautiful night, it was perfect the full moon was shining bright and so were the stars.

At Sabrina's dormitory, he gave her a kiss and she melted. Kenneth acted like a charmer that night, and he thinks he's slick. He knows how to calm a girl down. Sabrina calmed down fast.

Twenty-One

Its Pouring Men

Someone has captured Tanya's love. Someone she calls The Boss, who is six feet one. This person wears jeans and a polo shirt just about every day. Where the name came from is a mystery. Everything about this person is a mystery.

A phone conversation

You could hear her smile through the phone, she was so happy. "Hello, how are you doing?"

"Great, I had a lovely day," said The Boss. "I miss you. I hate that I only get to see you on the weekends. You're so far away."

"I miss you to. I'm feeling like our relationship is wrong. God might not approve of our relationship, but I don't want to break up with you. I don't think my friends and family will approve of us neither."

"It's hard for people to understand why I'm who I am or act as I act. I do need to meet your family."

"You will one day. Someone is calling. Let me call you back."

Tanya hung up on The Boss and took the call.

"How are you? I was just thinking of you and thought I would call," Patricia said.

"That's so sweet of you. I've been intending to call you, how are you? And the rest of the girls?" asked Tanya.

"Girl, everything is great for me. School is keeping me busy. Everyone is doing great!" replied Patricia. "Ellen is getting ready to get married."

"Really, I'll call her and give her my regards. School is keeping me busy too. You know I have a significant other, The Boss."

"That's great. I guess we'll meet your beau soon. Where did he get the name Boss from?" Patricia inquired.

"Girl, you know I never asked where that name came from.

Tanya is lying through her pearly white teeth. She knows she cannot tell the whole truth.

"Well, my friend, we all deserve to be happy. Do you have to do a lot of studying or writing?"

"I have to do both. Spelman is keeping me busy. I had to tell myself to relax."

"I have to do the same thing. I need to go my dorm mates are knocking on the door. Talk to you later friend!"

"Later friend!"

* * *

What's up with Rachel?

Three-way phone call

"Rachel are you coming back to Cedar Lake for Christmas?" Diane asked.

"No, I think I'll stay here."

"Aren't you going to be by yourself?"

"She'll be with her man," Ruth explained.

"What man? Diane responded. "We don't know a man."

"Stop tripping. I was waiting to tell you. But honestly, I don't mind telling the two of you. His name is Sam. I'm staying here to have Christmas with him and his family."

"Sounds pretty serious."

"Its real love. We strive to be patient and kind to each other at all costs. We understand love tells the truth. Now our relationship isn't perfect, but it's good." Rachel said.

"No relationship is perfect. Sounds like you have the right one. Congratulations on finding love ."

"Yes, congratulations," Diane said. "Are you going to decorate for the holidays?"

"You should. And cook dinner for him. Make it real special for the holiday season."

"That's a great idea. I'm going to do it. I probably should do it this weekend. Christmas is only ten days away."

"You probably should."

"I'll call you and let you know how it turned out."

* * *

Sam calls Rachel, its early Saturday morning

"Good morning."

"Hello, my love."

"Hello my Sam! What's up?"

"Do you want to go jogging with me this morning, and then maybe we can have some breakfast?"

"I'm always ready for a hearty breakfast. What time is it?"

"It's nine."

"I can be ready in about thirty minutes?"

"Perfect! See you later."

"Later Gator."

They hang up the phones.

* * *

While they were jogging, Rachel started huffing and puffing.

"Sam wait up, I'm out of breath."

"You can do it. I'll slow down a little."

"Sam I can't breathe; I feel like I'm about to fall."

Sam ran to her and grabbed her.

"Babe, I got you. Let's rest for a minute. We'll decide if we should continue. Let's sit on the bench."

They sat on the park bench for about ten minutes watching other joggers and watched the ducks near the pond.

"How do you feel?"

"Better!"

"You want to walk around the track real slow. Do you have asthma or anything?"

"I had asthma when I was a little girl."

"Honey, you might want to get that checked out."

"I'll go to the student health center tomorrow in between classes."

"I'll go with you."

"Sam. That's not necessary. I don't want you to miss class."

"You're tripping, missing one class isn't going to make a difference. I'll be there."

"If you must!"

* * *

The next day, Sam did go to the health clinic with her. The doctor gave her some asthma medicine. Rachel was so delighted her boyfriend made sure she was okay.

Marion and her man

Antonio is walking Marion to her dorm. They stopped at the steps of the building right next to the dorm.

"Stay outside with me."

" We have a full day tomorrow."

"Oh, honey, don't worry about that."

He grabbed her and hugged her, with her backside hugged to his front side.

He put his arms around her waist.

"It's a perfect night."

"Yes, it is."

"I'm glad I met you." Marion said as she turned around and stared at him.

"I feel the same way. I look at you and I can only imagine how blissful my life will be waking up next to you every morning."

"Antonio, that's so sweet."

"Ah babe it's the truth. You make my heart skip beats."

You're pouring it on thick. And I'm blushing. Keep it coming."

"I have to save some for another day. I'm going to let me queen get her beauty rest."

He kisses Marion on the cheek. "Good night."

"Good night!"

He watched her until she entered the dormitory.

* * *

Charles and Ruth

The following Saturday, Charles called Ruth.

"What are you doing?"

"I just finished washing and drying my clothes," she responded. "What's up?"

"Some of our friends are having a birthday party tonight. It's at their parent's house. Will you go with me?"

"I can use a break from studying."

"I'll pick you up at five pm. It's casual, not dressy."

"I guess we'll need to get a birthday present."

"Thank God for women. You remember everything."

"Target should be fine. It's right by the freeway."

"We shouldn't have to spend that much, right?" he asked.

"Correct, it's the thought that counts," she said.

"Well, honey, I 'll see you at five pm," he said.

* * *

Because of the weather, it took them awhile to get there. They were the last ones to arrive at the party.

Wana opened the front door. "Hello. Come in."

"Hello everyone," Charles said. Ruth smiled and waved.

"Hello lovebirds," John said. "Glad you made it."

"Hey John. Sorry it took us so long to get here. The streets are clearing slowly. A lot of ice in some places. But we drove about twenty miles per hour to be on the safe side."

"We're glad the couple of the year made it," John said.

Ruth is holding a beautiful purple and red wrapped gift. She turns to Wana. "This is for you."

"Thanks. I'll open it when I open the others."

"Now, lovebirds, tell us when you're getting married?" John said.

"Yes, when is the date?" Marcus asked.

"Listen, when we get married, you'll be invited."

"Can't wait until the big day comes," John said. "I better be the best man."

"You will, my friend."

"Everyone let's eat some of this food. Turning twenty-one is cool. I'm thankful God has been a great provider and guide for my life. He has given me friends and family," Wana said. "Lord, we thank you for this food, let it nourish our bodies, in Jesus' name we pray."

"I want some of that gumbo and the hot wings," Marcus said.

"Me too," John replied.

The guests were eating in the kitchen and the den.

Forty minutes later

"Please make yourself at home. Any friend of Charles is a friend of mine. I think of him as a brother. We would call him the baby, and big head. He was the last child in the neighborhood. We let him tag along with us. You have a man of character and integrity. We have two doctors in the house you a surgeon and he's pediatric doctor."

"I agree Yes we're both future doctors we met the first day of our internshp!" She responded. She glanced at the guys as they sat in the dining room drinking. *Ruth thought to herself, I hope that's his one and only drink.*

"Let me know if you need anything. If you want to, you're welcome to spend the night." Wana said.

"Thanks, I appreciate the offer. We might need to take you up on that offer."

"No problem. I'll be right back."

Charles walked over to his baby with a plate full of food. "What's going on?"

Ruth giggled as she looked at her beau. "You must be hungry. Look at your plate. How many glasses of wine have you had?"

"Yes, I was hungry, and the aroma of the food is breath taking. The hot wings and tuna fish are scrumptious. I've had two, my dear."

"Very appetizing. Wana just told me about your childhood. They called you big head. You're the baby in the group. She said we could spend the night. If you keep drinking, I think we should."

" I'm just being sociable. Let's go mingle and meet." He said as he stumbled when he took a few steps.

She watched him walk. He's stumbling a little.

"Hey come over here with us girls. We're about to watch a movie, it's a girl's flick."

"Here I come!" Ruth said.

The party is a hit. Everyone is having a great time. You can't hear yourself talking. People didn't start leaving until after midnight.

The party is over

She's sitting on the sofa in the den." Wana thank you for inviting Charles and I to your party. We were the last ones here and the last to leave."

Wana is picking up cups and paper plates the guests left. "You all have the longest drive back to your place. Please spend the night. I think he's has had too much to drink."

Ruth began to speak. "You noticed."

"Ladies I can drive. I've enjoyed myself. I believe my girl did too. But we're going to head out. I have something I have to do at church in the morning. Thanks for the invite. Thanks for being a friend and a sister to me."

You're welcome, my brother. I think you need to spend the night and leave early enough to go home and change clothes. You have had too much to drink."

"I'm fine. The wine I had has worn off."

"I believe you had more than three drinks."

"I'm fine " They walked to the door. They hugged each other.

"Bye," Ruth said.

"Bye!" Wana replied.

"See you later!"

He grabbed her hand and they walked to the car. He opened the door for her to get in the car. Then he goes to the driver side still stumbling.

Its hard for him to stay within the lines on the road.

About fifteen miles from Wana's house.

"Honey we should stop at a restaurant or that rest stop over there."

The car slides on some ice and went straight off the road and hit a pole. The car made such a loud noise it could be heard miles away. The electricity went out all over the area. They were knocked unconscious. Within a minute flashing lights were everywhere the ambulance and police cars were everywhere. The ambulance took them to the nearest hospital's emergency room. They ended up staying overnight.

The next morning about 6 am

Charles woke up. The nurse was in his room. "Where am I? Am I in a hospital?"

The nurse answered. "You and your friend were in an auto accident last night. Both of you were unconscious when you arrived at the hospital. Not sure if your female friend is awake or not. "

"Oh no! I hope she's okay!"

"Sir, I need you to relax. You just woke up. Everyone is fine." The nurse said.

"Can I see her?"

"No!" the nurse responded. "You'll see her once you rest and are dismissed from the hospital. I'll be back in an hour, please rest."

He tossed and turned for the next thirty minutes.

He thought to himself. Ruth and Wana told me to spend the night, but I was hardheaded. I hope my baby is okay. Lord forgive me I know I had too much to drink. I was drunk. I shouldn't have tried to be such a man. Please forgive and let my girl be okay.

He finally fell asleep for the rest of the night. He didn't see his sweetheart until the following morning. He was relieved when he saw her. She wanted to tell him I told you so but refrained.

"Good morning. I'm so thankful, we're alive and okay."

"Thank God!"

Charles thought to himself. Thank you Lord she's alright and she's looking good. I'll never have more than one drink again. I'll never drive drunk. I'll never be drunk with wine wherein it is excess.

Antonio is acting strange

One day Marion was washing her hair and didn't want to stop. The phone kept ringing, ringing, and ringing. Her roommate wasn't in. The phone rung for ten minutes.

Right about that time Marion was able to run and answer the phone. "Hello?" He's screaming at the top of his lungs. "I've been calling for the last thirty minutes. Where have you been?"

Marion began talking with water and shampoo dripping down her face. "Washing my hair."

"It doesn't take that long to wash your hair. Where have you been?"

" What are you talking about? I have a lot of hair. I wash it and condition it. That's a process."

"Who do you think you're fooling?"

"Honey, I don't know what's gotten into you. I can tell you don't have any sisters. You've never acted like this before."

"There's nothing wrong with me. I'm just trying to talk to my woman. Is there anything wrong with that?"

"No, you're just acting strange. I'm here, talk to me."

"I just called to say I love you."

"I love you too. Is that all that's on your mind?"

"I just wanted to talk to you." *He thought to himself. She better not have a man in that room.*

"Are you sure you're okay? I need to dry my hair."

"Go ahead and do your hair, call me when you're finished. "

"I will, love you."

"Love you too!"

Marion said. "I hope he calms down. Something is not right with him."

Twenty-Two

Bells Will Be Ringing

"Kenneth, I think we had better go down to the courthouse sometime this week, no later than next week."

"You don't care about having a wedding? Most ladies want a big wedding. I hope you don't regret it."

"I might regret it. But honestly, I don't want to have a beautiful wedding dress on with a big stomach."

"I understand. Let's get married!"

"Are you sure you don't want a wedding?"

"I don't mind just as long as I'm with you, my love."

"Yes, babe, as long as I'm with you too. I'm glad you're cool with going to the courthouse."

* * *

The Courthouse

A lot of people were getting married that day. The judge was in a rush.

They stood in front of the judge.

The justice of the peace said,"Hello Ellen Snow and Kenneth Womack. All of your paperwork is in order. Ellen Snow and Kenneth Womack, I now pronounce you husband and wife, by the power vested in me by the state of California. You may kiss the bride and exchange rings."

"Give me a kiss, wifey!"

They kissed for a long time. At least that is what the judge thought.

"Congratulations. Now can you move out of the way for the next person in line." The Judge said.

"Sorry judge thanks." She said with a big smile.

'Yes, sorry about that judge, thanks."

"That wasn't so bad. We're married now," she said.

"There were so many people getting married. I thought we were going to have to wait forever," he said. "When are we going to tell your parents?"

"The sooner I call, the better"

"That's true. Let's go out to eat. It's time to celebrate our new beginning."

"Fogo de Chao, that's a place I've wanted to go since I heard of it." she said it with love in her eyes.

"That's where we're going."

They headed towards their car, holding hands and looking in each other's eyes.

* * *

The restaurant

The restaurant was right down the street.

They waited to be seated.

The maître d' showed them to a table for two.

The restaurant has exquisite, unique, and beautiful decor. It has a beach theme, a lot of seashells in all shapes and sizes. "Thanks for bringing me here; this is a class act restaurant."

"You deserve the best. The ambiance is great."

The waiter walked up.

"Will you take our picture?" She asked.

"I'll take a couple, so you'll have several. Is it a special occasion?"

"Yes, it is. We just got married."

"Congratulations. You make a cute couple. Dessert and wine are on us."

"Thanks," Ken said.

"May I get you something to drink?"

"Water for now, no bring a coke too."

"Same here." Ken replied. The employee left. "I know you're glad we're married, but one day I want to make it up to you and give you the wedding you deserve and a honeymoon."

"Ken don't worry about that. I'm just glad we're married; I don't want to hear my parents complain or give you the blues. My father can get on your nerves."

"I want him to know, I'm not sorry. He needs to know I intend to treat you with respect and love."

"He can be stubborn. Enough of my parents. Let's enjoy our special day."

* * *

The Honeymoon Suite at the Hotel

To have had a court house wedding, their wedding day turned out to be a day to remember. They stayed at The Double Tree Hotel. The hotel had a pianist playing soft jazz in the lobby.

They entered their room. "Ken the roses are so beautiful. The candy bouquet is different. I'm taking a picture of them."

They recruited people to take pictures of them, and the rest of the night was a night to remember for the newlyweds. Ellen knew she had to share the news with her parents. She hadn't been home since Thanksgiving. She was scared because she'd been forbidden to see Kenneth.

The Next Day

"Hi mom! How are you? What are you doing?" Ellen asked.

"I just sat down to watch a movie," she answered. "What's going on?"

"Mother, Kenneth and I got married yesterday. We felt as though we needed to," she said softly, almost whispering.

"Did you say what I think you said?" asked her mother.

"Yes, mom. We got married yesterday," she answered.

"Why did you get married? You know your father isn't going to be happy. He's going to stop paying for your college." asked her mother.

"I'm pregnant," she said in a soft voice again.

"Oh my, you are? I guess you did the honorable thing. You just got up there and acted as if you have no self-control."

"I'm sorry, Mom. I love him."

"Now I understand why you didn't come home for Christmas."

"Kenneth wants to talk to you."

"Hello, I know this is awkward. Please don't fuss at her too much. You know it takes two to tango. It's my fault also. I plan to do right by her."

"I'm glad to hear that. I hope her father doesn't go through the roof. He told her she can't date."

"I apologize. I believe we'll be able to complete our goals. The timing might be off a little, but I think we can survive and make it," he said.

"I hope so," Mrs. Snow said.

"Again, I'm sorry you're upset. Do you want to speak with Ellen?"

He handed her the phone.

"Yes, Mom. It might be hard. I'm determined to get my education. I know I messed up. I know you're not ready to be a grandmother this early in your life."

"I truly hope so. I'm disappointed in you, my daughter. I must respect your decisions. You're legally an adult. Lord knows I have made my mistakes." replied her mother.

"We all have mom! No one's perfect."

She handed him the phone.

"We will survive. I do love her. All I ask is that you give us a chance and that you trust me."

"I guess I need to say congratulations," said Ellen's mom.

"Thanks," responded Kenneth. You want to talk to Ellen?"

"Yes, put her on the phone. I'm taking you at your word." Mrs. Snow said.

"Don't worry Mrs. Snow. Here she is!"

She took the phone from him. "Hello again mom."

"I told Kenneth congratulations. I just wanted to tell you congratulations and that I love you regardless of what has taken place." Mrs. Snow said.

"Thanks Mom. I love you too. Talk to you later."

Twenty-Three

Marion and Antonio

<u>Marion's apartment</u>

There's a knock on the door.

Marion asked. "Who is it?"

"It's me, your baby," replied Antonio.

"Just a minute," she replied.

"Okay, but can you hurry up?" he asked. "What are you doing?"

"Hold on! I'm coming!"

She opens the door.

"About time. Your other boyfriend here? What have you been doing? I tried calling you, you wouldn't answer the phone."

"I just got back about thirty minutes ago."

"Where have you been?"

"My roommate told me you called ten times!" she said with disbelief in her voice.

"I called only three times."

"Was there an emergency? Is everyone all right?"

"Now it is. I just needed to talk to you. I was feeling a little down. I knew you could make me feel better. Did you have any visitors today? Is that the reason why you wouldn't answer your phone? When I call, honey, I need you to answer the phone. No question. No discussion. I don't care what you're doing." His volume increased.

She paused and pondered to concentrate on what he's saying. "I think I washed clothes after I got home. I took a shower. I know I called home and talked to my family. What's wrong? You're extremely upset!"

He had an anguish look on his face. "They can wait. I'm number one. No one comes before me. Make sure you answer the phone before it rings three times. I don't have time for games. I'm not going to be second fiddle."

He's acting very possessive. Marion thought. "No one is playing games."

"I love you. I just want to be with you," said Antonio.

"I love you too," said Marion. *I'm saying this but he's acting rather possessive and strange. I'm not sure if I love him. I'm becoming concerned. I hope he's not abusive. Maybe its just a phase.*

Despite his weird, controlling behavior they did have a nice evening together.

Twenty-Four

Time for the Baby

The nurse urged her to keep pushing because the doctor will be there in less than five minutes. "Push, Push!"

"I'm pushing. I want this baby out of me. Help me Lord!"

The grunting, pushing,screaming and crying continued for a few more minutes, but it felt like eternity.

The doctor walked in the delivery prepared and ready.

The nurse moved over so the doctor could get in his position. "We only need a few hard pushes. I can see the top of the baby's head. Keep pushing." The doctor said.

"Come on, Sydney. Help your mother out. Keep pushing, baby." Kenneth said.

The doctor was in position to deliver the baby.

Sydney came out screaming as loud as she could.

"Thank God my baby Sydney is here!" Ellen said with a sigh of relief.

"Our baby, I'm so thankful." Kenneth said.

"Me too! So adorable, our precious baby thank God."

"Congratulations on your baby girl!" the doctor said.

"Thanks!"

***

The ladies were in the waiting room with both sets of parents.

The nurse entered the waiting room. "Ladies, Sydney is here. You'll be able to visit with them in about thirty minutes." "She's a pretty baby."

"I can't wait to see her. I know she's adorable." Ruth stated.

"Oh, thank God the baby came, and everyone is okay," Diane said.

"Ellen is a mom," Rachel said. "How many pounds?"

"Seven pounds, fourteen ounces," the nurse replied.

"Healthy too!" the girls said at the same time.

* * *

Forty minutes later

Ellen managed to smile even though she's exhausted. "My baby Sydney is here. She's so cute. I think she looks like me. Thanks for all the gifts."

"You're welcome!" Diane said.

"That's what friends are for." Ruth said.

"Yes, for sure. Thank God for a healthy baby and a safe delivery." Rachel said.

"Thanks for coming and it's nice to meet you all. Our baby is adorable!"

"I'm a grandmother at the age of forty, but who cares. Sydney, welcome to the world. I plan to spoil you rotten," Mrs. Snow said while she held the baby.

"Yes, you are mom, but you look good holding the baby." Kenneth said.

"Thank you so much. Everyone, you're welcome to stay. But I'm getting ready to go to sleep. I'm whipped."

"I guess the rest of us can get something to eat. How about Pappadeaux?" Kenneth suggested.

"I don't care what I eat. I need to get something on my stomach," Diane said.

"Follow me. It's about one mile from here."

"Wait a minute. Everyone can fit in the van," Mr. Snow said.

"Yeah, it makes sense for us to ride together," said Kenneth's father.

"Great idea!" Kenneth said.

Everyone went to the restaurant. They ate, talked, and got acquainted. They found out Mr. Womack and Mr. Snow liked to golf.

The girls surprised them by setting up the baby's room for them. Sydney had plenty of pampers, clothes, formula, and baby wipes. The girls stayed for a week to help out. It was a great success, great fun, food, and fellowship.

Twenty-Five

Rachel Sees Kenneth in Action

Ellen writes Rachel a letter one year later

I apologize for not being available when you call. Sydney keeps me busy. Kenneth is on the phone a lot, so the line can be busy. I decided to write, since it's hard to get you on the phone. And by writing, I don't have to worry about Ken eavesdropping. I have asked him about some lipstick and perfume. When he lies, he can't look me in the face. He has this movement that he does that lets me know he's lying. He denies everything. I don't know what to do. I'm so miserable. Please pray for me.

Enough of me, what's going on with you? I hope you met someone new.

Love you,

Ellen

The letter was received within three days. I guess I need to go to California to check on my friend. Let me check on the airline tickets. My poor friend.

***

Caliornia Time

Labor Day Weekend

Rachel is standing near the Delta sign on the sidewalk right outside of baggage claim.

The excitement showed when she began walking so fast to meet her friend. "Welcome to Los Angeles, California!"

"Hey, friend, thanks for picking me up."

They get in the car.

"Sydney is so cute. Hey cutie!"

She just smiles.

"She has plenty of energy."

"She's very busy."

"I understand busy. Where is Kenneth?"

"He's working overtime, on a Friday night. I don't know who he thinks he's fooling."

"He might be working overtime. Don't be imagining, give him the benefit of doubt."

"I'm not. You'll get a chance to see."

"I'm here to see the baby and you. I'll catch up with Kenneth, if he has time."

"Let's check out Hollywood, go to Beverly Hills and drive down Wilshire Boulevard. We can take pictures at the Wilshire Boulevard Temple. It's so beautiful. We should be there in about twenty minutes. Maybe you and Sydney can take a picture together."

"Let's do that and go see UCLA. And get something to eat."

They arrived at the Temple

It's a beautiful marble edifice with a glistening copper dome rising one hundred feet above the edge of downtown Los Angeles. It's decorated with an interior mural. It was completed in 1929. It's known as Congregation B'nai B'rith. It's the oldest Jewish congregation.

"The architecture is breathtaking. I have to get some pictures. Come on, Sydney, take a picture with Auntie."

She reached for Sydney and handed the camera to Ellen.

"That's a great pose. Strike a pose with me hugging my baby girl."

"Send me a copy of the picture! Maybe I can get them developed while I'm here."

Wait a minute—let me take a couple more poses."

"It should be a cute picture!"

"You and Sydney act like you've known each other forever."

"She knows I'm her buddy."

"Yes, Sydney does! Let's walk and drive down Wilshire Boulevard, then we'll get something to eat."

If that's what you want to do, we'll do that!"

* * *

They had dinner at Pacific Dining Car on Wilshire Boulevard, where they took more pictures. They talked about childhood memories, it was just like old times. Sydney was fascinated with Rachel and the people at the restaurant. They made it to the hous about ten pm. Kenneth wasn't home yet.

" I like your seashore looking drapes and the rugs to match. The blue is so pretty. It reminds you of the ocean. Your accent color beige tops it off. It makes your living room classy and stylish."

"Thanks, it's something I saw at JC Penney's and I had to have it. Excuse me for a second. I'm calling Ken at the office. He should've been home by now."

Ellen dialed the number several times. The phone rang. No answer. Feeling disappointed, deceived and getting worried, her emotions are all over the place. Some of his friends had called according to caller id.

She was lost for words, so she quickly changed the subject. "Show me my room, I think I'm going to bed. I've been up since seven o'clock this morning."

"For sure, honey." They walked past a hall closet, then the bathroom, both on the right. Rachel's room is in the corner of the house on the left. "There are towels in the linen closet inside the bathroom. Let me know if you need anything else. There are plenty of channels to watch on TV, the remote should be on top of the TV. Make yourself at home, my friend."

"Thanks, my friend, don't worry about him."

"You're so kind. Good night."

Everyone had eaten, taken a shower and sound asleep by by ten forty-five. Kenneth hadn't made it home yet.

Two hours passed. He wasn't home yet.

Four hours passed, no sign of her husband.

Six hours passed he wasn't at home yet. On the seventh hour he made it. Five-thirty am. California time, but eight-thirty Philadelphia time, Rachel happened to be awake. She was coming out of the bathroom. She saw him walk in the door. "Good morning, Kenneth."

Kenneth was startled. "Good morning and hello and welcome. I thought you were sleep. Please make yourself at home. I'll get with you later. I got to check on Sydney and Ellen."

"Thanks, I will." It was time to watch the news on TV. Shortly, after turning the TV on, she heard some yelling, swearing, and crying. *Oh, maybe this wasn't a good weekend to come.*

* * *

The Bedroom

"Shh, you'll wake the baby, and your friend will hear us."

"I don't care. It's five-thirty in the morning. You've been out all night. Did you forget you're married? Your job didn't hold you this long. You haven't been acting like you're married lately. I'm so disappointed in you!"

"Babe, you're tripping. I went out with the guys. I know I should have called the house. Everything was moving fast. I hadn't hung with the guys in a while. Please forgive me, sweetie."

"The only thing I know is its five-thirty in the morning! What guys?"

"Paul and John."

"Well that's strange, because they called here looking for you. They called twice. I wasn't here one time. Their names were on the caller id. Get your lie straight. The truth will come out."

Kenneth just stood there.

"I can't even look at you right now, Your lies come out of your mouth so fast." Ellen went to the bathroom.

Sydney woke up crying. "Don't cry, daddy's little girl. My little angel."

Sydney went back to sleep after Kenneth changed her and sung to her.

After returning from the bathroom thirty minutes later he had fallen asleep on one side of the bed. When she decided to lay down, it was on the opposite side, the far edge of the bed.

Ellen slept until nine am. She didn't realize it was twelve noon in Philadelphia.

Rachel was dressed, drinking coffee, and watching TV.

"Good morning, my friend. How did you sleep?" she asked.

"I slept well. I've been up for a while. I watched the news, some cartoons. I took my shower and I'm ready to go?"

"My husband is going to stay here and keep Sydney while you and I hang out today. We can visit Rodeo Drive in Beverly Hills and drive down La Cienega Boulevard. I want to take you to Venice and Santa Monica beach. Maybe we can roller skate. I'll be ready in an hour."

"Ready when you are."

* * *

One hour later, Kenneth and Sydney were still asleep. A short note was left for him to inform him of her agenda. *It would be nice to be shown the same courtesy and respect.*

"I'm ready. Let's hit the road. This is a treat for me. I've been busy being a wife, a mother, and a student."

"You deserve a break." The girls walked outside and got in the car. "Do you need gas?"

"No, I have a full tank. Did you hear anything this morning?"

"Yes, I heard it all. It's interesting how you caught him in a lie. I was up when he came in. My body's still on Philadelphia time. I think I scared him this morning. Something is definitely wrong."

"He should be embarrassed that you saw him come home late and heard us arguing. He's such a liar. I don't know what I've done to deserve this type of treatment. I know I shouldn't have gotten pregnant without being married. I asked God to forgive me. I need a miracle. I've been married a little over a year and a half, and I'm already having marital problems."

"Whatever you do my friend, don't give up. Keep calling him out. Don't let him walk over you. There's still hope, my friend. It can be a lot worse."

She throws her fist in the air. "My hormones act up so bad, there are times I just want to throw something at him or slap him so hard. I have dreams of throwing a skillet at him. He makes me so mad. I need help. Thanks for coming, believe it or not, your calmness keeps me calm."

"I'm glad to hear that. You're doing great. I probably would have hit him by now and ask God to forgive me later."

"I won't stoop to his level!"

"Trust me, it's not worth it, there are consequences to our actions."

"Thanks for reminding me my friend. I appreciate you."

She smiled and thought to herself. My friend is having a hard time.

They did have a great day and had a great time the whole weekend. There's a need for prayer, her friend needs clarity on how to handle this problem she's experiencing.

The friends are keeping their oath of remaining friends. That was nice of Rachel to go back to California to the aid of her friend. The girls have their share of problems as you see. From what I can tell through it all they seem to trust God in all the good and bad.

Twenty-Six

It's Tanya's Business

꩜

A couple of Fred's friends were hanging out at Cedar Lake Mall, outside the tennis shoe store. "Why is Tanya always with this girl?" Harold asked.

"Man, I don't know," John said. "I mentioned it to Fred. You know Tanya is friends with his girl, Diane. He said she's probably just a college friend. I told him it seems strange. Everywhere I go, I see them together. Man, I've been checking her out since middle school."

"I see them together in Atlanta and Cedar Lake. I asked Sandra. You know she's a gossip. She said she has a boyfriend no one has ever met this person called 'The Boss.' He goes to Morehouse, but none of our classmates have seen or met him. It's kind of strange."

"Tanya is fine."

"Yes, she is."

Later on that day

Meanwhile, Sandra was on a mission to find out what was going on with her. She called Sally. "Hey, this is Sandra in Cedar Lake. I was just thinking about you. How are you doing?"

"I'm doing fine. I have no complaints. College life is a lot of work, it's fun, and of course very educational."

"'That's great. How is everyone? I saw her from a distance. She's always with this girl and never a man or no one else ever. I thought she had a boyfriend."

"She does. His name is Boss."

"Are you sure? Have you met him?"

"Sandra, let me call you back, my other line is ringing."

Diane started talking as soon as I clicked over and without saying hello. "What's going on with Tanya? Harold and John called me asking me questions about her."

"Our friend must be the talk of the town in Cedar Lake. Sandra was on the other line asking me about her. I was glad the phone rang. She asked me, have I met Boss? I couldn't say anything. Thank God you called."

"I'm glad I called to! It's funny to me people always want to know what we're doing?"

"I don't have time to worry about others. It's too much going on in my life. My school, family, and my friend that keeps me busy."

"Yes, our schoolwork, our family, and my friends. There's always something going on."

You know what to keep it real, its kind of strange Tanya and her man."

"It is the truth will come out. We can't be consumed with it or make her tell us."

"So true, I hope we get to see each other soon my friend."

"Me too. We can meet in Cedar Lake or maybe you can come to Florida."

"We'll make something happen. Love you my friend. I was getting ready to study before the phone rang."

"Love you too!"

I've always wondered about the Boss also. Its a mystery. And the story continues.

Twenty-Seven

Patricia Writes in her Diary

What am I going to do?

I can't trust any man. Every guy I date, I accuse them of playing around. I don't know what's going on. I think what my uncle did to me has caused me not to trust men. He raped me on a regular basis in our basement. He threatened to kill me if I told. I never told anyone.

I have had ten boyfriends in the last three years. I can catch them but I can't keep them. I run them away. I don't rush to have sex, since that Bryan episode. I learned so much from that. I guess I'm growing in some areas.

I hope I don't run, my new beau Drew away, or I hope I don't throw him away. I hope this relationship last at least until Fred and Diane get married. He's very patient with me. I think I can do it.

Lord I knew help. Help me please! I wake up in the middle of the night, I have nightmares thinking I'll never get over my uncle. Lord I know only you can help me. This is our secret. I'm going to trust you Lord, heal me, and help me Lord.

Twenty-Eight

The Nerve of Windsor

It was a Saturday morning the last weekend of April, a networking brunch event just ended. Ruth wore a pink sundress. The event was at the school's university center. Windsor, a friend attended also, he's muscular, and strong. The women drool all over him. Windsor is like a brother to her. They've been friends since their freshman year in college.

"Windsor my car is in the shop! I don't know how I'm going to get home today." Ruth explained.

Windsor began speaking. "I have something to do in a couple of hours; I'm free now. Do you need me to take you home?"

She looked at her watch. "Yes, please. It's past noon. I guess we'd better go. Is it okay if I tell a few people goodbye?"

"Go ahead I'll bring the car up to the door to pick you up." Windsor said.

* * *

Windsor has a red Mazda RX-7 the seats are close in proximity. He drove along the Charles River so they can catch a glimpse of the sail boats, the tour boats, the joggers, and the beautiful scene driving parallel to the river. During the ride Windsor kept staring at her. The pink dress accented all of

170

her curves. Ruth didn't notice it because she was so busy enjoying the ride and the scenery.

The Apartment

Windsor stopped the car. He gets out the car and runs to her door to open it for her. "I need to use the bathroom." *I need to make a move on this girl, she's turning me on.*

"Sure, come on in. You're welcome to stay until your meeting starts at two thirty."

They go in. Windsor goes straight to the bathroom which is connected to her bedroom. She goes into her bedroom while he's in the bathroom. She puts on her house shoes while sitting on her bed. Windsor came out of the bathroom.

"Windsor! Zip your pants up you're exposed. I don't want to see you. You're not at home."

Windsor walked over to the bed. "Don't be scared. I'm not going to hurt you." Ruth tried to run away he grabbed her by her right arm and pulled her back to the bed.

No, you can't do this." Ruth tried with all her strength to get away.

Windsor had her on the bed, pulled her dress up and her panties down. Windsor had begun to try to take away her virginity.

The crying and screaming was loud enough for the neighbors to hear.

"Be quiet!" Windsor said in a demanding tone.

"Get off me. I'm calling the police. Oh Lord, I'm scared I can't believe a friend, a brother whom I trusted is trying to take away my virginity. Help me Lord; I can't get him off me. This isn't right help me push him off. Give me strength."

At that moment, she pushed him off and he landed on the floor.

"I hate you. Get out of my apartment! I trusted you."

"Don't act like that." Windsor got up off the floor started zipping up his pants.

"Get out!"

"I guess I had better get out of here."

171

Windsor made it to his car and drove off. *Maybe she'll calm down within a week. I may have lost a friend. We guys do some stupid things all for a moment of satisfaction. I couldn't help myself.*

Ruth ran to take a shower as she continued to cry. "I feel so dirty. How could he do such a thing? I feel nasty, I must take a shower and wash every body part he touched."

Tears streamed down her face as the water hit her body. The shower lasted twenty minutes.

I think I'll go to bed I'm so depressed, it's only one thirty in the afternoon. Maybe I can sleep it off. She got in the bed under the covers. *I feel so terrible. How can I face my parents, my father the pastor? It's embarrassing to think my friend tried to rape me. I'm so glad he didn't succeed. I don't know if I can forgive him. I know I'm supposed to if I call myself a child of God. Lord this is a hard one.*

The crying and praying continued.

Three days later

They have only one week of college left. Ruth went on about her business. She has avoided him.

Ruth came home to her apartment after class on Wednesday. She's greeted with twelve yellow roses at her door. "Who is this from? "The nerve of him to send me some flowers after what he did to me. I'm throwing these flowers in the trash." Ruth went into her apartment, and the first thing she did was put them in the garbage can in the kitchen.

Windsor sat at his apartment that evening hoping she would call him. Its ten pm. No call.

I guess she's still mad at me. If I was in her shoes, I would be mad too. I lost a friend being selfish. I guess I'll never see her again. I messed up; I need to think from now on.

***

One week after the Windsor incident

The Local Coffee Shop

Ruth is reading her Bible and drinking a cup of coffee at the Starbuck's not too far from her apartment. Windsor enters in. Ruth can't see him; her back is facing him. He hasn't noticed her neither.

Windsor walks up to the counter.

The waiter asked. "Can I help you?"

"I want a Grande coffee with hazel cream and some of that natural sugar."

"Will that be all?"

"Yes!"

"That'll be $2.50."

Windsor hands her the money and headed towards her still not aware she's there. Suddenly, he looked up and there's Ruth sitting there. *I'm going to sit down with her even though I know she's mad at me.*

Windsor sat down. "Hear me out."

"Just because you sat down doesn't mean I have to listen."

"I was so wrong for trying to take your virginity. To tell the truth, I've been attracted to you for a long time. You had that sundress on, and I got carried away. Please forgive me. I heard you say no. No means no. My hormones were telling me yes."

She looked at Windsor with a dead stare. No emotions at all.

"I deserve that look. What can I do to make it up to you? It's kind of ironic, a guy just took my sister's virginity I just happen to call her within hours after it happened. Since we're twins it's hard for her to hide things from me. I was already feeling bad but that really brought it home."

"Wow, I asked God to help me forgive you. God's word doesn't lie. You do reap what you sow. I have always thought of you as a brother. I had no idea there was an attraction." Unfortunately, I don't think our friendship will ever be the same."

"I realize that. I am glad you're willing to forgive me."

"Forgiveness is a process. God is helping me. I prefer to love you from a distance. And on that note, I'm leaving. Have a good day. God bless you." She gets up and leaves.

Windsor has a dumb and amazed look on his face.

Twenty-Nine

Wedding Bells

The rehearsal dinner

Patricia and Drew broke up the day after graduation, her time with Drew almost made it to Diane's wedding day. Her relationship with him was her longest yet. She might be growing in trusting people. The truth will come out.

Standing in front of the pulpit at the Cedar Lake Church

"Everything is going great," Diane said. "The music sounds right on key and perfect."

"The music sounded awful and loud. The soloist was singing in B, and the pianist was playing in the key of C," Yolanda, her first cousin said.

"It sounded fine to me," Ruth responded. *My friend has a strange cousin. I need to watch her.* "The girls and I said everything went great."

Yolanda stood with her hands on her hips. "I don't care what you and your girls think, it sounded terrible."

She ignored her cousin. "Thanks for a great rehearsal. We appreciate you. Now let's go to the fellowship hall and eat. The caterer has prepared several entrees, vegetable dishes, wings, salad, and drinks. I hope you like chicken."

"I like chicken," Sally said.

Patricia rubbed her stomach. "We all do!"

The wedding party walked to the rehearsal dinner. In the fellowship hall, the couple sat at the head table. The wedding party sat at the next two tables.

The food was served buffet style, and the line moved fast. The minister said grace, and everyone started eating.

"This food is nasty," Yolanda said, loud enough for everyone to hear.

And on the other side of the room her uncle was grabbing females and asking them to dance and there's no music playing. She grabbed them and did the waltz with them.

Everyone started laughing.

Patricia and Rachel looked at each other.

"Our friend has an interesting family the dancer and Yolanda." Rachel said.

"What's wrong with her and what is he on?" Patricia whispered.

"I don't know. Both are acting strange. I think she might be jealous and he might be drunk. Who does the waltz?" Rachel whispered.

"That explains her behavior."

Diane ignored Yolanda. Someone took the uncle outside. She was into her future husband. "Taste this, honey." She fed him a bite of chicken and vegetables off her own fork.

"Mmm," He said. "Tasty. The wings are delicious." "You want some more?"

"No honey. I don't want to eat all your food. I'll eat what I have on my plate."

"What's mine is yours!"

"You're right. Let me have some!" Patricia and Rachel walked up to them.

"What are you lovebirds doing?" Rachel asked.

"Don't answer, we see you feeding each other," Patricia said.

"We came over to tell you we had fun. And your cousin and uncle are crazy and weird," Rachel said.

"What can I say? You got to love them, that's my family. See you tomorrow. Tomorrow is the day!"

"Yes, it is," Patricia.

Most people stayed for about another hour and left because the big day is tomorrow.

* * *

<u>On the way home from rehearsal</u>
"Tomorrow is our big day." Fred opened the car door for her. She got in and he closed the door.

She opened the car door for him as he came to the driver side. "Honey, you've stuck with me through thick and thin. We made it through high school, college, and now the NFL. We've weathered some storms. We can weather anything that comes our way."

"Yes I did. I'm glad I did."

They smiled at each other.

***

He parked the car and they sat in the car to finish their conversation.

"Fred, I'm glad you chose the Atlanta Eagles instead of the San Francisco 49ers. At least we have our family close by."

"I'm blessed to have someone that wants me for me and not because I'm a football player. I know you'll make a lot of money being an engineer." It seemed like a kiss would be perfect timing and they kissed for about thirty seconds. It started out with a peck on the cheek.

"I still smile when I think of the time when we started dating. You 're my best friend. I feel so peaceful and safe when I'm with you. I thank God for you."

"You're right." Fred opened his door walked around to her side and grabbed her by her arm to walk her to the door. They walked slowly so they could enjoy the moment.

She looked up in the sky. "It's such a beautiful night, the sky is clear the stars are shining bright. "

"Yea babe it's perfect for you and me!"

They made it to the front door they stood there gazing at each other. Fred leaned over to kiss her again. They kissed for only thirty seconds.

She moaned and began to put her key in the door to go in. "Alright, I'm going in. We're about to start something."

"Tomorrow night will be the night. Eat your Wheaties."

"I'm ready."

"We'll see who's ready. Good night baby."

"Good night honey!" She closed the door.

* * *

Time to Jump the Broom

Her colors were teal blue and chocolate brown. The wedding party marched in to "Isn't She Lovely" by Stevie Wonder and "Baby Come to Me," by Patti Austin and James Ingram.

Her dad escorted her down the aisle, he looked so proud and happy. She chose "You and I" by Stevie Wonder as her processional. I must say my sister was the most beautiful bride in her lace and pearl dress. Her form-fitting dress had a V-shaped neckline.

The ceremony begins

Pastor Perry, Ruth's father, asked, "Who gives this woman in marriage?"

"I do!" her dad answered.

Pastor Perry nodded at her father and proceeded with the wedding vows. "Do you, Fred, take Diane to be your wife?" "I do."

"Do you, Diane, take Fred to be your husband?"

"I do."

"I now pronounce you husband and wife. Now you may kiss the bride." They began kissing, and they kissed for a long time. Everyone chuckled.

"Ladies and gentlemen, I present Mr. and Mrs. Fred Williams."

The music played, and the wedding party followed the bride and groom out to the reception.

Melody a classmate leans over to a friend, "She thinks she's something."

The friend, another classmate responds. "Yes, she does, she and her friends are full of themselves.

Eddie, Derrick, James, June, and Renee some of the sisters and brothers of Diane's friends were seated in front of those girls. Renee began to speak. "Some people always have something to say."

Eddie responded. "Its a shame, but the ceremony was very nice. She's a beautiful bride."

" Yes, she is!" June said.

"They're motioning for us to go to the fellowship hall." James said.

* * *

In the fellowship hall, the wedding coordinator had them line up to receive guests as they entered.

"You look so pretty," Mrs. Snow said.

"Thanks," Diane responded.

"Fred, you're looking quite spiffy in that tuxedo!" Mrs. Perry said.

"Congratulations, " Sean said.

They hugged Sean. "Thanks my friend." Fred said.

People kept coming down the reception line, congratulating the new Mr. and Mrs. Williams. Yolanda was still acting crazy. Everyone ignored her. It was her problem if she wasn't happy for her cousin. Everyone refused to allow her to mess up that special day. The uncle decided to sing to everyone today instead of dance. Everyone just let him have his way. He was showing his love and support for the couple in his own special way.

Because of the diversity of the guests, they served baked chicken, salmon, green beans, salad, and iced tea.

For the first dance, the band played a medley of songs by Earth Wind and Fire, the couple's favorite group. All the guests were taking pictures.

"Today has been such a beautiful day," Diane said to her sweetheart as they danced.

"It sure has. You're Mrs. Williams now."

"Yes, I am."

For the next thirty to forty minutes the bride and groom danced. People were coming to them to congratulate them and give them best wishes. Everyone made sure they ate.

Time to throw the garter belt and the bouquet

All the girls lined up to catch the bouquet. Diane was ready to throw it.

There were shouts from the crowd, "Throw it here! No, over here, throw it here you know I'm your favorite."

She threw it. "I got it!" Yolanda screamed, as she knocked the groom's cake table down.

There were conversations everywhere along with screams of shock.

"Is she hurt?" a wedding guest asked.

"Oh my God! "An elderly woman said.

"That's what she gets!" Patricia said, all the negativity she's been dishing out today towards Diane.

A gentleman asked. "Are you okay?" he proceeded to help her get up. "Let me help you up!"

Yolanda held her head down as she let the gentleman help her up. "My foot and bottom hurt can you help me to my car?" *I'm so embarrassed. I need to get out of here fast.*

The gentleman responded. "I'll be glad to help you!"

"Thanks sir." Yolanda started getting up slowly.

Diane and Fred made it over to her as she headed towards the exit. "Yolanda, are you okay?"

Yolanda couldn't look her cousin in her face. "I'm hurting I'm going home. "Congratulations! Go back to your guests. I'll talk to you later."

"Feel better!"

Sally had been standing next to her. "You're so nice. I would be saying that's what she gets for being so ugly."

Diane smiled. "I think she regrets her behavior. She couldn't look me in the face."

The wedding coordinator began to speak. " Hello everyone. It's time for the garter to be given away. Diane here's a chair, sit here. Come on and raise that dress up."

The men in the room started screaming. "Go Fred! Go Fred!"

"Throw it here. No, over here."

Fred threw her garter. "I got it," Sean yelled.

"Sean, your playboy days are ending soon," Harold said.

"Harold, those days have been gone a long time."

"You know you're a player!"

"Whatever you say." Sean walked away, toward Fred. Sean began speaking. "You have me thinking about settling down and now the garter. "

Fred put his hand on his friends' shoulder. "You'll know when it's time."

"I'm glad."

Time to wrap up

They walked up to their table. Fred began to speak. "Family and friends, we must leave. We thank you for all the love, and the gifts. We appreciate you. We ask that you keep us in your prayers. We love you."

Diane began speaking. " Thanks everyone for coming. You made my day special."

The limousine drove off with <u>Just Married</u> plastered all over it. We all threw rice at the car. Tears rolled down our parents' eyes. I'm overcome with joy. They really complement each other. What a blessing.

Thirty

Corporation Drama

~~~~~~~~~~~~~~~~~

Diane started a career at a small engineering firm, called The McDaniel Engineering firm. It's located between Atlanta and Cedar Lake. It has only thirty employees. There are fifteen men engineers and five women. The rest of the employees are the President, Vice President, and administrative positions.

Valerie interrupted a coworker during the board meeting. "Reginald how much time do we have to make the deadline for this project."

"Valerie, we have enough time."Reginald responded.

"I'm concerned because we didn't finish the last two projects on time. I oversaw those and since I'm assisting you on this one, I don't want this one to be late."

Diane thinking hard. "That's a legitimate concern, Valerie."

Mr. Hopkins, the vice president cleared his throat. You all don't have to worry about any projects being delayed anymore. Everyone will carry their load, or they will be terminated. So, go forth and execute the project."

"Thank you, Mr. Hopkins." Reginald responded.

"Yes, thank you. We will finish the software project as promised." *I'm so glad Mr. Hopkins said what he said. It was so much stress and confusion working on the last project. Too much bickering. And thank God only Samantha and Valerie* are working on this one. The others were so rude and disrespectful to me and the rest of the team. They were acting like high school students.

Mr. Hopkins grabbed his brief case and stood up. "I'm glad to hear that. The firm is counting on you. This meeting is over. Let me know if you need anything."

Diane stopped Reginald in the middle of leaving. "Reginald lets test what we have to see how it's flowing. Is this afternoon around three pm, okay?"

"Great idea. I'll see you then!" Reginald said.

Samantha spoke up. "I'll be there."

"So will I!" Valerie said.

"Great! See you later!" Diane said.

The Women Engineers meet– It's about one forty-five pm

The ladies walked in Sarah's office and took a seat. Her office has a beautiful view of Atlanta and Cedar Lake. Cedar Lake's skyline consist of rows of beautiful oak and pine trees. The Atlanta side shows skyscrapers with trees in the foreground. The ladies seated themselves in soft leather office chairs.

Sarah passed out papers to everyone. "Ladies as you know Math, Engineering, Technology, and Science (METS), a networking and educational organization for women, wants us to nominate a female engineering representative from the firm. I just passed out the nomination form and the requirements of the nominee. I believe we initially said it would be Diane. Are we still nominating her?"

Karen crossed her legs as she read the requirements. "I don't think she qualifies. She caused so much confusion during our last projects we had. And she's selfish. She works on all the projects with the men. Do you see she's always in Reginald and Dexter's face? I think she has something going on with them. I think she's blackballed us from working on any new projects."

Rita peered over her glasses. "I don't think she deserves to represent us. We need someone to be squeaky clean. She has blemishes. Yes, she's a big flirt."

Samantha cleared her throat. "We were slow about responding to what the project manager wanted. We didn't pull our weight. It's not fair to blame everything on her. And just in case you're not aware, she's happily married.

And finally, we just met her less than six months ago and you're saying all this. Give her a break. I think some of you are just jealous."

Sarah leaned towards Samantha. "There you go. We're not jealous. Can you be real sometimes? You know she told on us."

"We drove her to that. She had no choice. We need to acknowledge our wrong."

"Samantha we out number you. She won't be nominated. I nominate Karen." Sarah said.

"That's fine with me." Rita responded. "She thinks she's the queen of the office."

Samantha looked at all three of them. "You do what you want. But we must learn to be accountable for our own actions. We must leave that stuff in high school and work as a team. Let all that pettiness and immaturity die."

Sarah frowned. "We don't think she's capable."

"Yeah, right, you can call it what you want to." Samantha said.

Diane peeped her head into Sarah's office. "Hello Ladies, what are you meeting about?"

Sarah clears her throat. "We're just relaxing talking about how fast this year is going by and excited about our new careers."

"Yes, time is passing by and this firm is a great place to work. Ladies I know we haven't gotten off to the best start. I hope we can agree to work together and be successful regardless of any differences we may have."

Samantha leaned back in her chair with arms crossed. "Of course, we can do that. First, it's all about business.

"Yes," Sarah agreed.

"Great ladies. I'll catch up with you later."

Diane leaves.

Sarah makes sure she is down the hall by looking out the door. "That'll be the day. I don't want to be in her presence."

"Sarah you can do better!" Samantha said.

"I can but I won't."

"Unbelievable!" Samantha said.

Samantha shakes her head and begins to leave.

183

***

The new project ended up being very successful. It was peaceful and smooth. It ended on time. Its a good thing only Samantha and Valerie were the only ones from Sarah's group. They're professional and all about business. Diane's career as an engineer is blossoming.

Thirty-One

Patricia, Respect Yourself

<u>Patricia got a job at an accounting firm</u>

She entered the office and spoke with the receptionist. "Good morning, my name is Patricia Jones. I'm the new hire for the accounting department. I'm to report here, according to Mr. Washington."

"Yes, we're expecting you. Welcome," said Monica, the receptionist. "I'll call Mr. Washington. Make yourself comfortable. Get some coffee and have a couple of doughnuts."

"Thanks," She responded with excitement and nervousness in her voice.

"Good morning," said Becky Smith, another new hire, who was also waiting on Mr. Washington.

Mr. Washington is the vice president of the company. He's her boss. He's worked for the company twenty-five years. He's very active in the community and politics. He has a reputation for getting everything he wanted.

In the Breakroom, another new hire walked in

"Good morning. The coffee is strong. The doughnuts taste great," said Patricia.

"Is today your first day?" Becky asked.

"Yes, are you an accountant?"

"Yes," she answered.

"That's great. Congratulations to you."

"Same to you."

Mr. Washington walked up.

"Good morning, ladies. Are you ready to get started? "Your offices are ready. They're not the biggest, but they're yours."

They proceeded down the hallway walking on the beautiful gray tile and glancing at the different offices as they passed by. The hallway is about twenty feet long. Mr. Washington stopped at a door. "Ms. Smith this is your office."

"Thanks. Its so beautiful and well decorated for an office. It looks cozy and warm." she said. "See you later, maybe later on today."

"Patricia, your office is down the hall close to mine." Mr. Washington rubbed his hands across her back.

"Thanks for the opportunity. I planned to be an asset for the company." She said.

Mr. Washington didn't respond, he had his hand on her shoulder.

She was thinking. She was wondering why her office is down the hall. Why is he touching me? Not another man trying to take advantage of me. I'm not a plaything. I'm scared. Lord help me! I don't want to go through anything on my new job. What are they whispering about and why is everyone staring at us?

"Here is your office. You have the newest computer in the firm. I made sure you have the finest desk." Mr. Washington x-rayed her with his eyes.

"Thanks, Mr. Washington, for showing me to my office," said Patricia.

"You're welcome. We'll have lunch at least two times a week," said Mr. Washington. "I'll see you later."

"Thanks again. Good-bye," she said staring at him, looking puzzled and confused.

<u>Second Week of work</u>

Mr. Washington, wearing his navy pin striped suit enters. "Good morning, I forgot to tell you that you have a company car. It's being delivered today. Please test drive it today."

"Wow, I had no idea I would get a company car. Thanks sir." I'm getting all kind of perks. *I wonder if the other new hire is getting a company car. I hope so.*

* * *

Mr. Washington went back to his office for a meeting. He's running for a political office. He has a meeting with his campaign manager.

"Mr. Washington it's looking good. From the recent poll we took, it looks like you have a chance at winning the mayoral election." said Mr. Lewis, his campaign manager.

"Let's go for it! I do want to run for mayor of the city. My business experience and my connections should get me elected."

"Yes, they should," the campaign manager said. "I'm coming up with some great campaign slogans. I think we should make an announcement on Friday evening. It'll give everyone something to talk about over the weekend."

"Sounds like a plan. Let me catch up with you later," Mr. Washington said. "I'm going to lunch."

* * *

The following Monday, the announcement was made.

The employees are talking amongst themselves.

"Mr. Washington needs to calm down, if he's really going to run for office. He can't continue to have mistresses. It's obvious what his intentions are with her. Whoever gets the office next to his is his new catch. Her office is almost fit for a president." Joann an employee said.

"He has no new tricks. It's all going to catch up with him. When will he learn?" said Lindsey, another employee.

"The funny part, the new hire has no idea what's really going on. They fall right into the trap."

"They do!"

The office was discussing the campaign, Patricia, Mr. Washington all week.

* * *

Patricia's Third Week

Mr. Washington picked up his phone and dialed three digits. "Patricia, it's time for lunch. Meet me at the elevator in fifteen minutes."

"Mr. Washington, I have training in thirty minutes. I can't go."

"I've taken care of that. Besides you're in your third week of training, you should know your job by now."

I took the phone from my ear and just stared at it. This man is a trip. I don't want to go to lunch with him. I need to learn my job. I'm a smart girl, but there's a lot to learn. I guess I need to go so I can keep my job.

* * *

Lunch at a five-star restaurant

"How is the salmon and asparagus?" Mr. Washington asked her.

"The salmon is tender and so is the asparagus." she answered.

"Great! I'm glad, honey." He rubbed her legs under the table.

"Please don't touch my legs, Mr. Washington! I'm asking you to stop."

Mr. Washington touched her legs again. "Would you like some dessert?"

"No, no thank you," she responded nervously, her hands were shaking, and she started tapping her feet. "Can you please stop touching my legs? You're making me feel uncomfortable."

"You know you like it."

"No, I don't."

Mr. Washington became angry. He put his fork down and motioned for the waiter. "I'll get the check and we can go back to the office."

* * *

They headed to the car walking in a fast pace. He doesn't open the door for her.

She tried to make conversation. *My heart is beating so fast. Lord I'm nervous.* "So, I don't have to train anymore?"

"You've been exempt from training," Mr. Washington answered.

"Mr. Washington, I don't want to be exempt. Please don't do any extra favors. I want to make my own way. You don't understand, please leave me alone."

"You have no choice."

She holds her head down. Tears role down her eyes.

I feel so helpless. I don't want to lose my job.

The ride to the office was quiet.They were only five minutes from the office, but it seemed to take an eternity.

Mr. Washington grabbed her leg as he continued to drive. "Please don't touch me!" She demanded.

Mr. Washington ignored her. "You have to go along with everything I do. Why do you think you were offered so much money?"

"You're hurting me." They finally arrived in the parking garage. He parked the car.

He started caressing her again. "I didn't accept this job to be sexually harassed." She continued to cry.

"You go along with it or you'll be fired. This is a gift just for you." It's wrapped in an antique gold box with a red bow on it.

"I don't want any gifts. How much money did this cost? And what's in this box?"

"One thousand dollars and a pair of diamond earrings."

"I don't want them."

"You have no choice. Either you take them or get in your car and leave now."

She took the money and the earrings.

Both walked back in the building. She walked ahead of him by at least fifty feet, and she attempted to walk at a rather fast pace to get back to her office.

She went through the break room and maneuvered around the back way to bypass all the cubicles and of course coworkers. She made it back without anyone seeing her. She plops in her chair.

Do I wear the sign, you can do whatever you want to me, even if I don't want it? I tired of these men taking advantage of me. This is my first job out of college. I like this job. Lord what shall I do. I can't quit. I need to decide.

* * *

Three weeks later she went to lunch with him. Mr. Washington is very demanding and controlling. He doesn't take no for an answer. He drove about ten minutes away from the building. "Why are we at a hotel? Where is the restaurant?" Patricia asked.

"Come and go upstairs with me," said Mr. Washington.

"No, I'm not coming," She responded, so scared, she was shaking.

"Oh yes, you are!" Mr. Washington grabbed her and escorted her inside.

"Mr. Washington, I'm not going to this hotel room with you. I like the money and the diamonds, but I don't want them. Please take them back," She pleaded.

"I don't want that money. I don't want the diamonds. I want you. I'm going to have you," demanded Mr. Washington. "It's a little late to try to play like you don't know what's going on."

"You have no right. This is sexual harassment. I thought you were taking me on a business luncheon! Take me back to the office!"

"You aren't that naive. When you took the gifts, you said yes," answered Mr. Washington.

Mr. Washington held her close to him and pulled her toward the elevator.

"You could lose your job for sexual harassment." She attempted to get away.

He punched the elevator button. Somehow she managed to pry away from him and ran away as fast as she could.

The bellboy was standing by, and so were other guests. No one paid any attention to her. It wasn't the first time someone had ran through the lobby.

Mr. Washington stood at the elevator. He scowled; surprised that someone had escaped from his arms.

Outside, she screamed and hailed a cab. "Hey! Take me to 515 Park Avenue."

* * *

She made it to her apartment and cried all afternoon. The phone rang later that evening.

"Hello! "Patricia answered in a whisper.

" I apologize for my behavior," Mr. Washington said.

"I told you I didn't want to be bothered. I told you I don't want your gifts. You act like you didn't hear anything. My father has plenty of money and he has given me plenty of diamonds. Diamonds don't impress me."

"Please forgive me!"

"I will eventually, not ready to right now."

"I'll see you at work tomorrow."

She hung up the phone without saying goodbye.

Mr. Washington chuckled. She thinks that hurts me. She'll be alright. I'll give her some time.

* * *

All week, people whispered as she walked by their desks. When she went into the copy room or the break room, people would stop talking. Patricia felt awkward in the office.

* * *

Mr. Washington announced his candidacy for mayor. The next day, WCTV News ran the following story:

"Yesterday, we reported Mr. Washington of Nynex Corporation announced his candidacy for mayor. Today we have word that Washington has several mistresses. We received a tip from one of his mistresses, who declined to speak on camera but told us he has had a relationship with her for the past fifteen years. Our reporter Kip is reporting live from Washington's office. Kip, what have you learned?"

"Amanda, workers here at Washington's office have so far declined to comment." He stopped a worker leaving the building. "Hello, what is your name?"

"I'd rather not say," said the employee zipping by fast to avoid any more questions.

Kip asked, "What do you know about Mr. Washington's alleged affairs with women on the job? I know you know something."

"I have no comment."said another employee who walked away.

"We'll have more on that. Amanda back to you."

Amanda with a look of surprise. "Thanks Kip. And there you have it. The employees don't want to comment. Maybe someone will later."

Thirty-Two

The Other Woman

The Other Woman

Everyone is settling in with their new jobs and promotions. The Patricia problem is very dramatic, I know the diary will get back to that later. Now for some reason its talking about Fred and Diane. They're in Atlanta. In the heart of Buckhead, the couple decided to eat at Fogo De Cha.

Fred pulled up to the front door and went to the other side to open the door for her. He helps her out.

"Thanks honey."

The valet parker walked up to him. "Good evening."

They responded in unison. "Good evening."

Fred handed him the car keys.

"Here's your ticket. Enjoy your dinner." The valet attendant said.

They were escorted to their table as soon as they walked in. Fred helped his wife to her seat and made sure she was comfortable and then he sat down. They were seated in a booth in the far right corner of the restaurant.

The waitress came to the table within seconds. "Hello, my name is Shirley and I'll be your waitress this evening. She stood five feet eight inches, weighing less than one hundred twenty pounds. She had a brick house figure. Her eyes were big and light brown. She had the whitest teeth.

She's fine. Fred stared at her and adored her beauty and physique. "Good evening."

"What would you like to drink?" she asked as she continued to smile.

"For now, bring some water, no go ahead and bring some merlot." Fred responded.

"Hey, don't I know you. You play professional football, don't you?" the waitress asked.

Fred sat up straight, cleared his throat. "Yes, that's me. I was hoping no one noticed me."

My husband can be full of himself sometimes. He loves attention. I just shake my head.

"Don't worry about me. I won't advertise it. I do want your autograph."
Fred smiled. "No problem."

"Thanks. I'll go get your drinks." The waitress said and walked away.

She chuckled. "You were excited about that one. I guess she's rather cute. "

"Don't worry honey. I got it all under control."

"I'm quite sure you do."

A few minutes later

"Here are your drinks. Have you decided what you want to order?"

"We decided to have the Fogo Churrasco Experience." Fred said.

"Anything else?" The waitress asked smiling as wide as her mouth could go.

"That'll be it." He answered.

"You controlled all that smiling this time. I'm proud of you!"
I know!"

They ate their dinner and had a very relaxing time. The waitress did become more flirtatious throughout the course of the evening. The waitress brought the ticket to Fred.

"Thanks for everything." She puts the receipt on the table near Fred. The waitress said.

Fred and the waitress continued to converse.

She picked up the receipt without either of them noticing.

No, she didn't write down her number and gave Fred a picture of her.

She slid everything back without the two of them noticing.

"It was nice meeting you, but we have to go. Have a great evening."

"Oh yes, we have to go. Nice talking to you." Fred said. "Thanks for great service tonight."

"No problem, it was my pleasure." The waitress answered.

Fred took the receipt and the other items out of the receipt holder. She headed towards the exit holding her man's hand. Fred glanced at the receipt as he walked. His eyes grew big as he looked at the picture of the waitress.

Fred glanced at the picture again and put it in his wallet along with the receipt.

* * *

The Ride Home

"Fred you're going to keep the picture of the waitress in your wallet. Don't play dumb I looked at the receipt while you and the waitress were talking."

"Honey please stop. I planned to throw it away. I didn't want you to know that's why I put it in my wallet."

"Oh yeah. Give me the picture I'll throw it away. Give me the receipt with her number on it."

"I don't have a problem giving it to you. One thing I want you to understand is that groupies are everywhere. You can't stop them. I have handled them in high school, college, and now in the NFL. I avoid a lot of them because I don't hang out in the clubs like others do."

"That's good to know. But this one is on me. Hand it over when you stop at this red light."

Fred stopped at the red light. "Here you are . Take the picture and the number."

"The nerve of her." She took the picture and number and tore them in tiny small pieces.

" You're something else. Just trust me honey."

"You weren't going to say anything about the number and the picture?"

"I was going to tell you. I didn't want to spoil the moment."

195

"Too late!"

The Williams continued their drive home, it was quiet.

* * *

Oh, What a Thursday

Its 4 pm at the engineering firm

Hump time, working on a report that's due in thirty minutes. Her office phone rings.

"Hello!"

"Hey babe, just checking on you to see if you finished your project and to see what time you're coming to the game?" Fred asked.

"Hey honey. I'm almost finished with the report, but I need to review it before I submit it. That's going to get me out of here around 5:30. I wanted to go home and take a shower, but it looks like the shower is out."

"Ok. I understand. But I need to see your beautiful face in the stands."

"Don't worry honey. I'll be there."

"Thanks babe. Love you."

"Love you too, see you from the stands."

* * *

It's 8 pm

"Whew, I made it." Diane said out loud as she sat in her seat at the stadium.

The person next to her looked at her. "I'm glad you did. I like to see the regulars in their seat."

Fred happened to look up as soon as she sat down. He waved. She waved back. All of a sudden, she gets a tap on her shoulder.

"Hello," a young lady said.

"Hi."

"Do you remember me?" the girl asked.

"Vaguely."

The girl smiled showing all her thirty-two teeth. "I'm the waitress from the restaurant. My cousin is a wide receiver coach. I get free tickets all the time. It was so nice meeting you and Fred the other night. He's such a gentleman and a great player.

So disgusting. The nerve of her to smile at me after she flirted with my husband. "I remember now."

I would have never dreamed I would see this person again. Who would have thought she would be sitting behind me at a game? Lord have mercy on me.

* * *

Sitting room for family near the Locker Room

The players started coming out to meet family and friends.

Fred started walking towards his one and only baby, but is intercepted by the waitress. "Hey Fred, do you remember me?" she asked as she hugged him and kissed him on the jaw.

"Please get off of me!" Fred said with anger in his voice. I remember you, but I don't know you like that."

"Ah Fred, I thought we were friends." The waitress girl said.

"No," Fred said as he walked towards his wife. "Hey honey."

The waitress girl stood there looking confused.

A look of disgust showed on her face as she looked her husband in his eyes. "Fred you must get rid of her. She's a problem. She sat behind me during the game, trying to talk to me as if we're friends. Handle her or I will."

"Come on babe let's go." He grabbed her by the arm and began walking out of the room. "I told you I got this under control."

She looked at him and said nothing.

The following week on a Friday Night

The team members attended a birthday party for the coach. It's held at a five-star restaurant. Diane couldn't make it because of the firm and some deadlines she had to meet. The team could bring their family and friends. The wide receiver coach invited his cousin.

"Hello Fred," the waitress said as she seated herself next to him.

He turned to see who this female is. "Hi," he responded with unbelief.

The waitress leaned over to whisper in his ear."I don't know why you're so mean to me. You know you want this. I got a room upstairs. Don't worry I don't mind being the other woman."

"Listen, I'm happily married. I'm telling you leave me alone before I call the authorities, or even tell your cousin what you're doing."

Before he could finish his statement, she had groped him. Oh my. This woman has no shame in her game. Should I scream? No. I'm going to move her hand. I hope no one sees what's going on. It does feel good, but it's all wrong. Lord help me get rid of this woman.

Fred moved her hand just in time, because the coach was headed towards him.

The coach grabbed Fred's shoulders. "Hey Fred."

"Good evening coach." Fred said.

"Where is the misses? the coach asked.

"She couldn't make it. The firm had some projects to get out."

"We got to do what we have to. Tell her I said hello."

"I will."

The coach walked away. The waitress moved her left hand back in his lap, he just gave in and one thing led to another. Before the night was over, he was in her hotel room and had committed adultery for the first time. The waitress was elated. He enjoyed the moment, but in his heart of hearts he knew he had failed God and his honey.

* * *

Fred's Drive Back to his Home

I can't believe I did that. Now I must go home and face my wife. I know it was wrong it goes against my beliefs. I can't tell her yet. I'm going to lie. I hope I don't smell like her. What can I do to hide any smells? Let me check my clothes for makeup. Oh Lord, please forgive me for committing adultery. How could I have avoided this? Maybe I could have played it off by moving. Lord I'm so sorry. Now I must suffer the consequences.

* * *

Showdown
Its 11 pm

Fred pulled into the garage. He managed to find some lotion he uses to camouflage any scents he may have picked up from the waitress.

"Sweetheart I'm home."

A lathery shower was a must to get all the scent off of him. He took a fifteen-minute shower downstairs after he put his clothes in the wash machine. It's almost midnight.

Thirty minutes later

Diane walked down the stairs. "Man, you must have a burst of energy. Your shower woke me up. And you're washing. What's on TV?"

"Hey honey "Car Wash." I guess I do have some extra energy. You know every time this movie comes on; I have to watch it."

"Yes, I know. I guess I'll watch it with you. It'll be relaxing after a hard day work."

A commercial came on. "How was the birthday party?"

"It was nice. Coach looked like he was having a good time."

"Was I the only wife not there?"

"Oh no, quite a few weren't there."

"Good, was he surprised?"

"Yes, he was. Well, at least he looked surprised."

"How was the food?"

"The food was delicious, a little spicy, but very tasty. The movie is back on."

* * *

It's Not Over
Its 4pm on a Tuesday Fred beats her home

He went to the mailbox as he entered the driveway to his home. He began to sort through the mail before he got back in the car. There's a handwritten light blue envelope addressed to him. What is this and who could it be from, being addressed to me only.

Eagerness and anxious is an understatement, the envelope was opened suddenly. It said, Fred thanks for the other night you took care of all my needs. I hope we can do it again. Love your waitress friend.

This girl is crazy how did she get my address? Lord I have a problem. I need to throw this away or should I keep it as evidence. She's stalking me. This is unbelievable. Where can I hide this letter, in the glove compartment of the car, at the very bottom? For the most part she isn't a rambler.

Hiding the card is a must. An hour later she came home which is early for her.

He met her at the door and kissed her on the cheek. "Hello honey how was your day?"

"It was great the big engineering project we've been working on for six months was completed today. It was a major accomplishment for me."

He grabbed his wife by her arms and looked her in her eyes. "I'm so proud of you. Let's celebrate. I want to take you out to dinner."

" That's a great idea but I'm too tired to go out and eat. Maybe you can cook me a nice dinner."

"I understand, what do you want salmon, steak?"

"Surprise me honey. I'm going to take a shower and get into something more comfortable and relaxing."

"I like that," He said with a big grin.

5pm Friday

Diane beats him home, she whipped into the driveway, puts the car in park to get the mail.

She goes through the mail, checking each piece out individually. Mmmm, who is this from, addressed to Fred only and in a purple envelope and the address is Atlanta not Cedar Lake.

* * *

It's about 7:30 p.m.

He swung open the door to the kitchen after getting out the car in the garage. "I smell pizza. I hope you got my favorite. That supreme pizza melts in my mouth. "Fred said as he ran to kiss her on the cheek.

"Yes, I have supreme pizza. I got the mail this evening you have a purple envelope from some address I truly don't know. I figured you would."

She handed him the envelope.

He looked scared to death. "Oh, this is nothing. I think it's an invitation to a party one of the wives are throwing for a teammate."

"Are you going to open it up so I can put it on the calendar?"

"I'll open it later. I'm hungry now."

"I'll open it; you know how you are about forgetting things."

"No, not now. Let's eat and enjoy each other's company." He said with sternness in his voice.

"*Okay.*" *Boy is he acting strange. Lord I don't know what's going on, but it will be revealed.*

* * *

The letters kept coming on a weekly basis. They came sometimes twice a week. He made sure he beat her home every day. The waitress went to every game. At this time, Diane had begun to pray for her every time she saw her. But every time Fred saw her, he was sweating bullets.

* * *

Car Insurance Renewal Time

Diane answered the phone at her office. "Hello!"

"Hello Mrs. Williams, this is Beverly Terry your insurance agent. I'm calling to see if you want to add that other car you told me about. I believe you said your husband for some reason, or another has a separate policy on it."

"Yes, I do."

"Do you happen to have the vin number I can add it now?"

"No, I don't but I'm driving it today. I can get it when I go to lunch. I'll call you back after lunch. Is the price still the same price you quoted me thirty days ago?"

"Yes, it is. I look forward to talking to you. Thanks Mrs. Williams."

"I call you back after 2 pm."

* * *

Lunch time

Its lunch break. She began looking for the identification cards. For some reason she can't find the cards, she continued to look.

"What are all these envelopes with letters and cards doing in this glove compartment?"

Long streams of tears rolled down her face as she realized her husband had slept with the waitress. She discovered this woman had been writing him every week. Even though it hurt, she felt the need to read every one of them. Lunch was skipped because the letters were so long and risque. She decided to go home instead of going back to the office.

2 pm At home

"Lord I can't believe this, Fred and this woman have been perpetrating like nothing has happened between the two of them. He has committed adultery. Lord I just want to pack his clothes and move him out. I feel betrayed. He's been hiding this for over a month. How could he do this? Lord help me."

She cried and prayed all day long and went to bed early. She wanted to pack his clothes and put him out, but she knew she needed to talk to him first before she did anything irrational.

Thirty-Three

The Separation

~⁓⚬⚬⚬⁓~

Fred made it home

Fred walked in the kitchen headed towards the den where his sweetheart was watching Friday night TV. Fred is in a great mood, glad it's Friday; he's ready for Sunday's game.

Fred reached over to kiss her. Diane put her hand to his face.

She rolled her eyes at Fred. "Don't kiss me? Fred how could you sleep with the waitress?"

Fred trying to play dumb. "What are you talking about?"

"Don't open up your mouth and attempt to tell a lie. I read all the cards and letters she's been writing you."

"I've been keeping them as evidence, she's been stalking me."

"Did you sleep with her, that's what she said in her letters? She said she wants to do it again."

" It's not what you think?"

"I'm not having an affair."

I didn't ask that. I asked did you sleep with her?"

"She raped me."

"I can't believe this lie."

"She seduced me."

"I can't take it. Fred pack your bags and move out."

"I'm not moving out."

"Oh yes you are."

"No, I'm not."

"Stay then, sleep on the couch or in another bedroom. We'll live in the same house but be separated."

"Please forgive me. What did you want me to do hit her? She was so aggressive."

"You could have pushed her. How did you get to the place where you had sex? You're stronger than her. Currently, there's no forgiveness. I know what the word says. I'm hurt and disappointed."

"I don't know what I'll do without you."

"You'll make it. Please sleep in the master bedroom downstairs. I'm going to bed. Right now, I'm getting sick looking at your face."

Fred spoke under his breath "What am I going to do? I'm in the doghouse."

Friday night was the beginning of their separation. She lived upstairs he lived downstairs. She didn't cook, wash or clean for him. They're roommates. Fred continued paying the bill as he had been. Both kept the house tidy. Both were busy seeking the Lord individually on how to handle the situation. Everyone on the outside looking in would think they were the perfect couple. Only God can help them get through this problem.

* * *

Fred Tells the Truth

Fred prayed to God. Lord I want my wife back. I messed up. I guess I should tell her what happened. She knows I slept with that woman. I should confess so our marriage can be healed, please restore our marriage. I promised Lord I won't do it again. Lord I'm going to do my part to get her back.

* * *

The Restoration

Thirty days into the separation

I'll write a card telling her I'm sorry. I'll buy some flowers.

The plant was delivered. Fred put the card and the plant on the kitchen table.

When she came home from work, she looked at the plant and the card and kept walking.

"I hope he doesn't think he's going to get me back that easy with a card and some flowers. Lord I know your word says to forgive. It's so hard. Fred has disappointed me. I need a miracle to help me forgive him. I know God all things are possible with you. Help me Jesus."

The plant and the card sat there for two weeks. Fred kept the plant alive.

Fred prayed again, "Lord help me not to give up. The card and the flowers have been sitting on that table for more than two weeks. Lord I need her to pick up the card at least."

The next day 6 pm

Fred walked into the kitchen and noticed the card and planted were moved to the den area. "Thank you Lord she took the card and the plant. Thank you, Lord this is a beginning. I miss her, Lord."

* * *

Seated in the middle of her bed crying her heart out.

"I knew he did it. I don't care if she started it. He could have resisted. Only thing he had to say is no. We made it this far and never had this problem. Please heal my hurt God."

The 45th day

They're still separated.

Fred was up reading the paper. "Good morning lovely, have a great day at work. Please forgive me honey."

She headed towards the garage with keys in her hand not slowing down at all. "Good morning."

It's a miracle she's saying anything.

Fred thanked God. "Lord she said good morning. That's a start. Lord I made it through forty-five days of my wife not speaking to me at all. I'm going to thank you in advance for restoring my marriage."

* * *

Fred continued to write letters and cards assuring her she wouldn't have to worry about this again. He let her know how he planned to be more proactive if something like the waitress ordeal happened again.

It's the 62nd Day of the in-house separation

Coffee had been brewed and she was seated having her morning devotional. The coffee aroma is so strong Fred quietly comes out of the master bedroom.

He walked softly into the kitchen, but the house shoes he had on made a scuffing sound as he walked. She turned around as he made it close to the kitchen table.

"Good morning honey, the coffee smells so good.""

"Good morning." She responded with no emotions and a blank look on her face.

The brew of the coffee captured the room. He poured his coffee and put cream and a little dab of sugar in it. He headed over to the kitchen table and sat down at the table with her. She's reading. They both continue to sip on their coffee.

The coffee aroma filled his nostrils and taste buds as he took a sip of coffee ."What do I have to do to make it right with you?"

She looked at him and didn't blink an eye. "Why didn't you move to another seat? Why you didn't say no? I know she didn't drag you to the place where you actually did the act?"

"Hindsight, of course shows me how I could've avoided it. I should have gotten up. I could've stood up. It was packed. If it makes you feel any better. I did tell the wide receiver coach that his cousin has been stalking me. He doesn't give her tickets anymore. I've put a restraining order against her. I took the letters to the police station and showed them how often she writes me. I haven't seen her in over thirty days."

"The police don't care about a groupie stalking a NFL football, you know what they think? Who's to say you won't do it again. What steps are you planning to do to avoid it again? I've been thinking about a divorce."

" Please don't divorce me. I plan to be firmer. I should've given the waitress that picture back to her or left it on the table that night. I plan to be sterner when I'm approached. It's a hard lesson to learn."

She got up from the table and put the coffee cup in the sink. "That's great you have a plan and that you've put a restraining order on her. I hope that works. I'm not ready to reconcile. God will have to work a miracle."

It was time to leave for work, she grabbed her purse, her keys, and headed towards the garage.

To restore his marriage he knows the communication must continue. "Have a great day. I still love you."

She turned around and looked at her husband. "Have a great day."

The two of them began to have more short conversations, just being cordial to each other. Allowing his gentleman character to shine, he treated his sweetheart like a queen by writing love letters, cooking, and that's cooking all of her favorite foods.

Day Seventy-Five

It's a Friday night, resting in the den watching TV

She beat him home. He walked in, one hour later.

"I hope you haven't eaten. I have your favorite dish from Olive Garden. I got you their baked spaghetti with some bread sticks."

"My dear that's very thoughtful of you and your gesture is appreciated."

"I remember you love to eat Olive Garden. And to be honest sweetie, I want you back. I want things to be the way they were."

" I do miss you. I need to know you've changed before I can trust you with my heart. One of my favorite movies is coming on. Let's watch it together."

"Honey, I need for you to hang out with me. You'll see that I'm bolder about handling the groupies. Just give me a chance. I learned my lesson."

"I'll think about it.God is softening my heart. Its a miracle."

"I guess I need to be thankful, you're talking to me and don't mind being in the same room with me."

Yes, you need to be thankful. If it wasn't for God, I wouldn't be talking to you. Yes, it's all God. I'll think about hanging out. Maybe I'll go to a game."

"We have a game Sunday. I hope you make it."

"I'll think about it."

Sunday came

Diane came to the game and didn't tell Fred she was coming. She came during the second quarter to give him the impression she wasn't coming. That's not nice. She enjoyed it and realized how much she missed it once she was there. A visit to the locker room to meet Fred is a must, to see how he handles the groupies.

* * *

She's in a corner watching Fred's moves. Here he comes; boy the women are desperate and vicious. Look at them passing their numbers to the players. Oh, someone just gave him a number. Let's see how he handles that. He handed it back to her. He shook his head no. Oh Lord that's progress. The girl looked at him with an expression of no he didn't.

Thank God

Thank you, Lord. He continued to walk toward the exit door which is where I happen to be. Another woman gave him a number and it looked like a picture. I heard him say no thank you. He gave it back to her. Lord he's batting one hundred. He's bolder. Thank God. He's resisting them and turning them down and he doesn't even know I'm here.

Standing about eighteen feet from her, he looked in her direction and his eyes lit up like a lightning bug. "Hey honey, glad you made it." He hugged her so tight and didn't want to let her go. "Thanks for coming. Let's go get something to eat. I'm starving. You know I looked for you in the stands when the game began. I didn't see you. I thought you weren't coming."

" You're welcome. To be honest it was nice seeing you play again. I'm starving too."

"How about Bones or the Sundial?"

"I love the Sundial; I love the view. The food is delectable."

"Darling we have precious memories from eating there. We had birthday celebrations there. Great choice."

They made it to the Sundial. She went to another game the following week. Which was day eighty-three. By the ninetieth day of the in-house separation Fred was out of town playing. Her heart had begun to soften, she's spending more time with him and beginning to trust him more. God has helped her with trusting him. The realization she has discovered is the more you trust God you can forgive and move on. Her sweetheart made it back to Georgia on that following Monday. It's the ninety first day of the separation.

REUNITED
Fred walked in the door. " I'm home. I've been thinking about you every moment of the day. Can we end this separation? "

His sweetheart was in the kitchen eating a snack, she walked towards him in the den. She looked at him and smiled. "I want to say I do forgive you. I'm ready to be husband and wife again."

He grabbed her and squeezed her tightly. "I'm so glad to hear that. I thank God for answering my prayers. Honestly I didn't know what I would do without you."

"I realized I felt the same way. God had to change my heart. I was ready to get a divorce. I was so mad at you. And before you ask, we will be sleeping in the same bed from now on. We're one again. To God be the glory. It's a miracle, you just don't know how deep the wounds were. I was hotter than hot sauce."

"Oh, I know. God is faithful. I thank God we're married again not in title, but in word and deed."

" I do want to caution you. The images of you and that girl keep popping up. I have forgiven you. You must pray that the images leave. We will be starting from the beginning. The anger has gone and that's a miracle. "

"You have every right to take it slow. I understand. I messed up. I jeopardized our vows unto God."

"I'm glad you understand."

"Thanks for not getting your friends involved. You can tell them later, but the peanut gallery won't help us."

"Don't worry. This is between you, God, and I."

"Thanks, they can't know everything."

"This ordeal is too much to have too many people involved. I've had to fast and pray."

"Yes, fasting and praying is the key. I had to repent for committing adultery."

"I know you did."

Love is in the air. Wow, I'm glad my sister and Fred made up. I can't imagine them getting a divorce. We do think they're the perfect couple.

Thirty-Four

Will Bells be Ringing?

The food smelt like old greasy hot dogs and French fries. The restaurant was crowded.

Boss walked up to the counter. Tanya stood next to the Boss.

"How may I help you?" the waitress asked.

"I want two hot dogs. One plain one, one with chili and cheese on it, and some fries." "Is that it?" the waitress asked as she smacked on her gum."

"Yes!" the boss said.

" Here's a ticket; we'll call you when your food is ready."

They stood a few feet from the counter and started talking. Music played loudly up front it was hard to hear. A couple of songs played, the third song was it, "And the beat goes on" by the Whispers was on. People were singing and dancing.

Boss started dancing and moved closer to her. "Dance with me."

"No, you're embarrassing me."

"Relax, you're always uptight. Enjoy life."

"Number 55!" The announcer said as he spoke through a mike, in an extremely loud voice.

"That's our number."

Whew, I'm glad, don't have to dance in public. Tanya thought.

They got their food and walked toward the seats. "Let's go sit in that booth over there in the corner."

"A window seat, that's a perfect spot. We can look at all the interesting people as they pass. Thanks for the movie again and lunch."

"You're welcome." Boss responded and sat down.

"Let's say grace I'm starving."

Boss started praying. "Thank you for this food Lord, Amen."

Wow, that's short. Tanya thought.

"Tanya will you marry me?"

She looked puzzled. No, you're asking me to marry you at the Varsity. Nothing special about this place."

"I do want to marry you. I asked now just to see what you'd say. I know its not time even though we've been together forever. When am I going to meet your family and friends? The few times you went home, you played like it was an emergency or a last minute thing, so I couldn't accompany you."

"I'm sorry. I know it appears that way. But that isn't true. I promise, you'll meet everyone within the next year."

"We've been together six years. If your friends know about me, I know they want to meet me."

"It'll be perfect timing. Don't worry, let's finish eating these delicious hot dogs."

"It doesn't make sense. Honestly, I don't think you want me to meet them. This is the last time I'm bringing this up. You need to make it happen."

"I will!"

"I'm not playing with you!"

"Now relax and let's continue to enjoy ourselves."

Sounds to me Tanya is hiding something. Come on now, six years. Something just isn't right.

Marion is going to the Chapel

Marion and Antonio had been living together since their junior year in college. He asked Marion to marry him every year, and every year she declined. The time had finally come.

They flew to Las Vegas the week of Christmas.

Wedding Bells in the Air

"We can catch a cab to the hotel," Antonio said. "I guess we should check into the hotel and then get something to eat."

In the cab

He kissed Marion on the cheek. *Why is that driver staring at Marion. He needs to stop before I pop him upside his head.*

"We're here. That'll be $25.00." the cab driver said.

He handed the money to the driver as he stared him down. "Thanks! Let's get out of here babe."

Marion stood in front of the hotel taking in all her surroundings. "By 11:15 am tomorrow we'll be husband and wife."

"Yes, we will, why was the cab driver staring at you, he was eyeing you down?"

"What I didn't notice that. I was into you."

"He was staring. I wanted to say something, but I changed my mind."

"Yes, he wasn't important. We're the hot topic."

"You're so right."

"I'm excited. Antonio, our families and friends are going to be mad at us."

"They'll get over it."

"I don't know how I'm going to explain it to them, we've talked about being in each other's weddings. I'll write or call them when I get back home."

"You can do that. Right now, it's all about us, and no one else. I love you, Marion."

"I love you too."

***

They checked into the hotel and had dinner at a restaurant on the top floor that rotates; they could see the whole city.

" You've done an excellent job of picking the best hotel. The Excelsior is so classy. I love this view, the lobster, the saxophonist and his band."

"It's all for you, honey. You deserve all of this. I'm glad you like it."

"I hope and pray we have the best marriage ever."

"We will. You just need to do as I tell you. And don't ask any questions."

Marion's mouth dropped an inch. "We both need to do our part to make the marriage work."

"I agree."

<u>Wedding Bells-The Next Day</u>

"Honey, you look gorgeous. You're wearing that dress."

"Thanks honey. You're looking rather handsome in your midnight blue sheen tuxedo, cuffed white short, with that solid navy-blue silk tie."

"Are you ready?" asked the attendant. "Or do you want to wait until eleven am on the dot?"

"I'm ready. I want to get this over with," Marion said.

"Everyone lineup! The photographer is ready. My assistant will be your witness," the attendant said.

"Antonio, do you take Marion Rucker to be your lawfully wedded wife?" asked the officiate.

"I do."He answered.

"Marion, do you take Antonio Lawson to be your lawfully wedded husband?"

"I do," Marion answered.

They exchanged rings.

"I now pronounce you husband and wife. You may kiss the bride."

They kiss.

"We're married now," He said with a big smile on his face.

The photographer walked up to them. 'I want to take pictures. Stand right there and look into each other's eyes."

They looked into each other's eyes. They were glowing.

The photographer grabbed that pose. "Nice, keep that pose. I need to get different angles."

They took a few more pictures.

"Thanks for everything." Marion said. "We have that noon luncheon at Caesar's Palace."

"You'll enjoy that. It's elegant. They take pictures for you too," the photographer said.

Antonio walked up to everyone in attendance and began shaking everyone's hand. "Thank you for everything today."

The attendants threw rice. "Congratulations! Much success!" everyone at the chapel said as they walked towards the door to exit.

There you have it, Marion and Antonio are married. He sounds a little controlling.

Thirty-Five

Cat Fight

Ken and Ellen were in their apartment one Saturday morning, eating breakfast and drinking coffee. Their beautiful daughter woke them up at eight a.m. Sydney was almost four years old. She left the table because she was finished eating her Fruit Loops.

Ellen looked at Ken while she chomped on some bacon. "Who is Sabrina? You keep calling her name in your sleep. The first few times I let it slide. But it's been going on for over a month."

"What are you talking about? I don't know a Sabrina. You must be dreaming."

"I'm not! I heard you. I waited to make sure I heard what I heard."

"Honey, come on with the drama. Stop imagining things. I don't know a Sabrina."

"I've been carrying this card in my purse. It says Love, Sabrina. I found this on the floor when I was cleaning up. She gave you a card for your birthday. I trusted you. How could you do this to me and please don't deny it?"

"What are you talking about?" Ken grabbed his car keys.

"Where are you going? You can't stand the fact that you've been caught in your wrongdoing." she replied.

"I'm going out!" He slammed the door on the way out.

Ken went to the neighborhood park to try to cool off and sat on a bench watching the people ride their bikes on the trail. Parents pushed babies in strollers. People walked and ran.

Ken thought to himself. *I'm busted. I've told on myself. How could I be so careless, talking in my sleep and bringing that card home. How foolish of me.*

It was necessary for her to keep calm, this was accomplished by cleaning up and washing clothes. It helped her keep her mind off her husband, who had been cheating on her for over three years. She hadn't told Ken that she hired a private investigator who took her several pictures of them. The envelope with the pictures of them were on a table near her, of course she began scanning through them. It became evident real fast that looking at the pictures made her even more upset. She became angrier by the moment.

Now I wished I had not hired the private investigator. I feel horrible. But I had to know the truth. Kenneth has been living a lie all these years. Lord help me.

Four hours later, Ken returned.

Ellen is screaming so loud it's a piercing sound. "Where have you been? I've been worried sick over you. I know you're avoiding me. Ken you may as well admit it. You've been exposed."

"I've been at the park. I keep telling you, nothing is going on with any other woman."

"You've been at the park for four hours? Stop lying! Look at these!" she said. "I hired a private investigator. He gave me these pictures of you and Sabrina going to this motel. See! You can't deny these pictures."

Kenneth looked at her out of the corner of his eyes. "Hold up, you hired a what?"

"You heard me; I hired a private investigator."

"Girl, you've lost your mind."

"Don't try to put it on me, I've seen traces of lipstick on your clothes. You didn't even try to hide it. At least you could've been smart enough to take the shirts to the cleaners. I smelled perfume that wasn't mine."

He was turning red; you could see the anger on his face. "The lipstick on my collar is yours and that's your perfume you smell."

"Stop lying Kenneth. We need to separate. I trusted you, and you took advantage of my trust. Why? Where did I go wrong? What did I do to make you creep out on me? Am I not pretty enough? Am I too fat? What is it? Am I satisfying you in bed?"

"Look, woman. I don't know what you're talking about. You're acting crazy!"

She began to cry. "I can't trust you. I'm so hurt. Sydney and I are leaving."

"Why are you leaving? If anyone should leave I should. Where are you taking Sydney?"

"Don't worry! We have somewhere to go. Too many memories here. I have to get away!"

"Come back!"

She grabbed Sydney and begins walking out the door.

Sydney stretched her arms out for her daddy. "Come on daddy; come go with mama and me."

She kept walking.

"Mama, why daddy not coming."

They got in the car and drove off. Sydney began crying.

* * *

Ellen called Rachel.

The phone rings she answered. 'Hello!"

"Hello, my friend I left Kenneth. Rachel, he has a mistress. Her name is Sabrina. They've been dating since college, while I was pregnant with Sydney. I'm moving out. I can't stand to see his face. I've cried so hard I have a headache."

"Friend, I hate this is happening to you. He should be ashamed of himself. You need me to come out there?"

"No, you're doing enough right now. You're listening. I appreciate it. Keep me in your prayers. Only God can bring me through this. Love you, my sister.

I got to go. I thought I could talk about it, but I can't. I'll talk to you later."

"I understand. Love you more, sis. I'll be praying for you."

***

The next day, she went by her house to pack some more clothes. She walked in and heard some noise in the bedroom. She walked closer to investigate, walking slowly and quietly to their bedroom and turned the light on.

"Kenneth what's going on? Woman, you better get out of my bed! Get out of my bed, you hussy! Ken, get out too! The nerve of both of you."

She grabbed the covers off him and this woman. "This must be Sabrina! Get out of my bed!"

Sabrina jumped out of the bed, picked her clothes off the floor, and started running while trying to put her clothes on.

"You're a big liar and a deceiver, Get out! Get out now."

Sabrina managed to put her dress on before she made it outside. Ellen followed and chased her out of her house. Kenneth ran after them.

Kenneth thought. *I've been caught. Lord help me. I've messed up.*

The girls were pulling hair, tearing clothes off of each and screaming as loud as they could. It was a horrible sight.

The neighbors were running outside to see what's going on.

Mrs. Gray, a neighbor dialed 911.

"The operator answered. "This is 911."

Mrs. Gray responded. "My neighbors are creating a disturbance in their front yard. They're fighting and rolling in the grass, screaming at each other. Hurry!"

"911 operator responded. "A unit is on its way."

"Thanks!" Mrs. Gray said.

Ken tried pulling her off Sabrina. "Stop it! stop it! Sabrina please!"

"Leave me alone Kenneth, before I punch you in the nose." Ellen said as she continued to fight. She's furious.

They kept fighting.

Sirens from the police car were flashing and heading towards the Womack's place.

By the time the police officers arrived, they had been rolling on the ground like two cats fighting for at least ten minutes. They were pulling each other's earrings off and pulling hair. Some of the neighbors tried to stop the fight, but the girls swung at them.

The police ran towards them.

The police officers grabbed the girls. "What's going on?"

Ellen was so furious that her face had turned red. "I came home to get some clothes; I found this witch in my bed with my husband. I politely yanked her out of my bed. My husband denied he was having an affair. I started seeing evidence of her lipstick, and some other stuff. He lied."

The officer asked Sabrina, "What do you have to say?"

"I plead the fifth. I have nothing to say," she responded.

"You can't plead the fifth. Is this true?" The officer demanded.

Sabrina straightened her clothes. "Yes, he's my man. He was mine's first!"

"He's not yours if he's married," the officer responded.

Ellen looked disgusted. "You're dreaming!"

"Today, I'm going to give all of you a warning," the officer said. "If we have another call to come here, we'll put all of you in jail. This warning will be documented in our system. I need all three of you to sign your warnings. Go get your license."

Kenneth handed his license to the officer.

Sabrina went to her car. Ellen got hers out of her purse in the house.

Police officer wrote out Kenneth's warning. "You need to do better. You have to make better decisions."

Ms. Sabrina Woods, after you sign your copy, I need you to leave the premises and don't step in this yard again or you'll be arrested. Do you understand?"

"Yes, sir!" replied Sabrina still breathing heavy. "I'm leaving now."

.

The officer finished writing his report. "I'm leaving now, Sabrina is gone. She was part of the problem. Please don't let me have to come back. Do you understand that, Ellen and Kenneth?"

"Yes," Ellen said.

"Yes, sir." said Kenneth.

"Good, no more calls to your residence. I mean it." The officer got in his squad car and drove away.

She put her fist up in Kenneth's face. "Get out of my way before I hit you!" Thank God only Kenneth could hear her.

"Wait, wait, I'm so sorry. I lied to you. I apologize. Can you forgive me?" asked Kenneth.

"You lied to me. I don't trust you anymore. How long have you been seeing her? Why am I asking you, I know you have been seeing her since college. I'm so hurt. Talking about deception."

"Six months," Kenneth lied,

"Well, that's funny. While we were fighting, she said she met you the second semester of our freshman year. You've been dating her since our freshman year in college. You told another lie. Call me when you're ready to tell the truth."

Ellen got the rest of her clothes and left without saying one word to her husband. I forgot to mention Sydney saw all of this. She cried during the while dilemma. One of the neighbors was watching her during all the fighting. Kenneth had a puzzled look when she left. Why is he puzzled this is the mess he created.

In one night, he lost his mistress, was just short of going to jail, and had a fight with his wife. The men in his family always had other women in their lives other than their wives. It was a generational curse. Poor Ellen was hurt and confused. She felt like her life with him was a big lie. This marriage needs a miracle.

Thirty-Six

Rachel In the Spotlight

Rachel decided to be an author. She happens to be very successful with her writing and speaking engagements. Her writing began when the girls made a pact in elementary school.

The phone rings

"Hello!"

"Hey Rachel, I have you booked for several bookstores this month. It conflicts with your television interviews. The TV stations aren't budging. One of them is screaming in my ear. He's rather rude. I think you'd rather do the TV shows correct?" Mr. Gibson said.

"Why is he screaming? "

" The bookstore events are out of town. He's concerned if you'll be back in time. He has everything planned. He thinks we're messing up his schedule."

"Tell him I'll be there."

"I think I'll let you call him. He's so disrespectful. I'm about to give him a piece of my mind. I don't want to mess anything up."

"My other line is ringing. Can you hold on for a minute?"

"No problem."

She clicked over to the other call. "Hello!"

"This is Mr. Jennings from WGXA radio station. We were given your name by our TV station. From my understanding you did an interview with our affiliate and it had great ratings. We want to do an interview with you within the next couple of weeks."

"I would be delighted!"

"Great, will two weeks from today be a great day?"

"Let me glance at my schedule," Mr. Jennings it's looking good."

"I'll put you down. I'm looking forward to it."

"Me too. Is there a specific topic?"

"You're the topic, just be yourself!"

"Sounds like a plan. Good-bye! "Rachel clicked back to Mr. Gibson.

"Mr. Gibson, I'm so sorry. A gentleman called about a radio interview. Did we need to finalize anything?"

" Call this man before I scream. His name is Brandon Bloom. I'm usually cool calm and collective , but this one here , is something special. I have some contracts for some other gigs I need you to sign. I'm going to mail those to you. There are so many dates, it would be best for you to look at them."

"I'll call him. You sent the information last week. I'll look for the contracts in the mail. Thanks for holding on the phone for me. I'll call you when I get them. Don't worry I'll calm Mr. Bloom down. He won't disrespect you anymore. Don't forget I have an interview on Friday with one of the major networks. I'm feeling like a real celebrity."

"Thanks you are a celebrity, you're just humble."

"Thank you so much."

* * *

After one of the interviews

After the interview aired."You did so great on the interview." Ruth said.

"I did? I was so nervous."

"We couldn't tell you were nervous."

"My knees were shaking. I was sweating like a pig."

"I couldn't tell. You represented Cedar Lake very well."

"Thanks. Did the others see me?"

"I talked to them while you were on TV. We were screaming."

"Thanks for supporting me it means a lot to me!" Rachel said.

"That's what friends are for. Keep us updated. Love you my friend, Gotta go!"

"I will do. Love you too!"

Thirty-Seven

Changes for Diane and Patricia

⁘

Fred had a fair season with the Atlanta Eagles. It was time for a trade. He went to play for the Pittsburgh Hogs. They moved to Nottingham, Pennsylvania, into an eight-bedroom house with a swimming pool and a movie theater.

The House
   "This is a dream come true," she said. "What else can I ask for?"
   "Baby, you're the best. You encouraged me when things started going down with the Eagles. You forgave me and stayed with me."
   "Don't start!"
   "It was a traumatic time for me. It's a miracle our marriage made it during that troublesome period."
   "Come on honey, I don't want to argue. We made it pass all the drama. You're spoiling the moment."
   "You have a point."
   "Our new endeavors will include the success of your engineering firm."
   "I'm hoping it all works out. I know God works miracles."
   "The firm will be a success and a blessing. You have all the skills and knowledge. And with God on our side you can't go wrong. Just trust God."
   "You're so right. I'm not going to worry. It'll be a success. I'll trust God.

Thanks honey."

Fred leans over trying to avoid falling over some boxes. "You're welcome."

" I need to start unpacking a few boxes. We have a few hours before the reception starts."

"I'll help you."

She walked towards a big box near the window. "I'll start with this box."

Fred started opening the box in front of him. "I'll start where I am. We have a lot of boxes."

"Yes, we do."

She opened another box. "Check this out! This is one of our wedding gifts from Ruth. Our engagement and wedding pictures displayed in this crystal frame. I'll always cherish this. I miss them. Life can be bitter but sweet."

"Ruth has exquisite taste. Baby, look at this —my trophies from tenth, eleventh, and twelfth grade year."

"We have a lot of memories. I better keep unpacking before I start crying."

"Aw, honey. Give me a kiss." They kissed.

"Thanks honey." She hugged her husband.

* * *

Three hours later, at the Pittsburgh Hogs campus, they entered the reception hall.

"Hello, Fred," said Coach Harvey, the wide receiver coach. "We're so glad you decided to join our franchise. We know you'll be an asset to us."

"We're glad to be here. I plan to make a difference. I'm excited about this opportunity."

"I'm glad to hear that. Let's go check out the buffet bar. I heard it has everything a man's stomach can hold," Coach Harvey said. "Kool and the Gang is the entertainment for tonight. Just let your hair down and relax. You have plenty of time to be serious."

"I see you did it up. There's lobster, caviar, shrimp. I'm going to dig in. Please excuse me," he said.

"Help yourself. We don't want to throw anything away."

Kool and the Gang took the stage and played "Celebrate."

"Wow, we had better eat so we can dance."

They made sure they put plenty of food on their plates.

"Well, well who do we have here?" asked Mr. Timmons, the owner.

"Hello," said the head coach, Mr. Huddleston.

"Hello," Fred said. "It's a pleasure seeing you, Mr. Timmons and Coach."

"The feeling is mutual. We're glad you chose our franchise." said Mr. Timmons.

"Enjoy yourself. I'll see you on Monday, if I don't see you any more tonight." Coach Huddleston said.

They headed to the dance floor but was cut off before they could make it.

"Fred, welcome to the team, but I want to tell you you're not going to start. No new person is taking any starting position. You must sit it out your first year." Mark, the starting quarterback said.

He sneered at Mark. "Time will tell it all."

Mark looked at him with disgust. "Yes, it will. Watch yourself."

"I want to dance, no time for nonsense. Please remind me to call Patricia tomorrow. She has a lot going on."

"You're right babe. The proof is in the pudding. And I will remind you. Let's dance."

✳ ✳ ✳

Where did she go wrong?

"Breaking news," the anchor said, "Prominent business leader Mr. Allen Washington, a candidate for mayor, is being investigated for sexual harassment. Investigators say he took these ladies on trips and bought them extravagant jewelry. Stay tuned for more on this story. This is Warren Morris, Channel 7 evening news."

Her affair was on every TV station, radio station, and in every newspaper in the city.

Despair and distraught showed all over her face and she's pacing the floor. "I should have broken up with him. Everyone knows about he and I. I'm so embarrassed. I should kill myself. This is devastating. And who are these other ladies? He's been cheating on me! The nerve of him! The media is calling us the Three Musketeers plus one. I'm the plus one because I haven't come forth. Who can I turn to? I'm so depressed." Patricia said out loud. "I know who I can call."

She grabbed the phone and started dialing. Ruth answered.

"I have no one to turn to. I need someone to listen to me. I haven't told you the whole truth about this guy I've been dating. He's the vice president of the company, and he's married. I was too embarrassed to admit he's married. It's on the news here and in all the papers."

"I'm here for you Pat. Have you stopped seeing him and told him it's over?"

"No not yet!" She continued to pace the floor. "What do I need to do to make it right?"

"First of all, don't beat yourself up. Just make sure you repent for having an affair with a married man," she said. "Stop the affair immediately!"

"I'll repent. I know I must ask God to forgive me for allowing him to take advantage of me. I was scared I would lose my job. The money is so good. I was tired too of fighting. I need more fight. I was terrified not just scared. I can't let men run all over me. What is wrong with me? I should have turned him in."

"You can't fear people like him. Do you still work for the company?"

"Yes, I do the news report said he's been suspended. I don't want to go to work tomorrow. My other line is ringing, hold on. No, I'll call you back."

Pat clicks over to answer the other line. "Hello!"

"Hey, I hate to be the bearer of bad news. We're moving you to another office until this story on the news dies down." Her immediate supervisor, Mrs. Rutledge, said. "And you'll be moving to a new department, at our other branch thirty miles away."

"I'm glad I get to keep my job," She answered.

"I'm not at liberty to say much."

"Thanks so much!"

"You're welcome. I'm so sorry for all of this."

"I hope it dies down soon."

"It should! Good-bye!"

"Good-bye!"

Patricia calls Ruth back

"Hello!"

"That was my supervisor telling me that I am being transferred to another office. I didn't say I was guilty or nothing. She said they want to let the story die down."

"Wow. That's a miracle."

"I'm glad God forgives me. I wouldn't know what to do if he didn't. Boy, you do reap what you sow. Mr. Washington is suspended indefinitely. I'm just as guilty as he is. I went on trips with him. I accepted expensive gifts every year, for every birthday, Christmas, and Valentine's Day. The first couple of times he made a pass at me, I managed to be strong. He even took me to a hotel about four years ago. I got away. But no, he wouldn't stop chasing me. Finally, I gave in. We had sex in his office on more than one occasion. He would say the right things and do the right things. But in my heart of hearts, there was emptiness, because I knew he was married. I should have said something instead of wanting to hang on to my job at any cost. And how many men leave their wives for their mistresses?"

"I don't know any. You were involved. Pat, it looks like God has shown you favor and given you grace. You're embarrassed, but I believe that's something you can get over."

"I'm thankful."

"God is a forgiving God. Hey friend, I must go. The girls want to get together soon. Look for a call from the group soon. Everything will be all right. I love you."

"Love you too."

The next day she reported to her new office. She ignored all calls from Mr. Washington.

Thirty-Eight

Kenneth had a Stroke

Ellen was in the lady's restroom at work, crying.

Margaret, a mentor, friend, and coworker had been waiting on her for ten minutes. She goes into the ladies' room. "Young girl, what's taking you so long? Are you okay?"

Sobbing hard, she answered, "I'm all right."

Margaret hugged her. "Are you sure? We can talk about it at lunch. Let's walk to the Chick-fil-A. We can talk then."

"Let's go." She wiped her eyes and began to walk out of the bathroom. She kept talking as they walked towards the elevator.

Margaret punched the bottom for the first floor. They got on it. It's empty.

Margaret put her hand on her left shoulder as the elevator was traveling downward.

They got off the elevator continued through the lobby.

"Let me start from the beginning Margaret. Four years ago, Kenneth had this woman in our bed. The girl and I ended up fighting. The police came. It was so embarrassing. He lied several times saying this Sabrina person didn't exist. That day was a nightmare. To top it all, my husband had a stroke this morning . I feel so bad. He kept asking me to come back to him. I just found out he's been under a lot of stress on his job. I feel so guilty." She explained.

They continued walking and talking on their way to the restaurant. "You made it through that nightmare. God is faithful and he's a healer. I pray that God heal Kenneth's body." Margaret said.

"This weekend he asked me to come back to him as his wife. I told him I will think about it. He's in ICU. I would hate for my daughter to lose her father. She loves her father. I don't know what to do. Our daughter is nine years old. She wants her daddy. She asks me at least once a week. He can't die. I don't want him to die. I still love him. Margaret, to be honest, I don't trust him. Let me change that, I trust him most of the time. There are times I start imagining he's with another woman. Right now, I just want him to be healed, nothing else. The other woman issue, none of that matters if he dies. He can't die, Margaret. This is unbelievable."

Margaret hugged her. " Jesus took thirty nine stripes for Kenneth. Lord I ask you to send your healing angels to Kenneth's room. Let a miracle occur. Please fix it where he doesn't have to have physical therapy." Margaret said.

"Thank you Lord for healing my husband. Thank you for humbling my heart and me."

Margaret I think I'm going to leave and go to the hospital and sit with Kenneth. I have peace now that I've cried and talked to you. I believe God wanted me to surrender my will, die to my agenda. Let old stuff die. He needs me, his wife. Thank you so much for listening, calming me down, praying for me, Kenneth and Sydney. Thank you Lord and thank you for sending Margaret to me."

" You're so welcome. I'll be praying for you. Will you keep me posted on what's going on with you? I believe God will heal Kenneth and your marriage. It's not a coincidence that I heard you crying in the bathroom." said Margaret.

"Thanks again! I've never been through anything like this in my life."

"Take it one day at a time!"

"Thank you so much!" She hugged Margaret.

Thirty-Nine

Going To Jamaica

Its evening time about 5 pm. Someone began knocking on the door.

Sally was freshening up.

"Who is it?"

Thomas posed so she could see him through the peep hole. "It's your knight in shining armor!"

" You can use your key. I'm in the bathroom."

"I forgot I had a key." He came in and checked out her place. She has great taste, seems like she made some changes. "I hope you're almost ready. Our plane leaves for Jamaica in two hours."

"It'll be about a minute." He took a seat on the sofa and started watching a rerun of Family Feud.

Five minutes later

Sally entered the living room.

He looked up from the TV "You look fabulous, my darling."

"Thanks, honey. And so, do you!"

"Let's go have some fun."

Surprise Surprise in Jamaica

Thomas had taken Sally shopping to make sure she had a flowing white dress to take pictures in. He purchased a white linen suit. It was suppose to be for a dance or something in Jamaica. Her dress is a dress you can dress it up or dress it down. The attire is for their wedding what a beautiful surprise. They both were ready to close off this engagement and get married but little did she know what her babe had prepared.

12 noon wedding time

Thomas walked her down the aisle that had rose petals on the ground. Sally's mom, and three sisters are in attendance, all of her girls are there, Fred and Kenneth, Eddie, Mr. and Mrs. Patterson, Diane's parents, Tanya's parents, Charles, Ellen's parents and Patricia's parents, and Uncle Richard.

"How did you do this without me knowing? I can't contain myself. You all got me good!" Sally said.

Thomas begin to speak. "I know this a surprise of a lifetime. We've been planning or trying to plan a wedding. I got tired of you trying to figure it out. I recruited your girls they helped me plan this. Can we get married today?"

"Yes, we can!"

The girls are lined up next to a minister.

"Come on Sally! Come on!" they said.

Sally got in position and so did Thomas.

The minister began the ceremony.

The tour guide for the catamaran cruise was standing there waiting for them to say I do.

"Come on everyone lets go celebrate the newlyweds on the cruise, time for dancing eating, and so on and so! One Love, welcome to Jamaica man!" the tour guide said.

Everyone started following the tour guide and they hugged Sally and Thomas as they headed towards the catamaran. Sally was smiling from ear to ear.

They had a photographer taking pictures from the beginning to the end.

"Thomas thank you so much, you did such a great job."

"I guess was the head honcho and they did the legwork. They did a great job. Wait until you see this boat. It's nice and big. And you deserve every bit of this. "

"I'm so happy, we're married now."

"Yes, we are!"

The boat ride accomplished two things the wedding reception and site seeing. The first stop was the Bob Marley Museum.

Charles, Thomas, Kenneth,and Fred loved this place. These guys love music, sports, and cars.

"This man was gifted like no other. Just think if he would've lived past 36 years of

age. " Fred said.

"He was a musical genius."Charles said as they walked through the museum.

"I'm loving our tour guide. He's singing every Marley song."

"He's singing my favorite, "Is This Love." I think about my girl Ellen. Man I will never let her go. We've been through the storms." Kenneth said.

"Yeah man, I love that song I can the same about Diane. Man, she's everything. It will be to death do us part."

"Kenneth, I heard about your early adventures in your marriage. Ellen wasn't playing with you. She fought her battles and didn't wait on God. I'm glad you all reconciled after that fight man."

"Ya Mon, that's why I can do my reggae dance and thank God for my babe. She's forgiven me. I want to be the best husband. Man she was there for me when I had the stroke. Look at her that pretty smile, everything about her I love."

"Our girls are a beautiful bunch. They look they're having as much fun as we are." Thomas said. "I'm glad they came up with the idea to do our wedding different. A vacation and honeymoon altogether."

"Yep, they're beautiful inside and out!" Charles said.

And being a NFL player, Diane stood by my side while I handled a few groupies. Thank God for her. And yes guys we have some jewels."

"Fred, some of that stuff you run into as a player you just can't help. "

Thomas said.

"You're so correct. For the most part, there a group of girls that find there way in to our parties, locker room areas. They're regulars who are very aggressive."

"I can imagine. Gold diggers. I'm so glad you and Diane made it through."

"I'm grateful you and Kenneth stayed with Ellen and Diane. We guys have our own gang or buddy system going on."

"Yes we do!" Thomas said. Thanks guys for coming to my wedding celebration. It means a lot."

"Nothing but love and support. That's what we're suppose to do." Fred said.

"That's right!" Charles said.

"Ya mon, nothing but love and support." Kenneth said.

Thirty minutes later

The tour guide started talking. "The tour will end in five minutes. Its been great being your tour guide. Your van is pulling up to take you to your boat. Inna Di Morrows."

"See you tomorrow also, Inner Luv," Kenneth said.

The tour guide chuckled. "I hear you!"

Everyone headed towards the van.

The newlyweds grabbed each others hand.

"You guys looked like you were having the time of your life."

"Yes, it was a nice time with the guys. You girls looked happy."

"You know it. My girls through thick and then."

Thomas helped his wife onto the van.

At the resort

"Hey guys Sally and I are going to freshen up. We might see you for dinner. Remember we're newlyweds, just married and this is part of our honeymoon. We know you all can entertain yourselves."

Everybody waved or chuckled. Some said "Later!"

We understand!"

Okay Newlyweds!"

"See you later!"Sally said with a big smile.

The Next Day at Ocho Rios

"Wah Gwaan!" said the tour director.

"What's up with you Mr. Tour Director. "

"Hello my friends, welcome . Let's go to Ocho Rios. Dunns River Fall & Park here we come. Put your seat belt on lets go. It's about a two hour drive."

"Here we come Dunn's River!" Sally said.

"Yes, we're on our way!" Patricia screamed.

"Lord encamp your angels about us in Jesus name we pray." Ruth prayed.

The tour guide began speaking. "Go to sleep relax. I'm going to put on some Bob Marley, "One Love" is coming up first."

The music was playing not to loud and not to soft. The parents of the girls were seated up front. Sally's mother looked so happy and relaxed. The conversation seemed so jovial and light-hearted.

Sally whispered in her husbands ear. " Babe when I was in high school, I never dreamed that when I got married my mother would attend my wedding. This is a miracle weekend, babe. God is so good."

"Yes, God is good. I'm glad there is a 365 degree turn around for your relationship with your mom. Its hard to believe she was capable of that."

When we began our amend, I found out she was treating me the way she was treated and she was unhappy. She didn't realize what she had done until I went to college early without her being involved."

"I'm so glad God healed your relationship with your mom. Babe lets take a nap. We have a fun long day ahead of us."

Dunn's River Falls Park

"Here we are, be careful on the Falls, let's have fun. I will guide you," the guide said.

Patricia, Rachel, Marion, and Tanya ran to the Falls like it was an amusement park ride with a long line.

"Dead wid laugh," the guide said. "Where are they rushing too. "

"Those four will keep you laughing, especially Patricia and Tanya. Just keep watching them." Sally said as she and Thomas got off the bus.

Yes, you're gonna be dead wid laugh for the rest of the trip." Thomas said.

The couples stayed together because the guys wanted to help their wives up the falls. You climb rocks that about two to three feet tall with the water flowing down on them. The falls are beautiful, you must be careful and wear the correct shoes.

Patricia, Rachel, Marion, and Tanya had already started up the Falls with the other tour guide.

"Talking about being adventurous, this is it." Patricia said.

"The life for sure!" Tanya said.

"Refreshing and relaxing." Marion said.

"The cool breeze flowing through my hair is so right. I feel like I'm flowing in the wind." Rachel said.

"After we get up to that landing let's take a picture the four musketeers." Patricia said.

"Great idea!" Marion said.

The newlyweds were very cautious as they stepped on each rock to avoid falling.

"I must say this is invigorating. Somehow it seems like this is something we really shouldn't be doing just because this is what people do." Sally said.

"Wow, I was thinking the same thing, babe. That's why I'm watching our every move carefully."

Whoosh! Whoosh! Whoosh! Whoosh! The four musketeers fell into the water.

"Oh my God, I hope they're not hurt." Sally said.

Fred and Diane who happened to be near, started pulling them out of the water. Tanya was flapping in the water. All you could see were her arms.

"Tanya relax I got you!" Fred said. "The water is only three feet deep."

"Whew, the only thing I know is I fell and I'm getting out of this water!" Tanya replied.

Yes, you are!"

Kenneth and Ellen helped Patricia and Rachel. Ruth and Charles helped

Marion.

Everyone made it to an exit area to the left of the falls.

Ruth and Charles went into their medical mode.

"Does anyone have any pain?" Charles asked.

'I do!" all of them said at once.

"My toe looks crooked and it hurts." Rachel said.

"My finger hurts." Tanya said.

"Let's find the infirmary and some ice while we're on our way!" Ruth said.

Ruth and Charles took the girls to the infirmary. The rest came off the waterfall and decided to get something to eat while waiting.

At the restaurant

"I truly hope the four musketeers are okay." Thomas said.

"Me too!" Sally said.

Mrs. Perez seated next to Thomas and Sally. "They'll be fine. At the most they might have to wear one of those shoes or put a soft cast on their fingers. I raised four daughters and have seen all types of injuries. Talking about my daughters, reminds me I have a son now. I welcome you into the family. Its about time I have a son."

"Thanks mom! I feel very welcomed. I'm glad to be a part of the family."

"You make me smile, Thomas." Mrs. Perez said.

Diane started talking. " I don't know about you all, but I've done enough shopping and seen enough of Jamaica. And now that the four musketeers have these minor injuries I think the last night here we should enjoy each others company. There's plenty of entertainment at the resort. Let's just sit it down. What do you think?"

"I agree! You know the newlyweds don't mind." Sally said.

"No we don't mind," Thomas said. "Hopefully the girls will be back soon."

Yeah, we'll make sure they're fine and get them settled. We can freshen up and come down to eat and enjoy the activities at the resort." Ellen said.

Fred began speaking. "Yes, I think we should relax. I have enjoyed myself. Hats off to the newlyweds, Congratulations! Thanks for doing something different. I wish you many years of a happy marriage."

"Thank you so much Fred." Sally said.

"Yes, thank you, Fred!" Thomas said.

The girls did suffer minor injuries. Everyone did relax for the rest of the evening. The newlyweds of course rested for the evening and ordered room service. They have things to do.

Forty

Ashamed and Not Ashamed

Tanya arrived home from a barbeque. She started entering her apartment and immediately turned her head to the right, because she heard someone running up the steps.

The Boss was at her door and out of breath from running. "Where have you been?"

A couple of neighbors were just coming home, they looked at their every move.

They continued to watch as The Boss shoved Tanya in the apartment. "You heard me! Who told you to go to somewhere without me?"

"I didn't think you wanted to go," Tanya answered.

"Why would you think that?"

"It was a barbeque. Well there were families, husbands and wives, with their children. I thought you might feel uncomfortable."

"I don't believe a word you're saying. I think you're ashamed of me."

"No, that isn't it."

240

"You don't have to worry about me anymore. It's over. Don't call me. Don't come over to my house. We've been dating for nine years and I haven't met any members of your family or your childhood friends. Go play with someone else."

The Boss left, slammed the door, got in the car, and drove off speeding.

Tanya ran to catch up. "Wait!"

The Boss was gone like dust in the wind. The car made a lot of noise, it sounded like thunder.

Tanya went back in the house and started crying on the sofa. There was no one she could talk to about this situation unless she told them everything. She wasn't ready to tell her secret about who the Boss really is. She sat on the couch in front of the TV and cried. She called The Boss all night long, but no answer.

* * *

The next day, Tanya was at her new dental practice.

"Dr. Patterson are you okay?" asked Cynthia, her receptionist.

"I'm fine," "I just have a few things I need to iron out. Thanks for asking."

"Are you sure? I called your name three times and you didn't respond."

"Yes, sorry about that. I was thinking. What time will the next patient arrive?"

"Ten-thirty."

"Okay."

All of her calls were ignored. No answer.

During this time she didn't return any of their calls. She didn't want to talk to her friends while her heart was bleeding. The Boss had gone out Friday night looking for a new love, but no such luck.

At noon, the phone rang again. Tanya answered.

"I'm truly glad you're still among the living."

"I am. It's been a crazy week."

"What's going on?"

"I have about thirty new patients. I probably need to hire another dental hygienist."

"The fact you need to hire people is great. Congratulations. Is everything okay in your personal life?"

"Everything is great!"

"I'm glad. I could've sworn God was showing me something else. You seemed troubled and depressed. The others might be calling you. You know how we do. We realize it's time for us to get together. We're behind schedule."

"Thanks my friend, my sister. Yes, we're behind. Love you too!"

They hang up. Tanya's phone rang again.

"This is Diane, Is everything okay?"

"Yes, Ruth just called me too. I had a busy week with my patients. My dental practice is growing; my customers have been referring people to me."

"That's great news. I knew you would be successful."

"How is Pittsburgh treating you? How is Fred? Your job?"

"He likes the new franchise. I like it too. They've been great for us.
The engineering firm is doing great."

"You go girl. You deserve it."

"Thanks, my friend. I miss everyone. The snow is a lot to deal with. How is your love life? I'm ready for you to get married."

"My love life is fine. I want to marry The Boss, but it's complicated."

"Who cares what people think. I do want to say, you've been on my mind a lot lately, and I thought I was discerning trouble with you. You know we haven't met this person yet. I'll keep praying for you. At times it seems like you want to hide him from us."

" I need to sort some things out."

"I'm concerned about your safety. I hope nothing crazy is going on."

"Don't worry. We'll talk later. Good-bye."

"Good-bye!"

They knew she was lying to them. They respected what she said .

Forty-One

Sally is a Hero

"Sally, what's up girl? How you doing?" Ruth couldn't contain the excitement in her voice.

"Nothing much, getting ready for our Thanksgiving dinner tomorrow."

"I hope you're making your mac and cheese dish."

"Girl, of course! I can't come without it."

"Sally, I just spoke with Diane. She's planning a Super Bowl party in New Orleans, if Fred and the Hogs go to the Super Bowl. It's looking very promising. She wants her friends to be in the nice suites of the football game where all the parties are. Put it on your calendar."

"I will. I hope they make it. Those suites always look like fun when you see them on TV."

"Yes, they do. What's up, with you?"

"My cousin Helen hooked up with a drug addict. She married him about five years ago. His addiction has caused them a lot of problems. She was addicted and trying to stay clean. She ran away, now she's living with me. He found out she was living with me. He comes over the house after midnight disturbing us and the neighbors. He just want to use her as a runner for his drugs. He doesn't care about Helen. He's a user that only thinks of himself. I let him in one time and he stole money out of my purse. I can't get any rest. She's an emotional wreck. I'm trying to encourage her. It's been going on for about a month. I've overslept at least three times this week. I think I'm going to tell her she has to leave. I'll help her move into her own apartment."

"I'm sorry to hear that about Helen. We can help others, but we must make sure we're not hurting ourselves. You can't lose your job."

"Yes, I think so. I love my cousin, but this situation is a handful. Please pray for me. My cousin is coming, and her husband drove up right behind her. I must deal with this."

"Talk to you later, I got you in my prayers."

They said good-bye and hung up.

Helen ran into the house

"I think I need to call 911. Ricky followed me all the way over here. I need to put a restraining order on him. He won't leave me alone."

"I think you need to. It's getting worse. You want me to call?"

There's a loud knock on the door

Ricky banged on the door. It got louder and louder. "Open up the door, Helen! Open up."

"Rickey, you need to leave. I'll call the police if you don't leave. You know I don't want to do that."

"I'm not leaving until I see her. She has a package for me."

"No, she doesn't. Please leave, Rickey."

He kept banging on the door.

"I'm calling the police."

Sally dialed 911.

"Hello, what's your emergency?" asked the dispatcher. Sally began speaking with frantic in her voice. "There's a man banging on my door. I told him if he doesn't leave, I was calling the police. His wife is separated from him. She's staying with me. He wants her to come out. I told him she doesn't want to see him. He refuses to leave."

"I have your address as 919 Elm Street. We'll have someone there in less than five minutes."

"Thanks!"

"Helen!" Rickey screamed.

"Rickey," the police are on their way. You need to leave if you don't want to get in trouble."

The next thing she heard was a car taking off fast. Rickey took off right before the police arrived.

She heard another bang on the door.

"Who is it?"

"It's the police. Someone called in and said there's a disturbance."

"Yes, I did!" Sally opened the door to talk to the police.

"Is everything okay?" The officer asked.

"Yes, officer, he just left less than thirty seconds ago. I did tell him I called the police."

"That was a smart move on his part. We like peaceful resolutions."

"Thanks for showing up. His wife Helen and I were frightened."

"Here's my card. I'm Officer Walker. Call me if you need anything."

"Thanks again."

Helen walked to the door. "Yes, officer thanks. I'm scared for my life. I've been thinking about taking out a restraining order."

"You should, if you feel your life is in danger. Just go down to the station and file a report. Don't procrastinate!"

"Thanks, officer. I will."

"Call us if you need us."

"We will."

Sally closed the front door.

"Helen, you have to file a restraining order. Rickey needs help, and we can't allow him to do something crazy."

"I know, it's priority. I'm not going back to drugs. God has delivered me and I'm so grateful. Right now, I want to go to bed. I have a long day tomorrow. Good night. I guess we need to turn the alarm on."

"Good night, Helen."

Forty-Two

Marion in the Hospital

Marion Goes to Baptist Hospital

Marion ran out of the house. "Help! Help!" She screamed as she ran to her next door neighbor's house. "Help! Help!" She banged on the door.

"Marion, is that you?" Mr. Banks asked.

"Yes, open the door, Mr. Banks. I've been hurt. Can you take me to Baptist Hospital?"

"What happened?"

"I fell."

"You look horrible. Let me get the car. We have to hurry." "I'll meet you at the garage door."

Blood dripped down her face and from her mouth. She made it to the car. Mr. Banks was nervous. He almost forgot to let the garage door up. He backed out the car and got out to help her get in.

Antonio, her husband, approached the car. Come home now. I can take care of you. Where are you going? You better come here! I'm the man of the house. You're making it hard on yourself."

Mr. Banks ignored him, put the pedal to the metal and drove off.

Mrs. Banks watched the ordeal. The nosy neighbor Mrs. Coleman called her. "Banks, what's going on over there with those young folks? She had blood all over her. I bet you that husband of hers has been beating on her."

Mrs. Banks began speaking. "Stephen took her to the emergency room. When he gets to the hospital and gets settled, he'll call me."

Mrs. Coleman interjected. "He did, she always have a black eye. She tries to cover it up with make-up."

"We'll figure it all out. We want her to be alright!" Mrs. Banks said.

"For sure, keep me updated." Mrs. Coleman said.

Emergency room being treated

"Check her pressure! The bandage and gauze are helping the bleeding. As soon as the bleeding stops, let's wrap it up," Dr. Moody demanded.

"Her pressure is normal. I have the bandage to wrap her up." Nurse Betty responded. "You're a walking miracle. All that blood you lost, you should be dead."

"Nurse Betty. I'm blessed. I'm blessed to be alive. I could have died." Tears ran down her face.

"You know, you're correct. God spared your life. We're bandaging you up, your wounds will close and heal appropriately. Your swelling will go down when the pain medicine gets in your system. The police have been called. It's obvious you've been abused."

"No, please, no police!" Marion screamed.

"We're obligated to call the police. Dr. Moody will admit you. The police will interview you later today."

"Oh no, I don't know what I'm going to do. Please don't. He'll kill me! I beg you, please don't!"

"You need to stay away from him. He sounds dangerous."

Mr. Banks entered the room. "What's up? Is she going to be alright?"

"Yes!" Nurse Betty said." She's a walking miracle."

"God is good. I appreciate you Mr. Banks. You saved my life."

"You're welcome. You know we had to call the police."

"I wish you hadn't. He's a perfect gentleman."

"No, he's not. Any man who hits a woman isn't a gentleman." *She is delusional.* Mr. Banks said.

"I just don't know what to do."

" You need to handle this before it gets worse. That's what you need to do, young lady."

"I'm so scared."

"My wife and I will be by your side. I need to call her. I'll be back."

"You can use the phone in this room."

"Oh no, I'll use the phone in the hallway. I don't want to disturb you. I need to make several calls."

The phone in her hospital room rang.

Marion answered. "Hello!"

"Honey, how are you?" Antonio asked.

"I'm fine considering," She answered.

"When are you coming home?"

"I don't know, maybe tomorrow."

"I have a surprise for you. I want to come to the hospital."

"No, honey, it's not in your best interest to come up here."

"Why is that, did you call the police?"

"No, I didn't."

"Well, I should be able to come!"

"Don't. It's not a good move for you to visit me."

"What do you mean? You're making me mad!"

"Don't be mad."

"I'm coming up there." She hung up the phone.

The phone rang again.

"Don't come up here. They filed a police report. You might go to jail. They're saying I have no choice."

"How could you do that to me? It was an accident! You know I love you. I didn't mean to hurt you."

" I have to go. The doctor just came in."

"Young lady everything is coming along. The wounds will heal on their own. I'll probably release you in a couple days."

"Wow, that's great news!" Mr. Banks said as he entered the room.

"Yes, it is," Marion answered.

She stayed at the hospital two more days. The neighbors were right there to take her to their home. The hospital reported the domestic violence.

* * *

Marion gets in the back seat of Ms. Coleman's car

"Mrs. Banks, I really appreciate all that you and your husband are doing for me. Honestly, I'm scared to go back home."She said.

"We didn't think it would be safe to go back to the house. We've arranged for you to stay with me. Your husband won't have a clue you're right across the street from your house." Ms. Coleman responded.

"So, you'll have no worries," Mrs. Banks said. "I think it'll be wise to move or leave."

"I don't know how I can repay you."

"You can repay us by getting some help."

"I'm so scared. Can you help me find some help? I should say Lord help me!"

"Don't worry we're your angels!" Ms. Coleman said.

"Thank you so much. You all knew all along what I've been going through! I feel like crying!"

"I've been praying all this time!" Ms. Coleman said.

"I've been praying too; we knew something was not right." Mrs. Banks said.

"Thank you, ladies." Rachel said.

A few minutes later they pulled into the garage. Its good that Ms. Coleman keeps her cars in the actual garage. That way Antonio can't see anything.

Forty-Three

Super Bowl

Everyone had their fingers crossed hoping the Pittsburgh Hogs are going to the Super Bowl. So far, they were undefeated. The Hogs were in the playoff game. If they win it, they will go to the championship.

Less than two minutes to go.

Patricia called Diane at home.

Of course, she wasn't there, she was at the game.

She left a message on the answering machine.

"Oh, my friend, looks like we're going to the Super Bowl. Only forty-five seconds left. The Hogs have possession. I know you'll call us with the details. Love you, my friend. I'm excited."

Everyone except Marion left messages about the Super Bowl and the festivities.

A couple of days later they all got on the phone, except Marion.

"All right," Diane said, "Are you ready to party? Fred has arranged for all of us to come to the game. We have a suite."

"I've never been to New Orleans. I want to experience Bourbon Street and the French Quarter," Tanya said with expectancy in her voice.

"I bought my ticket right after Thanksgiving. I decided I would go to New

Orleans regardless." Ruth said. "I've never been to New Orleans neither."

"Wow, sounds like you're ready!" Diane replied.

"Has anyone talked to Marion?" Ellen said. "I've called her several times since Thanksgiving. She hasn't returned my call. Antonio answered the phone every time."

"She called me," Sally said, "but she called while I was at work. She told me to tell everyone she's okay."

"She was the first one I tried to call. I got her answering machine. I hope she makes it," Ruth said.

I thought she moved into her own apartment." Patricia inquired.

She did Sally responded. "Maybe she moved back in or he's just over there all the time. She's not telling the whole truth."

"I'll call her. Feel free to bring your husbands or your boyfriends. As you know Fred will be there."

"Too late, I told Kenneth it's a girls only weekend," Ellen said.

"I did too," Ruth replied.

"I guess it's a little too late for the guys to come," Patricia replied.

"Well girls, I guess I'll reserve two rooms for us at the Ritz Carlton. Fred has to stay with the team. All right, it's a girl's weekend. I'll call Marion to see what's going on. It won't be the same without her."

The next day during work hours, Marion left a message for Diane. "Hello, I got your message about meeting in New Orleans. I'll be there. I just bought my ticket. Girl, I need a break. I can't wait to see everyone. Talk to you later."

New Orleans

"My girls are here!" Sally crowed as she walked into the Ritz Carlton in downtown New Orleans.

They ran to meet her. "Hey !"

Tanya embraced Sally. "We're getting ready to experience part of the French Quarter on Canal Street. Come go with us!"

"I want to taste the creole cooking, gumbo, etouffee, and boudin," Sally responded.

"I have two suites for us, right next to each other. The team is having a big party tonight," Diane said with excitement in her voice.

"Sounds like fun!" Rachel said.

"The rooms are side by side. Let's go to our rooms and put our bags up, we can catch the parade on Canal Street."

"Time to party!" Rachel said.

The girls got on the elevators and went to their rooms. The rooms were decorated with the most elegant, classy French style furniture. The rooms had several martini gold antique tables, Cote d'Azur sofas and UN grand lit beds, double French beds. It fits with the culture of New Orleans. They were ready in less than thirty minutes. New Orleans jazz was heard all over the lobby, a band was jamming.

"What a good time, everyone is dancing everywhere!" Marion said.

"Get down Pat!" Ruth asked.

Others in the lobby joined in.

Everyone took pictures.

Pat almost out of breath. "This is fun. The music is great."

"New Orleans jazz is the best!" Rachel said as she danced in the crowd.

A stranger walked up to them and started dancing.

"Oh my!" Marion began dancing with him. He was dancing very provocative. He got closer and closer. "Ladies it's time to go!"

Rachel ran out the lobby door and the others followed.

The stranger stood in the lobby looking lost. "What did I do? Why did they leave?"

The other guests kept dancing.

* * *

The parade had just begun

They ran to the street.

Dancing began again. "I love the New Orleans sound."

Marion waved a handkerchief in the air. "Me too."

Rachel lined up behind Ellen dancing.

"Wow, did you see that woman? She was all over that man." "She's almost naked too," Sally said.

"They say anything goes on in New Orleans," Patricia said.

The music and dancing in the street continued.

They started singing, "Oh when the saints go marching in."

Ellen pointed. "Look over there, they're second lining across the street."

"What is second lining?" Tanya asked.

"They dance and walk with parasols and handkerchiefs. Watch me y'all. How does it look?" Ellen asked.

"You got it, do it girl. You got it! Go ahead and join them!" Tanya said.

"Look at that man on those stilts." Sally said. "That takes skills."

"I don't see how they can walk on those things," Rachel said.

A band is coming, they're playing My Cherie Amour by Stevie Wonder."

Tanya stared. "They're marching with some tight precision."

"Yes, they're on beat, looking really sharp!" Ruth said.

Marion why are you so quiet? Patricia asked.

"I'm sleepy," Marion said.

"I noticed you're quiet too. I hope that's all it is." Diane said.

"It is, I had to wake up early to catch a plane here." Marion explained.

"Marion. We'll leave you alone. Check this out, this is my favorite, the little dancers. So cute," Ruth said.

"Do they make you want to have one?" Diane asked.

"No, not in a rush for that. I just like looking for now."

"Let's get something to eat. This cafe looks like it serves all the Cajun dishes. I'm starving," Patricia said.

"Cool! I forgot I hadn't eaten since yesterday afternoon," Marion replied.

"Mmm, that's not good," Sally replied. "Why not Marion?"

"No reason at all, just been busy!" Marion replied.

Everyone shook their head in unbelief.

Marion, looked frustrated. "Come on, give me a break."

"For now!" Rachel said.

They walked into the restaurant. They were helped instantly.

"Follow me!" the hostess said.

They followed the hostess.

"Did you see that plate of food that waitress had. It looked mouthwatering." Marion said.

Tanya was checking out the restaurant. "I did. I love the wood decor and the aqua blue and chocolate colors."

They sat down and looked at the menu. The restaurant was very casual and relaxed.

"I want some gumbo, crab legs, and etouffee," Patricia said.

Ellen glanced at the menu items. "I want some boudin."

"I'm ordering shrimp and lobster," Marion said.

"Marion, now it's time to talk! Where in the world have you been? We've haven't talked to you since November," Tanya asked.

"You never answer the phone," Ruth said.

"I called twice," Sally said.

"I've been busy," Marion replied. "Real busy."

"Is everything okay?" Tanya asked." I do remember what you told us."

"Has he been treating you right?" Patricia asked.

"Yes, he has. Everything is peachy," Marion answered.

"Well, my friend, that's interesting. Why has Antonio been calling us looking for you, if everything is okay?" Tanya asked.

"You all make me sick. I can't hide anything from you."

"Marion, you can't lie to us. We always find out. He was looking for you. He called all of us," Ellen said.

The server came and took their orders.

"Now back to you, Marion, don't think you're going to get off that easy," Diane said. "Remember I'm the big sister."

Crocodile tears rolled down her face. "Okay, my friends. Things have not been great with us. I had to move out."

They hugged her tight.

"You can tell us later," Rachel said. "It's a miracle you got that out."

"Okay friend." Marion sniffled and wiped her eyes and nose.

"You feel better," Sally asked. "Hard cries always make me feel better."

"We're going to change the subject and when you're ready we can continue." Rachel said. "Girls, I had a problem this week. I had this book signing I didn't want to do. I found out about it from a casual friend. I didn't want to accept it. I accepted and changed my mind. Then changed my mind again. I kept changing my mind because the girl who invited me is so unprofessional. You know I didn't want to be bothered. My godmother helped me with finally going. She said I must go. People need what you have to offer. You have to die to self, it's God's agenda not yours."

"It was hard, I know," Ellen said. "I'm glad you did it."

"Me too," Ruth answered.

"I'm glad I died to my agenda and did what God wanted me to do." Rachel said.

The waitress arrived with the food.

"It smells tantalizing," Tanya said.

"Yes, it does," Ellen said. "Now let's say grace."

Rachel led the prayer. "We pray to you God who art in heaven, we thank you for this food we're about to receive. We ask that it be of nourishment to our bodies. And Lord please strengthen Marion during this trying time in her life. Please lead and guide her. With you God all things are possible. I ask that you encamp your angels about her. We thank you in advance. In Jesus' name we pray, amen."

"Amen!" everyone said in unison.

" This shrimp is very tender and tasty," Marion said

"Was the book signing a success?" Tanya asked.

"It was a real success. I got seven other bookings as a result of going there. I'm glad I was obedient."

"I'm glad, you deserve it." Tanya said.

"Much success on those future book signings," Marion stated.

"Thanks Marion." Rachel replied.

Marion sipped her drink. "You're welcome. I hope Fred and his teammates win the super bowl. I don't understand football in detail, just the basic. Do you think they have a chance?"

"They have the best offence and defense in the league."

Tanya wiped her mouth. "That would be pretty cool. Fred will get his first super bowl ring!"

"We hope so, that's every player's dream! I think he deserves it."

"We need our brother to get his ring, Lord Jesus," Ruth said.

"Yes!"

"Girls, can we change the subject? I'm starting to get worked up and nervous. I need to stay relaxed for Fred."

Ruth responded immediately. "We got you and understand. What about some dessert?"

Sally motioned for the waitress. "Can we have a dessert menu?"

Ellen started licking her lips. "I hope they have a brownie a la mode with ice cream. I can taste it now."

Sally started daydreaming. "I have one better; I can taste the peach cobbler and ice cream in my mouth."

The waitress came back with the menus fast.

"They got it!" Ellen said with excitement in her voice. She pointed to the brownie to show the waitress.

Tanya anxious to speak blurted out. "I want the peach cobbler with ice cream! "

"Got it! Anyone else?" asked the waitress.

"Can you bring four peach cobblers and four brownies, both with ice cream?" Patricia asked.

The girls continued to eat their and had meaningful conversations.

* * *

Let's ride the trolley

"Does it bring us back to this spot?" Marion asked.

"Yes, it does, it takes you all over the city," the bus driver answered.

"How much is it?" Tanya asked.

"It's free!" the bus driver answered. "Jump on girls let me show you the city!"

The girls jumped on.

"I would love to come here for the Jazz Festivals," Rachel said.

"It sounds like a lot of fun." Tanya replied.

"The people here have a lot of fun. It's a great place to relax and let your hair down. Antonio, almost killed me. He beat me up so bad I had to go to the emergency room. Presently, we're separated. We've been apart since the Sunday after Thanksgiving. That's when it happened," Marion explained.

"We knew something major had happened," Ruth replied.

"We panicked for a while," Patricia said.

"No need to worry. I had three angels helping me out. My next-door neighbors the Bank's and Mrs. Coleman. They took care of me as if I were their child. I have my own apartment. I don't know if he's changed or not. I can't tell if he's putting up a front. Honestly, I think he hasn't changed."

"That's not good Marion," Ellen said.

"What about counseling?" Diane asked.

"He doesn't want to do that. He said everything is fine."

"That's a red flag, my friend!" Sally said.

"She's right Marion, that's a red flag," Tanya replied.

"It sounds like he needs help. You're not a punching bag."

"I know, but I love him. I miss him sooooo much. We have dated at least twice a month since I moved out. He treats me as if I'm someone he just met."

"Sure, he's on his best behavior. From my understanding of abusers," Rachel cautioned, "They have periods when they're extremely what you may call perfect and then they're extremely abusive. They have honeymoons. Be careful."

"I will."

"You promise?" Rachel asked.

"I promise," Marion replied. "Let's pay attention to this tour. I don't feel like crying."

"You know we'll be watching you and checking up on you," Rachel said.

"Thanks for sharing, Marion." Sally said.

Game Time!

Super Bowl Sunday 8 pm

The game has started. It's the third quarter. The girls are eating and having a ball. It 's a nail biter. Both teams are playing well.

"A win tonight would be a win for my husband's career. Go Hogs! Go Fred!"

"Go Hogs go." Everyone is excited.

Sam the announcer begins to speak. "The Hogs are playing defense like never before."

Greg the other announcer interrupted." I'll say, they act like they want it bad. But you can't sleep on the Cowboys!"

"You got that right!" Sam responded.

"Mmm good!" Marion said. "The food is filled with Cajun Creole seasoning. This taste of New Orleans is Delicious!"

Tanya replied. "Very tasty!"

Greg came on the loudspeakers again. "The ball is thrown. It's caught. The Cowboys are on the fifty-yard line. They got a first down off that play."

Rachel jumped up. "Defense Hogs!"

"We're funny, yelling defense, and the team can't hear us." Marion said. "I'm just having a great time. It's so relaxing."

"Marion, you need to have a blast. Just let your hair down. Relax," Sally responded.

Marion smiled. "Thanks, honey."

"Marion, are you going to remain in your apartment?" Rachel asked.

"Yes, my friend. I'm not sure it's safe to go back to him."

"I'm glad you realize that," Sally said.

"Don't mean to eavesdrop! I am too," Ellen said.

Game is moving along

Sam, the other commentator, called, "Touchdown Dallas! The Cowboys made sure it's not going to be a shutout! Less than five minutes left into the fourth quarter."

Clock is <u>ticking</u>

Greg the announcer began speaking loudly over the microphone. "We have one minute left in the fourth quarter. Both teams are playing great defense."

"They're playing defense," Sam said. "The Hogs forced the Cowboys to fumble the ball. Before that fumble it looked like Dallas was getting ready to score."

"This is a great game!" Greg screamed thought the mike.

"Yes, it is. It's fast pace; the clock has been running down fast." Sam responded.

Rachel resumed. "It's hard for me to talk when the commentator comes over the loudspeaker. It looks like Fred and the team will pull it off."

Greg blurted out. "Touchdown! The Hogs have scored their third touchdown with less than forty-five seconds left in the game. The Hogs kick for the one point. The kick makes it in. The Cowboys have one time out left. The Hogs have one time out left."

Diane looked nervous, "Come on Hogs, only twenty seconds left.

" The Hogs kicked the ball to the Cowboys! They get it at the five-yard line. Cowboys can't decide what they're going to do. The first play seconds to go!"

Sam began speaking. " Its second down with nine yards to go. The ball is in play. The quarterback is sacked. The clock is running. The cowboys are taking their time about getting to the line of scrimmage. It looks like it's over the clock is at five seconds. They're ready now. The quarterback throws it long for number 27 Woooooo! Almost intercepted. Pass incomplete. Game over! Pittsburgh Wins!!!!"

They're screaming like never. "Go Pittsburgh! Yeah! "

"Thank you, Lord, my baby has a ring! Go Pittsburgh!"

It's Party time in New Orleans

The girls ran to the field to celebrate with Fred.

Diane was the first one there. She ran to Fred." "Congratulations honey. You deserve the win."

Confetti was everywhere. Everyone was happy. The Cowboys congratulated the Hogs. It was like a party on the football field. The sportscasters were interviewing everyone.

Forty-Four

Skiing at Alpine

⸺ ❦ ⸺

Television time for Rachel's friends

Diane, Patricia, and Ellen are on a three-way call.

Patricia began to speak. "Everyone doesn't get to travel. One thing, I like about Rachel is she broadens her horizons. She met Christopher by traveling to these ski races."

"I agree." Diane said. She's getting an education that's more than just books. As a matter of fact we can say by being in Europe she's making history and geography come alive."

"The girl is focused. She gave up the fashion industry and decided to focus on her writing and through her travels, this is where she's landed. At the Alpine Ski World Cup. This competition has been around since 1967. Rachel always believed she has plenty time for a man. But men are not foremost on her mind. They don't consume her thoughts."

"I wish I could be like her." Patricia said. "I'm always ready for a nice man, my future husband."

"He's coming." Ruth said.

"Yes, he is." Diane said.

"I appreciate you all. You're the best."

261

"Do you see what I see? Rachel is standing right next to the cameraman."

"I see her. This is so nice. She's in Europe and we get to see her. "

At the race

Dressed in all white from head to toe looking like a millionaire, Rachel is standing next to the cameraman and Americans are standing on her right side. Fresh apple cider filled the air, it made you think its warm, when its actually twenty degrees below zero. The air was filled with some strong vodka coming from a guy standing behind the cameraman. Why is that drunk people have to always show out and act like they have no home training.

"You Americans, that Christopher guy isn't going to win," the drunk man said as he bumped into the cameraman.

That bump didn't move the camera or the cameraman.

"Hey you, the one dressed in all white, you hear me. No one from the USA is going to win!" This time he stumbled and bumped everyone a lot harder.

"Can you move out the way and stop bumping me and my camera?"

"Who do you think you're talking to? You're not the boss of me!"

Rachel began speaking. "Sir, I think you need to move. He's probably going to call the police. And you're rather unruly. I came to see the Christopher guy, my boyfriend win this race. I want you to move so I can watch him in peace."

"Snow White all dressed in white you don't tell me what to do!"

"Very funny. Please leave!" Rachel begged.

At that moment the drunk's bottle of liquor wasted on the camera.

The guy was livid. "Enough I've had it. I'm calling the police and security. You've ruined my clothes and my camera is wet. I hope your liquor hasn't messed up my equipment."

The drunk pushed Rachel, the cameraman and the other Americans one by one. He's rather strong. Or is it the alcohol.

"I'm going to call the police now for harassing me and causing me to fall." Rachel said.

"For sure!" The cameraman said as he got off the cold snow.

Rachel began to walk away. "I'll be back with the authorities."

Back in the United States

God is so awesome did you see what I just saw. We need to pray. Rachel is upset and walked off. She and the cameraman fell and it looked like words were exchanged. We need to pray, we can't have our friend have any problems while overseas." Ruth said.

"I noticed it also." Diane said.

"I saw it too! Lord please protect our friend , we ask that you encamp your angels about her in the name of Jesus."

"In Jesus name we pray! Amen!" the girls said in unison.

Rachel on her journey to get the officer

Wait a minute, by the time I get back to that spot I would have missed the race. And I'm in another country. I don't need any trouble. Let me stop here and watch the race.

Rachel stopped because she realized the race had started about a minute ago.

The announcer was talking, "Christopher Smith is getting ready to go downhill. He has to beat 1:53:24 to be in first place. He's in position. And there he goes. Looking good. He's the only American in the race. Oh no, his time is 1:53:26, almost beat the 1:53:24. That might put him in second, I hope not third place."

"I hope that time gives Chris at least second place." Rachel said out load. She's talking out loud to herself. I think she's excited.

The next skiers time was 1:54:00, the next one was 1:53:28.

"There you have it folks Christopher is in second place, Banks is in first. Congratulations to you both. Either way it goes, I wouldn't mind having any of their winnings." the announcer said.

"Yes, that's my baby! Congratulations!" Rachel screamed.

"Congratulations to you and Christopher." A lady next to Rachel said.

"Yes, congratulations!" The ladies on the other side said.

"Thank you so much! I'm glad he placed! My heart was skipping some beats."

One hour later at a winery

"Cheers to Christopher Smith for his win today!" the owner of the winery said.

Chris went up to the mike. " Thanks everyone. It was rough out there. I'm thankful I came in second place."

The owner began speaking, "Thanks for allowing us to be one of your sponsors. And because of that the patrons and I raised $10,000 for you! Thank you so much for helping our business grow. You're appreciated."

"Words can't express my appreciation. I have a dear friend, my girlfriend who flew over here to support me, Rachel Walker."

Rachel stood up. "Hello, everyone."

"Nice meeting you!" everyone said.

"Nice meeting you also. Thank you!"

Later on Rachel and Christopher had dinner and celebrated even more.

Forty-Five

Is This Move Temporary or Permanent?

They met at Longhorn Steakhouse, a new restaurant in Cedar Lake.

Marion just finished putting their name on the waiting list. "Do you believe we're all together?"

"I don't. We have such busy schedules," said Ruth.

"It's a miracle," replied Ellen.

Tanya walked in wearing her black and white jogging suit. "Hello everyone!" Everyone looked up. "Hello Tanya!"

"Back together again," Tanya said.

"It's great to see everyone. We've been trying for two years to get together," Sally said.

* * *

The waitress took their drink orders.

"What is your most ordered item on the menu? The ribs on that table look tender," Patricia said.

The waitress tapped her pen on her pad. "The ribs are our best seller. Our steaks are a hit. You might want to try a combo. Honestly, whatever you choose you won't be disappointed. I'll be back with your drinks in a minute."

"When are we going to meet The Boss? Can we see a picture of him?" Sally asked.

Rachel chimed in. "Yes, Tanya we're waiting."

Tanya answered with agitation in her voice. "You will in time."

"Patricia, how are you doing? How is the job?" Ruth asked.

"Everything has quieted down. I'm glad the Washington ordeal is over. I won't date another married man ever again."

"God rescued you." Ruth said.

The waitress brought the drinks and bread to them.

"We're glad it's over!" said Marion.

"I regret it. I'm using that experience to help others. For a while, I was beating myself upside the head. Girls, I want to thank you for your prayers. Enough of me. Rachel, how is the book coming?"

"It's coming. The speaking engagements keeps me so busy I don't get that much time to work on it. The main theme is women loving themselves regardless of whether they have a man or not."

"I can't wait to get my autographed copy of your book!"

Marion put a dinner roll in her mouth. "Me neither. I'm proud of you. I'll buy ten of your books, my friend. How is Christopher."

"Your support is appreciated. He's fine. We're just friends. We broke up six months after his event. He's full of himself. I found out he's not my guy. Ellen, how are things going for you?" *Marion is on the late show why is she asking about Christopher.*

Ellen thrown off guard. " Lately, I've been kept like a queen. I'm walking in my beauty. Kenneth seems to be coming along and has recovered well from the stroke. "

Diane was eager to comment. "Relationships take work. It's a matter of us choosing to make it work. "

"We haven't heard from Sally and Marion. Come on girls. What's going on?" asked Ruth.

"The students are great," Sally said. "I love them. One thing I realize this isn't my stopping point. I'm enjoying being a counselor. Words can't express the love you showed me ladies by helping Thomas prepare our wedding.

Friends to the day I die."

"I enjoyed every minute of planning your wedding.That's great news about your new job. You can inspire the children on a more personal level," said Ruth. "I knew you had something special going on."

"Sally we enjoyed planning your wedding. Thomas is very good at delegating. Jamaica was plenty of fun. What about you Diane?" said Rachel.

"We're great right now. You know Fred and I had a few challenges early on. We dealt with the ladies flirting. He knows how to handle them now, thank God. We have peace in our home. It has been an interesting ride. I don't think I would trade this journey! And on that note Ruth when are you and Charles getting married, you've been engaged for a minute? "

"Yes Ruth what's up with you, You've been asking us what's going on. Give us an update." Patricia said.

Ruth chuckled as she began to speak. "We got married right after the New Orleans trip. We had a private ceremony in my fathers office. He married us. There were only five people in attendance. Tanya came I asked her not to tell you all. It happened all of a sudden. We were here in Cedar Lake. We decided to do it because our schedules are so hectic. We didn't have time to plan a wedding."

"I'm a little disappointed. I do understand having too much to do."Rachel said. "Congratulations."

"Its your wedding you do what you want. I'm not happy about not attending a wedding but I am happy for you." Patricia said.

"I wanted to see you in your dress. But I know the dress has nothing to do with the marriage. I think you and Charles will have a great marriage. Congrats, my friend!" Diane said.

"Congratulations Ruth! Tanya did good keeping this a secret. Tanya you're loyal like that!" Ellen said. Tanya smiled.

"Yes, congrats!" Sally said.

"I'm happy for you Ruth." Marion said.

"Thanks Sally and Thomas inspired us. The private ceremony was nice." Ruth said.

"I hear you Ruth. Marion we need an update from you." Rachel said.

" We're still separated for now. I need to move. He found out where I live. He drinks and when he drinks he becomes so mean."

Ruth seated next to Marion. "I'm so sorry to hear that."

Rachel put her hand on top of Marion's. "Has he sought help?"

"No, he doesn't think he has a problem."

"That's not a healthy situation," said Rachel. " Do you have a plan? You can stay with me."

"I appreciate your hospitality. I'll let you know. I thought I was safe having my own apartment. He stalks me and he bangs on the door. He causes a big disturbance. It's so embarrassing."

Rachel looked Marion directly in her eyes. "Just show up. I want you to be safe."

"Thanks for the invitation. I'm so nervous," Marion said.

"Marion, we're here for you! Please take this check for two hundred dollars," Ruth said.

"Here's a check for five hundred dollars," Diane said." You know we're praying that everything will work out."

Patricia moved her right hand towards Marion. "Here's a hundred dollars."

"Thanks girls, this will help. I'll have to leave my job."

Diane hugged her. " More than likely. Another city, state will be a great move."

"Thanks, everyone. I thank God for you Rachel." tears rolled down Marion's face. "I know I need to get away from him."

"That's a step in the right direction," said Ellen.

"We need for you to be alive," said Diane.

Tanya nodded in agreement. "Marion. We don't want to go to a funeral. Many people end up dead because of domestic violence."

"Marion pondered her thoughts before she spoke. It's hard to explain. You're on the outside looking in. Let me tell you, I feel totally insignificant and humiliated. I have a hundred reasons to stay and a hundred reasons to leave. Can we change the subject, sometimes its too much?"

Ruth chimed in. "We can change the subject and finished eating and drinking. Everything is going to be alright."

* * *

Marion did prepare to go live with Rachel. But she talked to her husband all day long every day. It would be a miracle to pull this move off.

Marion stays with Rachel

"You made it! Come on in! Make yourself at home! Your room is upstairs on the right."

Marion put her luggage down and started looking and walking around the house.

"I love your house, the red brick is so rich, the winding staircase, the built-in bookshelves in your den. Thanks for letting me stay. I needed this place to get away. Antonio has been calling all day."

"You did the right thing."

"Thanks."

"Go ahead and get settled. I cooked some chili. Come down and get some when you're ready.".

"I'll be down in a minute."

Marion's cell phone rang. "Hello."

"Where are you?" He asked.

"I'm moved out of the city. Your abuse is unacceptable. I'm tired, Antonio."

There's intense rage in his voice. "What do you mean? "I don't abuse you. You need to be home in twenty-four hours."

Marion doesn't say anything.

He screamed through the phone. "Hello? Hello! No, she didn't hang up on me! She has a lot of nerve!"

He was furious with her for hanging up on him. He called at least twenty more times, but Marion didn't pick up.

He busted a hole in the living room wall. Then he went down the hall screaming and put a hole in the hallway wall. "Who told her to move? Wait till I get my hands on her."

He went to the liquor store and drank himself to sleep. He drank so much he urinated in the bed. He woke up depressed.

***

Marion yelled downstairs." I'm going to take a long shower."

Marion take a twenty-minute shower.

She began drying off.

Marion looked at the phone on the dresser as she continued to dry off. "How many times has he called? I'm turning this phone off. I can't get any rest with him calling a million times a day."

"I'll be down in a minute to have some of that good smelling chili." Marion yelled again.

Chili Time

"This chili is delicious. It's perfect for a day like this. It's so comforting."

"Thanks Marion. I'm so glad you're here."

"That's an understatement. I'm glad I'm here to."

"Everyone is glad that you're here. What does your family think of Antonio, Marion?"

"They don't know. I felt like it wasn't necessary. My friends know and that's enough."

Marion to keep it real we are concerned about you. Our friends have sent money to me to make sure you have everything you need. We want you our friend to be safe. Domestic violence is no joke. I hope you understand the consequences and what has happened to thousands of women. We love you. We like having you alive my friend."

"I appreciate everything you've done. I don't take you all for granted. I guess I've been believing for a miracle. I want Antonio to change."

"God performs miracles, but he doesn't think he's doing anything wrong and that's a problem."

"Wow thanks for not sugar coating it!"

"No time for that, this is tough love."

"I understand and thanks."

"I've said all I want to say. Let's watch a movie."

"Sure!" Marion said as she propped her feet up.

They watched a movie and then they went to bed.

The next morning

Antonio is about to go crazy. I know she's with one of her friends. I'm going to call every one of them.

I 'll dial Diane's number first. The phone rings.

She is *in* the kitchen cooking. "Fred get the phone. Never mind I can get it." *I'm not answering the phone, as she looked at the caller id. I don't know what Antonio wants but I'm not about to find out. He hasn't called our house in over a year.*

He's getting annoyed. He started rubbing his fingers through his hair as he paced the floor. *They won't answer the phone. I'll let it ring for at least twenty times.*

"I thought you were answering the phone."

"I was but its Antonio."

"He's something else. I guess he's going to make us answer the phone. Help him Lord."

"Honey, you don't know the half."

"My, my, my, I think I know enough."

"And believe me you don't want to know anymore."

He shook his head.

Meanwhile at Patricia's house

Her phone started ringing.

Its her goal to make it to the phone before the answering machine picks up. "Hello!"

Hello this is Antonio. "Do you know where Marion is? I've been trying to reach her."

I should've checked caller id before I answered this call. "No I don't. I'm quite sure she'll call you back soon. She's your wife."

He started yelling. "Girl you're so wrong. You're lying. You know everything that's going on with each of you."

Who can he call a liar? "Goodbye Antonio!" She hung up the phone very quickly.

He stared at the phone. *I told Marion her friends are full of themselves.*

Marion and Rachel relaxing on the patio. The next evening

Marion is relaxing in Marion's wicker chaise. "It's a great feeling to sit here and in a peaceful tranquil setting."

"All for you my friend. You deserve some peace and quietness."

'That's an understatement. I'm so tired of books, pots and pans, shoes and whatever thrown at me."

"Wow, Marion he didn't consider he could hurt you."

"He has bouts of rage. People don't think when they're that mad. It's very scary. The miracle is that I haven't had a nervous breakdown. Thank God. I don't wish that kind of rage on anyone."

"Marion it's a miracle you're alive."

"Our house looks like a mess. They're holes in the walls. Blood stains on the carpet. I would clean up in the beginning, I stopped after a while. That's why I didn't invite you all over."

"Marion, we understood. We wanted to come over at times to beat him up. We were going to bring bats, hammers, big sticks and beat him. The plan kept failing; we could never get together at one time."

"That's so thoughtful. I'm glad your plan didn't work. I would hate for my friends to get in trouble. And enough of my problems. Let's talk about you."

The phone rings

"Ah shoots the phone is ringing. I don't feel like running to catch it. I'll let the answering machine pick it up. I can hear who it is from here."

"Hey, I just wanted to give you a heads up. Antonio is calling all of us asking where you are Marion. I told him I don't know. He called me a liar. I hung up the phone after that."

They heard the message from where they were.

"I guess we'll let the answering machine answer all the calls. Who wants to be bothered with Antonio?"

"Relaxing is all I want to do."

Forty-Six

She's Gone

~~~

Marion lived with Rachel off and on for two years. She would go back to Antonio then come back to Rachel. Marion had been at her house three months this go round. Antonio was begging her to come back home.

On Tuesday morning, the sun shone brightly. Rachel got up and went to work. Within an hour, Marion left. Antonio had convinced her to come back to him.

She left a note:

Thanks again for your hospitality. My stay here has been so peaceful. It has been a place of refuge for me. I don't know what I would have done without you. I don't know how I can ever repay you. I'm going back to live with my husband.

Love you always,

Marion

***

"Oh my. No! Let me call her on her cell phone. I hope she answers. "I'm glad no one is here to hear me talking to myself. I can't dial her number fast enough. She's going back to her husband. She's not answering. Let me call everyone."

She called Ruth first. "Marion has gone back to her husband."

"She's a grown woman. We've tried to warn her and tell her he needs help. You and I both knew it was just a matter of time for her to go back. But hasn't she gone back to him several times? What's different about this time?" asked Ruth.

"This time she left a note. I'm scared for her. I believe she'll talk to you. Please call her," Rachel said. "While you're trying to reach her, I'll call the others."

* * *

I don't know why the girls keep calling me. If I want to talk them, I would. I'll call them once I get there. I have about an hour before I get there.

She was determined not to answer their calls. She talked to Antonio over the phone, from the minute she left Rachel's house until she drove into her driveway.

Antonio came running outside to meet Marion.

Honey, I missed you so much," Marion said.

"Baby, I missed you too." He smiled and kissed her. "I'll get your bags."

"Thanks, sweetie." Marion blushed.

"I cooked some spaghetti and meatballs for dinner. I bought some wine for this day; the day I knew you would come back home. It's time to eat. Go wash up. I'm starving," he said.

Marion washed up.

"The food smells good!" Marion said.

"I cooked it just for you, you're my queen."

Marion blushed. "Thanks baby!"

They continued to eat.

One hour later in their bedroom

Antonio is kissing and caressing his wife. "I'm so glad to have you back. I missed your loving Marion. I'm going to do right by you."

"Antonio, you know what to do! It feels just right! I'll never leave you again!"

"Good, no more talking, let's enjoy this."

* * *

Meanwhile,

Rachel's phone rang.

"I know you told us Marion left you a note and left. But have you heard from her?" Diane asked.

"She won't answer my calls. "

"Girl, I'm concerned about Marion."

"Hopefully she will call one of us."

Days passed and no response from Marion. Months passed, no word from Marion.

* * *

She's Gone

Ruth started reading the local newspaper in Marion's town. One day, she found the following headline:

Headline News in the Paper

Third Young Lady Killed by Significant Other; Domestic Violence on the Rise Marion Rucker Lawson has been killed by her husband

"Oh no! She's dead! He killed her!" Ruth cried, as she read Marion's local newspaper. She began dialing Marion's parents.

Mrs. Francine Rucker, Marion's mother answered the phone as she sniffled. "Hello!"

"Hello, Mrs. Rucker this is Ruth. How are you?"

"My baby girl is gone. She's gone."

I didn't want to start the conversation off about Marion. But I was reading the newspaper in the city where Marion lives."

"Yes, my baby is gone."

"I'm sorry to hear that. I'll be praying for you."

"The neighbors saw Antonio kill Marion, so he was jailed immediately."

"No one could make her stay away from him. Everyone at the hospitals knew her. She would never file charges."

"I know, my baby is gone!" Marion's mother said as tears rolled down her eyes.

"Yes, my friend is gone! I'm here for you."

"Thanks, I'm getting off the phone now. I'll talk to you later."

"We'll talk later."

* * *

All the girls went home for her funeral. The girls are wondering how they're going to make it through. They always tried to reach out to her when she was having problems. The girls and Marion's parents wore purple, her favorite color, in honor of her. All types of flowers and plants, yellow roses, white lilies, green ivies, and gladiolas filled the sanctuary. They received many cards from residents of Cedar Lake. The services were packed.

***

At the burial site, the minister said, "We commend her body back to God." ashes to ashes dust to dust to be absent from the body is to be present with the Lord."

Mrs. Rucker seated between her son James and her husband Bernard whispered loud enough for both to hear her. "Our baby girl is gone."

James touched his mom's shoulder. "Yes, mom, she is. We have to do something to honor her."

He put his arm around his wife. "Yes, we do. My little girl is gone."

Tears ran down all their eyes, including Derrick who sat on the other side of his father.

Mrs. Rucker's sister came up to her and hugged her. "Sis, we're going to make it through this."

Ruth and Rachel approached Derrick and James. "You know we're here for you, we're coming by the house."

"Thanks." Derrick said.

"We also want to thank you for trying to save her from that nut! I'm glad he's in jail. "James said with anger in his voice.

Rachel replied. "Unfortunately for him, jail is the best place for him now."

"I guess we need to pray for him. Even though it's hard right now." Ruth said.

"That's the right thing to do! Like you said it's hard." Derrick stated.

Everyone kept coming up to them as they were heading towards their cars.

* * *

The girls stayed at Marion's parents' house for several hours after the service.

"Ladies, thanks for coming by," Derrick said.

"You know we're going to be here for the family." Rachel said.

Derrick nodded. "Do you want anything to drink?"

"I'll have a Coke. I know I need water."

"It's like a link will be missing," Ellen said.

Derrick had a serious look on his face. "I'm glad that crazy husband of hers is in jail. He's reaping what he has sown. I want to put my hands on him. My only sister is gone."

"We want to put our hands on him too!" The girls said all at the same time.

"Thank God he's locked up. God's protecting him from us," Ruth said.

James walked in.

"There are so many people in the house. That's a blessing. Your family is loved," Tanya said.

"We thank you all for coming. We appreciate you."

"We wouldn't have it any other way," Sally said.

"Let's think about something to honor our sister. I don't want her death to be in vain." James said.

"Sounds good James. We'll pray about that." Ruth said.

"We'll pray! It has to be something of significance." Rachel said.

Ellen walked up. "Derrick and James, we don't want to hold you up. We know you have a lot of guest to talk to. We will share you."

"You're right. We do need to mingle. We'll be in touch about that honoring thing. Please eat some of the food. We have plenty of it." Derrick said as he hugged the girls and walked away.

"Give me a hug!" James said flirting as he always does.

They hugged.

A couple of hours later

Ellen walked over to Mr. and Mrs. Rucker. "I think I'm going to head to the house. You all need to rest. I'll try to come by tomorrow."

"You're right, we should leave." Rachel said.

"Yes, we will leave. We'll back tomorrow to help you out."Diane said.

Everyone started hugging, kissing and saying their good-byes.

* * *

Coping with Grief

The girls walked down the street toward their parents' houses. Ruth's parents were on the front porch talking, so the girls stopped by.

"Hello, my children, it's always a pleasure to see the girls!" Mrs. Perry said. "Come in and sit for a minute!"

"Mama, everyone was on their way home. They just wanted to say hi," Ruth said.

"I'm taking your mother's offer up." Diane said.

The others agreed.

"Come on in, girls. I have some chips and dip. We can watch a movie. You know it'll be like old times," Mrs. Perry said.

"Make yourself at home!" Ruth said.

"Mrs. Perry, do you need any help?" Rachel asked.

"No, honey. You can talk to me while I put the food out."

"I can get the paper plates, napkins and cups together. Do you keep them in the same place?"

"Yes."

"Mrs. Perry, how do you handle the loss of a loved one?"

"Well, I must say it's a process. It's not always easy. You really must trust God. That is how I made it through."

"Did you do a lot of praying and crying?"

Mrs. Perry is smacking hard on some chips. "Yes, I did. I cried a lot. Especially when I lost my mother and a brother. Our family is very close. Mr. Perry was very helpful but there were times he wasn't available. I had to ask God to lead me step by step."

"Did you feel guilty at all?"

"No, I can't say I felt guilty, because I always believed in giving people their flowers while they 're alive. Do you feel guilty or responsible for Marion's death?"

"Sometimes I don't think I did enough when she stayed with me right before she was killed."

"You can't hold yourself accountable. You have no control over the fact that Marion decided to go back to her husband. She made that choice. Don't beat yourself up!"

Rachel took a sip of her coke. "I guess I'm so overwhelmed in grief I didn't think about it like that. Thanks, Mrs. Perry. It was meant for us to come by here tonight."

"Mom, what is taking you and Rachel so long? Did you forget about bringing us some snacks?"

"I'm so sorry. Your mom is helping me out ."

The conversation continues in the den

"One thing I discovered during my periods of grief is that no one grieves the same. You must talk about it. Talking about it helps you heal. Trust God. Pray. My favorite scripture during that time was cast all your care on him because he cares for you—1 Peter 5:7. I will turn your mourning into gladness: I will give them comfort and joy instead of sorrow—Jeremiah 31:13. Trust in the Lord with all thine heart and lean not unto thine own understanding—Proverbs 3:5. There are so many Scriptures I can give you.

You will find your own to stand on. I had to seek counsel because there was a time period when I lost about thirteen relatives in three years. I lost family members on my mother's side and my father's side. I thought I wasn't going to make it. People were pleasant in the beginning. But they didn't want to talk about it after a while. I couldn't worry my husband. Don't be embarrassed if you need to seek grief counsel. Grief is no joke."

"Wow, Mrs. Perry, you made it through. I hope I make it through. We won't be the same without her. It's like we have a hole in our group," Patricia said.

Ellen began drinking her lemonade. "It's hard for me to accept."

"Honey, you will in time. I had that problem. It was a hard pill to swallow."

"Mom, I miss her so much! I was getting a guilt trip. Daddy had to console me on that. He told me I did everything I could do. She had choices. It's not my fault."

"Your father told you right. You can't be mad at her. Antonio had a choice also. We need to make wise decisions in life. The Scripture says the wages of sin is death!"

"Thanks, Mom."

"You're welcome."

" Sally said, "You mean we'll grieve differently. We won't grieve the same amount of time."

"Yes, expound on that because we're so different,"Sally asked "Are you saying we might not be able to depend on each other because we might be at different stages?"

"Each one of you had a different relationship with her. When you want to talk about something you experienced with your friends might not want to talk because they just finished crying an hour ago and she's just getting herself back together. Yes, as close as you are, you will grieve differently," Mrs. Perry said.

"That makes a lot of sense. We can't get mad at each other because someone isn't available," Tanya responded.

"Thanks for expounding on that part. We have to be understanding of each other," Rachel said.

"I have to keep it real with you young ladies. God had to help me when my mother and brother died. The Lord showed me to keep my parents' legacy going by continuing to teach the Word and love people. God saw my tears. He told me to walk in faith day by day. Day by day, through the help of God, I got better and accepted the passing of my mom and brother and other family members."

"I guess acceptance and faith are very important on this journey," Tanya said.

"Yes, they are. You can make it, don't worry! Just trust God. Now let's eat," Mrs. Perry said.

The girls ate and watched comedy movies. They needed to laugh. They stayed over Ruth's house until two in the morning.

Forty-Seven

Thirty-Nine Stripes for Ellen

She trusts God to heal her.

Ellen is dusting the living room furniture.

The doorbell rings. "Who is it?"

"I'm the delivery man for the local florist!" The gentleman said with plenty of bass in his voice.

"I'll be there." She made it to the door and opened it. "Hello how may I help you? "

"I have a delivery for Mrs. Womack."

She took a bouquet of red and yellow roses from the guy, "Very pretty!"

"Ma'am, can you sign for them?"

"Sure!" Ellen put the flowers down. She reaches for the clipboard to sign for the flowers.

"Thanks. Enjoy your flowers!" The delivery guy leaves.

"I will." Ellen said as she closed the door and began reading the note on the flowers. "I knew it; it's my hubby, so thoughtful. I'm calling him." She begins to dial his work number.

Phone rings. Kenneth answers. "Mr. Womack speaking how may I help you?"

"Oh baby! Thanks for the beautiful roses. They lifted my spirit. Thanks for being an awesome vessel of God. It's God's way of saying you are healed. These roses are right on time."

"Yes babe, you're healed. I must go. Love you! Bye!"

"Bye!"

* * *

One Week Later

Kenneth walked in through the garage door, puts his briefcase down on the kitchen counter. "Mmm, something smells inviting. Smells like chicken."

Ellen entered the kitchen. "Good evening, honey."

He noticed her demeanor, he reached for Ellen and hugged her. "Don't worry honey, regardless of what the doctor says we believe you walk in divine health; you're healed of cancer. God is good and faithful. Whatever you're cooking it sure smells intriguing."

Ellen leaned back to look into Ken's eyes while still wrapped in his arms. "Thanks for being so supportive. I love you for that."

"Babe don't worry we're going to beat it. We'll trust God to see us through this. The surgery will turn out fine. Thank God."

A quick second later, her head landed in the comfort of her husband's chest, tears rolled down her eyes. "Yes, we will trust God. He's faithful."

"We're going to thank him in advance. Let's eat. I'll fix your plate, you have a seat."

"You're so kind. I guess I 'll take a seat and rest for a change."

"Rest is important, let's say grace and eat this delicious food you have prepared!"

They enjoyed a rather romantic evening together. Love has everything to do with it.

* * *

After the surgery

Kenneth is in the room. Ellen is asleep. The parents went to get breakfast while she slept.

The doctor entered the room. "Mr. Womack, I see your wife is still sleep."

"Yes, she is."

"I'm up. How did we do doc?"

Doc begins to speak. "You were the easiest patient I had. I truly believe we got all the cancer out. I don't believe in God. But your surgery makes me think there is a God."

"Thank God for that. God is awesome! He is a healer."

The doctor smiled. "I'll say that's appropriate. I'm not going to hold you. I do want to follow up with you in two weeks. Get some rest Mrs. Womack."

Kenneth interjected. "She will. Thanks for everything."

One week later

Time to tell her friends.

The phone rings.

"Hello," Diane answered.

"Hey Diane, this is Ellen. How are you doing?"

" I'm fine, what's going on?" Diane asked.

"You have a moment."

"Yes girl, anytime to talk to you. What's up?"

"Diane don't be mad. I've been going through something. I'm just getting around to telling you. I had an ordeal with cancer. Praise God it's all gone. It all happened so quickly. Just pray it remains gone."

"Really, I've been praying for you a lot in the last thirty days. Now I understand. It's done in the name of Jesus. Jesus took thirty-nine stripes for you and by his stripes you're healed."

"Thanks Diane. I needed that. I'm trusting God. I'm not going to lie; it's been hard at times. I have had some anxiety attacks; thank God he saw me through."

My friend, I'll pray that God will give you peace that surpasses all understanding. I know you've been busy dealing with this, but I wish you had told me sooner."

"Thanks Diane. Praying for me means a lot. I'm sorry I didn't tell you.

Everything did move kind of fast."

"I understand. I'm a little disappointed, but I'm okay. I'll start calling the others when we get off the phone."

"I appreciate it. Love you!" Ellen said.

'Love you more. Talk to you later." Diane said as she hung up the phone.

* * *

Showing Support

Within the hour of Diane's call they start dialing Ellen's number.

The answering machine comes on and Patricia leaves a message. "Hello, Diane told me about your surgery. Just wanted to let you know I'm praying for you. And if you need anything, I got it. Love you. Call me when you get a chance."

Phone rings. Sally called Ellen.

"Hello!" She answered as she awoke from her nap.

Sally began to speak. "If I woke you, please forgive me."

"I'm awake. Nice to hear your voice."

"Same here. First, I'm praising God your body is healed. God is good. My friend, I'm not going to fuss at you, but please know you can count on me."

"Friend, I know. I was extremely busy. I was tired a lot. It all went so fast. Please forgive me."

Sally smiled. "You're forgiven. I'm going to let you go back to sleep. You sound like you're talking in your sleep. Love you my friend."

"Love you too! I'll talk to you later."

She slept through the night. Kenneth has left for work.

Ellen began talking and praying out loud. "Oh my, I have ten messages. I need to listen to them. Oh Lord everyone is so sweet. Lord thank you for some awesome friends. Thank you, Lord, for being so faithful. Thank you for healing me."

She assured the girls she was fine and not to worry about her. She was healed totally of cancer. The girls believed her and trusted God she was healed. The support they showed to Ellen is what friends are supposed to do.

Forty-Eight

Carmen Got Away

⁓⦵⦵⦵⁓

"What's going on, Patricia?" Rachel said. "Did you get my letter about the foundation and being on the board?"

"Yes, the idea about the foundation is right on time. Before I opened your envelope, I just saw CNN news about a lady who cut off her husband's private parts. I was thinking Marion should have done that—maybe she would be alive. She's on trial. She claims her husband abused her and made her have an abortion. He was also unfaithful. Wasn't Antonio all of this and more? Experts say she will probably be found not guilty. Just thinking about her not being here makes me mad. And the way she left. I'll be glad to serve on the board. I'm sending two hundred dollars."

"You know I want to bop Antonio upside his head or put the guys on him to give him a beating. They might not let him live, so I changed my mind about that. I read in a book about how to channel your anger into something positive. Our mission is stopping domestic violence and educating everyone on the dangers of it. All of us will be on the board of directors. I scheduled a kickoff meeting Memorial Day weekend in Cedar Lake. Do you think you can make it to the meeting?"

"I'll be there."

Derrick has started getting all the paperwork together. We need bylaws. I believe we can start reviewing and coming up with each member's duties in advance. We can define our mission. Ellen said we should provide a place for women to run to. We need to have clothing and food on hand at all time, because some wives may have to leave their husbands and not take anything."

"Rachel, this is going to be great. She's looking down from a great cloud of witnesses saying thanks, friends.

" This foundation is going to help a lot of women. I'm glad her brothers are helping!"

* * *

The Event

"Greetings family, friends, officials of the city, and the news media, my name is Derrick Rucker. I'm the brother of Marion Rucker. We're here today to honor her memory by launching the Marion Safe House Foundation. All the family and her close friends want to channel our anger in a positive way. We have Rachel, to thank for that. She came up with the idea. The main areas we'll focus on is education, lodging, food, and counseling. We'll provide lodging. Those places will never be disclosed because you know it can be very dangerous for the victims. All donations are tax deductible. Right now, I want you to hear from Rachel, the CEO of the foundation."

"Thanks, Derrick. Good evening, everyone. My name is Rachel Walker. I was a friend of Marion. The girls and I were talking about our grief and how to channel it the right way. I kept thinking of certain Scriptures about grief. One of my favorites is a beatitude that says blessed are they that mourn, for they shall be comforted. God is comforting me and my friends. She had places to stay, as a matter of fact she stayed with me several times. We know that everyone might not have a place to run to. That's the reason we started this foundation. Please pick up the information we have about the foundation, and make sure you get some food. Let's make this foundation a success. Thanks for coming!"

The people mingled while Boney James music played in the background.

The networks were there to interview Rachel. An ABC News reporter asked,

"This is a very noble thing you're doing in honor of her. What does Antonio think of this?"

"We have no idea what he thinks, and that's not important. Our focus is on this foundation. Please excuse me."

Rachel walked away. The reporters followed, shouting questions.

"No more comments. I must help. Thanks for coming," Rachel continued to walk away.

The place was packed. People stayed to the end, and everyone seemed to enjoy themselves. The foundation reached its financial goal. Marion's family and her friends were very pleased with the outcome.

<u>Safe Hose Foundation In Use</u>

The Saturday morning before Mother's Day

Foundation hotline phone rings. "Hello, answered the operator named Gail." how may I help you?

"My name is Carmen; I need to leave my husband. He pulled a gun on me and my children today and several times before. The police, child services, the hospitals, and neighbors know everything. I've been so depressed. He has broken both of my arms. The police have been to the house at least twenty times for domestic violence. I would love to get information about the Marion Foundation."

"There are a few spots left. I can get you and your children in within twenty-four hours. I hope you're serious; you will have to leave everything behind. You'll be starting over."

"I am, tell me what to do."

* * *

Carmen called the foundation the next morning while her husband was at work. Everything started moving fast.

Four hours later a plain dull gray Chevrolet Impala came to Carmen's house. The driver didn't get out the car. The license plate was dusty and dirty on purpose. Carmen came running out the house with folded up garment bags in her arms. Carmen and the driver headed toward the school to pick up the children.

The school office

Enters Carmen into the office

"Hello, I need to check my children out early," Carmen stated, as she remained calm with her heart beating ninety miles per hour.

The office worker responded, "I can help you and your name is? I need some identification."

"Carmen Reed." She gave her id card to the lady.

The worker responded; Mrs. Reed I'm contacting both of your children's teachers right now.

"Thanks," Carmen responded as she held her hands to keep from fidgeting.

Five minutes passed which seemed like a lifetime.

The children entered.

"Hey mom! "They both yelled as they entered in.

"Hello darlings hurry we have to make your appointments."

"What appointments?" Her son Chuckie asked.

"No doctor's mom," the daughter Alexa stated.

"No questions let's go. Thanks ma'am." She grabbed her children by the hand and walked fast to the car.

They made it to the car in record time and they're on their way to the foundation.

Thirty minutes later they're checked in

"Why are here mom?" The children asked.

"We will be staying here for awhile."

Chuckie was checking out his new location. "Mom I'm glad you finally decided to leave daddy. He needs help. I was tired of him hitting you. I wanted to beat my daddy up."

"Me too, mommy. I was tired of him beating on you too. He's mean."

Carmen grabbed her children and hugged them tight. "We're safe now."

Three days later

Breaking News

Police responded to a suicide murder today Johnathan Reed killed himself today. He left a note apologizing to Carmen his wife and two children. According to the police they had been to the house numerous times for domestic violence complaints. The neighbors had a lot to say about witnessing the abuse. It was always loud when he went into a raging fit. His wife and children apparently left him a few days ago. What a story.

Carmen thought to herself. *I can't believe he killed himself. Wow!*

The foundation has helped its first victim. The girls and Marion's family are pleased the foundation is being used.

Forty-Nine

Never Knew a Love like this Before

The Friday after Thanksgiving

Patricia walked into Starbucks to get her favorite peppermint coffee. It's her favorite coffee during this season. A nice handsome, tall, gentleman was standing next to her ordering the same thing.

He received his coffee and began to leave the counter. "I see you like the same coffee I do. It's my favorite this time of year."

"Mine's too. It brings in the holidays."*I'm checking this man out from head to toe, he's wearing this nice black and white jogging suit, that fits him right nicely.*

"Are you sitting in here, if so, do you mind if we sit together this place is so small?" The gentleman asked.

Patricia smiled. "No, I don't. It's small, but rather cozy and comfortable."

He assisted her to a seat. Then he sat down. "Oh, by the way, my name is Gordon." He reached out to shake her hand.

She responded by shaking his hand. I'm Patricia. "It's a pleasure meeting you."

"Same here. Are you from New York?"

"No, I'm from Cedar Lake, Georgia right outside Atlanta. Are you from here?"

"Yes, I'm from New York, I work in Manhattan, but I live in Yonkers, New

York. I ride the train up here."

"I love New York. The first time I came to visit I knew I wanted to move up here. I attended college here."

"That's what happened to a lot of people. What college did you attend or are you attending?"

"As she inhaled the peppermint aroma of her coffee she began to respond. "I attended Columbia University."

"I did too. What was your major?"

"Accounting."

Gordon laughed. "I can't believe it. Me too. What year did you graduate?"

"1983!"

"Ah hah! I gotcha on that one. I graduated in 1981. When you took all of your accounting classes I was gone."

"Yes, I was taking those sixty hours all business majors had to take."

" I have to meet some buddies to play basketball with. I would love to keep in touch with you. May I have your number?"

Oh, my I'm a little hesitant. I don't know this guy, but how am I going to get to know anyone if i don't respond properly. "Yes, its 212-778-9595."

"Thanks, I'll call you this weekend. Maybe tonight. Do you think it'll be okay if we catch a movie one day?"

"It's possible."

Gordon got up out of his seat. " I look forward to talking to you. Good-bye!"

"Same here! Good-bye!" Patricia said as she watched him walk away. He's a hunk with a brain and appeared to be a gentleman.

* * *

Gordon called Patricia the next day. They went out on a date that weekend. This was the beginning of a new phase in life. They have a lot in common they both like sports, theater, travel, family, enjoy friendship, accounting, and they serve the Lord.

One month passed everything is going smooth, two, three, four, five, and six months have passed no confrontation or problem yet. That's a miracle considering her history with men. The question is does she trust them now?

* * *

It's a spring afternoon in Central Park exactly seven months from the date they met.

Gordon and Patricia are having a picnic lunch; they have a cute picnic basket with turkey sandwiches, potato chips, bananas and strawberries. The food was very filling and rather tasty. Gordon planned the lunch, for dessert they have a slice of velvet cupcake big enough to feed two.

Gordon started feeding the cupcake to Patricia. When he knew that she was getting close to his surprise in the cup cake. He took it away from her so she couldn't see the item.

"Gordon the cupcake is delicious why did you take it from me?"

Gordon dangled the cupcake in her face so she could see the sparkle.

Her eyes got big. "Is that what I think it is?"

"Patricia will you marry me?" Gordon asked as he took the ring out of the cupcake.

Patricia touched the ring and just stared. "This is for me Gordon! You want to marry me? I don't deserve you Gordon, I've done some awful things."

"All have sinned and come short of the glory of God. We all have a past. Will you marry me, just say yes?"

"Gordon, I say yes, yes I'll marry you. It has to be next year Gordon."

"Next year will be perfect darling."

"Gordon you're everything I ever dreamed of in a man."

"Honey, I feel the same way. You're like a dream come true."

"Gordon you think you're slick, how did you know my ring size?"

"One day I was over your house and you had some rings on both hands. You took them off and laid them on the coffee table. I politely picked the one you wore on your ring finger and took it to the jeweler."

"That was smart. How did you know what type of ring I wanted?"

"You told me; you probably didn't realize what you were doing. At times we were out for dinner and you noticed rings on different people. Sometimes you would comment especially if they were shining bright. I caught you glancing at rings when we were out. And one day we passed by a jewelry store and you said what was cute and what was ugly to you. I pay attention."

"I see, very observant."

"You're going to be the future Mrs. Gordon Sparks."

"Yes I am."

The couple left Central Park, both ecstatic about getting married next year. Gordon drove her home and walked her to the door as a gentleman would do. The night ended on a positive note.

The following morning
Gordon's apartment
Gordon is in the living room reading the sports section of the newspaper with his feet propped on the coffee table. I'm glad my girl said yes. For a minute it sounded like she would say no, just because of her skeletons. Shoots I have skeleton, I guess we need to talk about it. We've talked about a lot, but this is a conversation we need to have and have it soon.

The apartment, she's lying in the bed
I need to tell Gordon about my history, so he'll know what he's getting into. I want him to know everything. I can't have him going into our marriage without him knowing my secrets.

Gordon called his sweetheart.

The phone rung. "Good morning,"

"Good morning dear, did I wake you?" Gordon asked.

"No, I'm relaxing for a change."

"That's a smart move. Can we do lunch after church today?"

Of course, I don't have anything planned. Are you coming to pick me up?"

"Yes, I'll see you at ten thirty. Be ready honey."

"Gordon I will."

The couple did go to church. The service was very uplifting. The message was about things we go through and how God uses it for his glory. The things we go through will help others. It lets others know they can make it through if you made it through. You're a witness for God. The scripture text was all things work together for the good of them who love the Lord and are called according to his purpose.

* * *

At the restaurant

They placed their order. Both had water and sweet tea for their drinks.

Gordon sipped some of his tea. "Baby, you got me thinking, you said something about things you've done in the past. Well, I realized after I left you last night, I need to tell you something. In high school some buddies of mine we decided we wanted some liquor, so we broke in a liquor store and stole liquor. It was the week that we graduated from high school. We got caught. It was a felony robbery charge, but our lawyers got it dropped to a misdemeanor since it was our first offense.

A shocked look was all over her face. "I can't believe it."

Babe I was going to be a criminal. The misdemeanor stayed on my record for seven years. I almost lost my scholarships. Hanging with those boys got me in trouble more than once."

"They were the wrong crowd."

It didn't seem like it at the time. But looking back, they were the wrong crowd. I went to a party with them. I met this girl. She wanted me, I didn't want her. She got mad and said I raped her. That was the summer between the eleventh and twelfth grade. Thank God that didn't make it to court. She ended up telling the truth."

"It seemed like it caused you to grow up and realize who your friends are and to ask God for wisdom."

Sweetheart, I can go on and on. God performed miracles on my behalf. The robbery should have been a felony, and the misdemeanor was dropped."

"Yes, he is. He has healed me. I received healing. Gordon for the longest I didn't think I deserved true love. Throughout my adult life I would date guys and it wouldn't last long enough for me to share with my parents or my friends. You see Gordon, when I was in high school, I had an uncle who molested me and it caused me not to trust people especially men. I allowed people to take advantage of me. I had a boss who initially coerced me into having a relationship with him. He was married. I was scared to speak up because I didn't want to lose my job. Gordon, I had to forgive my uncle and my boss. God taught me how to walk in being fearfully and wonderfully made. I don't have to accept abuse from anyone."

" I would have never guessed all of that happened to you. You have a very healthy self-esteem now. It's amazing how God waited until you were healed, and I learned how to use wisdom and then he brought us together."

"I'm glad I was ready, because I was tired of all the broken relationships. I told my uncle I forgive him. I haven't seen my old boss, he was fired, and I was moved to another department. God knows how to make all the crooked places straight. I feel better now that I've told you."

"I'm glad you shared. I feel better too. What we've gone through babe we can use it to help someone else."

"Yes, Gordon, it was something."

"My dad helped me a lot. I think I embarrassed him at first, with him being an assistant pastor. I guess initially he was hurt. I'm glad he encouraged me through those situations."

"Gordon, I thought you weren't going to want me, after I told you my history. There were times I was so embarrassed. But I learned a lot of people have gone through similar things. After meeting some of them it has helped me throughout the years."

"Honey, please, who am I to judge. I'm glad you've been through things, which show me you know how to work out problems. You know how to trust God."

"Thanks Gordon. I know I can't judge you neither. I'm glad you've gone through some things too. Trusting God is the key."

"Amen!"

They ate their food and continued to enjoy each other's company. A load has been released off both. The conversation today took them to another level of closeness and trust towards each other.

The Next Day, Patricia's at home

She began peeling off those work clothes she had on since six am in the morning. She dialed Gordon's number.

Gordon answered the phone as he glanced at caller id. "Hello Princess.

"How was your day?"

"Mines was great. I kept thinking about my future wife. Thinking of you made it even more beautiful. And yours?"

"It was a little hectic, but when I thought about you my day became easier. I enjoyed our conversation, but I have so much more to talk to you about."

"Honey don't fret. Let it all flow like yesterday. You don't have to tell me everything at once. One question, have you ever killed anyone?" Gordon asked jokingly.

"Gordon, stop it with your jokes, silly, no I haven't killed anyone. I just want to tell you everything."

"Baby don't worry. I trust God and the Jesus in you. God is faithful."

"Thanks Gordon. You always know what to say."

Well baby doll, I just got in. I'm going to cook dinner, work out downstairs in the gym, and I'll call you back later."

"Ok, honey."

They continued to spend time with each other. They shared more when the conversation flowed as Gordon said they should. They grew more in love. They decided to get married sooner. Time to begin looking for her dress. She sent invitations to her immediate family and of course her friends. Only fifty people were invited.

The day before the actual Wedding Day

A Hurricane hit the east coast Thursday afternoon, shutting down airports, trains all along the east coast.

* * *

Ruth called Patricia

Ruth left a message for Patricia. "Hello, this is Ruth. I can't believe this is happening. I can't get a plane to New York until 8 pm Saturday. I might be able to drive or the train."

Another message: "Pat, this is Tanya. I can't get out of Atlanta to come to New York. This hurricane has messed everything up."

The girls left their messages. But the show must go on. She was disappointed her friends couldn't make it.

Her parents made it in town on Monday. Diane drove because she lived closer to New York. Rachel was able to make it from Philadelphia. Ruth somehow made it from Boston. If anyone would make it would be them. They can come by train and car.

* * *

The ceremony

Patricia stood beside Gordon; wearing a silk white dress that came to her knees she wore white satin pumps with a white laced veil. She was a picture of beauty. Gordon was rather handsome arrayed in his black tuxedo with his black and white ascot tie.

The minister performing the ceremony began to speak. "Gordon do you take Patricia to be your lawfully wedded wife?"

Gordon stuck his chest and answered proudly. "I do."

The ministered continued the ceremony. "Patricia do you take Gordon to be your lawfully wedded husband?"

She smiled and spoke loud enough for the back row of witnesses to hear. "I do."

"I now pronounce you man and wife. You may kiss your bride."

The small crowd smiled. The couple began to exit as the witnesses stood up and the musicians played a melody of songs.

One witness said. "They look good together."

Diane, Ruth, and Rachel smiled at their friend and her new husband.

Rachel said. "They make a cute couple."

"They do!" Diane said."

"Yes, they do." Another friend said.

* * *

They took pictures while the guest made it to the reception. It took about thirty minutes to get pictures of the immediate family, Diane, Ruth, Rachel and the groom.

* * *

The couple made it to the reception and sat down at the head table.

A full blown orchestra played at their reception.

Diane and Fred came up to the main table to hang and talk to the couple. "You're such a beautiful bride. Gordon welcome to the family. You and Pat should come to Pittsburgh to see us when you can.

Fred made it over to Pat and hugged her and shook Gordon's hand. "Congratulations. Yes, you're invited to our home, feel free to come any time."

"Thanks Diane and Fred. I'm glad you made it."

Gordon said, "I'm glad to be a part of the family. We're starting our new life together."

Rachel and Ruth walked up to hug the bride and groom.

"I'm so glad you all made your way through the storm. It means so much to me! Thank you so much, I love you."

"We are too! I glad the train is still running." Ruth said.

"Congratulations friend." Rachel said.

"Come on ladies we are in the way of the other guests. We'll talk to you all later." Fred said.

The Cedar Lake girls enjoyed the wedding. They're a beautiful couple. Everything was perfect.

Never Knew a Love like this Before

Fifty

Tanya is Missing

Three days before the girls are scheduled to go on their Houston trip. The girls phones are ringing off the hook.

"Hello," answered Diane. Hello Diane this is Anita I work under Dr. Tanya Patterson. She hasn't called in to tell us what to do about her patients. We'e had to tell them to come back tomorrow or reschedule. We tried calling her parents, there is no answer. She has your number listed as an emergency number and Ruth.

"Oh my, you haven't heard from her all day, its 3 pm. Have you called her friend named the Boss?"

"My other coworker is trying to call that person and Ruth. She has always checked in with us even when she's running late."

"I'll try to contact her parents and check with our other friends to see if they heard from her. We're suppose to leave in a few days to go on our mini vacation. Do you think she left early to go there?" Diane asked.

"Thanks, can you provide an update to us? And I don't think so." Anita asked.

"We will and you do the same if you get an update." Diane asked.

Diane started calling people for some reason no one was answering the phone except for Ruth.

"Hello!" Ruth said.

"Tanya's office called you?"

"Yes!"

"I thought I would call you so we can be strategic about trying to locate Tanya." Diane said.

"I'll call our buddies. You call her mom, and dad.

"Lets check back in at 5 pm."

"I will. Lord let her be alright." Ruth prayed.

Ruth dialed Sally's number. "Hello, good evening," Sally said.

"We have to find Tanya as of 3 pm today she didn't show up at her dental practice. No one has heard from her. No one knows the The Boss's number. If you know any other friends she may have. Please call them."

"Oh no!" Sally said. "I do have a couple of numbers I can dial. I'll let you know if I find anything.

Five hours later

Tanya's friends were calling everyone trying to locate their friend.

The girls called each other so that everyone of them were on the call. Rachel asked "When can we file a missing persons' report? "

Patricia began to answer. "I think after twenty four hours. I 'm filing it as soon as its time."

"That sounds about right maybe forty-eight, let's go with twenty-four." Ellen said.

"Where can she be?" Diane asked. "I can't believe we don't have The Boss's number?"

"She didn't want us to meet him." Sally said.

"That's so true! Ladies I have to go Charles is calling me. We're going to pray for our friend." Ruth said. "I love you, guys. Talk to you in the morning."

"We all should try to get some rest!" Rachel said.

"Goodnight!" everyone said in unison.

***

<u>7am the next morning</u>
No news of where Tanya could be.

<u>8 am</u>
Calling the Cedar Lake and Atlanta authorities.

"Hello," the policeman said.

"Good morning, I need to file a missing persons report. It is Dr. Tanya Patterson, she is from Cedar Lake, Georgia. No one has seen her since Friday afternoon. She didn't show up to her dental practice on yesterday. She has an office in Cedar Lake and one in Atlanta."

"Please describe her." Patricia started describing her. "Hello my partner just received a missing report on your friend. We'll put a news bulletin out on her. We will find her don't worry."

"Thanks,we truly hope so. Please provide an update in twelve hours."

"We will if we have anything. Good-bye!"

"Good-bye!"

The phone rang as soon as she hung up. "Hello and good morning."

"Good morning, did you file a missing person's report?" Rachel asked. Great because I was going to, if you didn't."

"Rachel, someone beat me to it. It was probably Mr. and Mrs. Patterson. Its too early to call them. I'll wait until 10 am."

"Do you think we should we cancel our trip to Houston?"

"Rachel I don't know, we still have two days. I hope we find her before Thursday."

"Me too, I hope she's okay. My other line is ringing. Let's talk around noon."

"My phone is ringing too. Noon it is."

Patricia clicked over to the call coming in. "Hello."

"Good morning my friend. I spoke with Mr. and Mrs. Patterson, they called a missing persons report in this morning. The residents of Cedar Lake are gathering together to pray at 12 noon and 6 pm. Ruth's' father Pastor Perry will lead it. I think I'll pray with them at that time." Diane said.

"I figured her mother and father did file a report. The police officer said someone was filing one with his partner. I'm going to pray too. Rachel was asking should we still go to Houston, I said I don't know."

"I don't know either, if we should cancel. postpone, or what. I just don't know. I hope our friend is safe and sound. I guess we'll wait on see. We probably should do a lot of praying, talking about this situation can get you upset or keep you upset."

"I agree. I guess we can talk late this evening. Love you my friend."

"Love you too."

<u>12 noon</u>

Everyone that knows Tanya prayed.

6pm They prayed again corporately. Still no word from Tanya.

<u>10 pm est Tanya's friends are on the phone together</u>

Sally began to speak. "I have been overwhelmed with peace the last hour. I thank God. I take it to mean Tanya is okay. I'm hoping that means we will hear from her soon."

" Me too. I have peace too." Ellen said.

"Same here!" Patricia said.

"God is good, me too!" Ruth said.

"Praise God, he has given all of us peace. We will hear from Tanya soon. The guys want to go to on the trip. I need to go. I need a vacation, but right now Tanya is a priority." Diane said.

"I packed last week, but right now, I'm not excited." Rachel said. "I'm glad he's given us peace."

"Let's talk tomorrow. Good bye!"

"Good bye!" Everyone said.

<u>Its Wednesday at 1 pm</u>

Everyone had corporate prayer in Cedar Lake and across the United States where all Tanya's friends lived. Still no word from Tanya. Everyone is thanking God in advance for bringing Tanya home safely.

6pm No Tanya

10 pm No Tanya

The girls talked for a minute. They haven't cancelled their trip. Somehow everyone's plane is scheduled for late Thursday evening. Everyone went to bed after their short phone call.

Midnight Thursday morning

Diane's phone rung. "Hello!"

"Diane this is Mrs. Patterson. Tanya called a few minutes ago. She and her friend went on a last minute trip to the islands. She send her apologies for scaring everyone and not informing you all that she won't be going with you all this time. She's out of the country. Something isn't right. I don't understand why my daughter would leave her patients hanging like she has. Tanya has never been this irresponsible. Please continue to pray. "

"Thanks for letting me know she's alive and fine. I'll tell the others. We will continue to pray."

"Thanks Diane. I'm going to bed now. Sorry for the late call, but I know you wanted the update. Talk to you later."

"Ladies, Tanya has been found. Boss and her decided to go to the islands. Tanya felt the need to call her mom. Of course, she won't be going to Houston. She sent her apologies. The Patterson's want us to continue to pray for their daughter I told her we will."

"I'm glad she's fine. Its very inconsiderate what she has done to everyone. Especially her patients. We do need to pray." Ellen said.

"Unbelievable is all I have to say!" Patricia said.

Sally began speaking. " I'm shaking my head! "

"Thanks Diane. I'm going to bed. See you later on today!" Rachel said.

"Yes!" everyone said and hung up.

***

The girls did go on their mini vacation. They had a great time without Tanya. Everyone was surprised but not surprised she pulled this stunt. Tanya does strange things when it comes to this Boss person. She leans on the irresponsible side. None of the girls have heard from her. Everyone decided life goes on with or without Tanya. Remember they have never met this Boss person. Everyone resorted to lets just continue to pray for her.

***

Six months passed

Rachel was at home watering her flowers and plants on a Friday evening when the phone rang.

"Hello."

"Hello Rachel, this is Tanya. I'm calling to let you know I'm okay. I want to thank you for being patient with me. I hope you have forgiven me. Tell the girls I love them. The main reason I called is to tell you that The Boss died two weeks ago. It was a very small ceremony."

Rachel spoke with empathy in her voice. "Tanya, I'm sorry to hear about your loss."

"Thanks, my friend. The relationship was all wrong; I did it for so many years I hope God forgives me. I don't know who I am. I was in a controlled relationship. I thought I was insignificant. Deep down inside I was embarrassed and didn't want you all to meet the Boss. I've been so depressed. I have nowhere to turn."

"Don't beat yourself up. We all kind of figured your relationship was unhealthy. That's why we kept asking questions. We have different ideas of who The Boss was. Right now, that's not important."

"Rachel, you're always making a person feel better. I'm really pathetic," said Tanya. "I do apologize for the panic I caused six months ago."

"You scared us. We forgave you. We've been praying for you," replied Rachel.

"Thanks for your prayers. I wanted to say something to you girls when the controlling part of the relationship got out of hand. Please don't tell the girls all my business. Just tell them the Boss died. I'm not ready to answer a lot of questions."

"If you want them to know, you'll tell them. Is there anything I can do for you?"

"Just pray. I'm going to try to go to sleep now. I'll call you tomorrow."

Yes, Tanya get your rest. Love you! And we'll talk tomorrow!"

"Love you too!"

Rachel called all the girls to tell them. Thank God she was able to leave a message.

One hour later

Ruth dialed Tanya's number; the phone rang.

The phone just rang.

Thirty minutes later

Diane called. Tanya didn't answer.

Every one of the girls called. Tanya answered none of their calls. The girls didn't fret because they've grown accustomed to not talking to her. They just pray.

Fifty-One

Patricia's Skeletons

Diane's office phone rings

"Engineering this is Diane, how may I help you? Diane said.

"This is Patricia?"

" Hey girl," Diane squealed with excitement in her voice.

"Hello, my friend. How are you?"

"I'm great. I've been working hard at the office. And how are you?"

"I need to talk. Diane, I have secrets I've never told anyone, but Gordon. I was so embarrassed, so I kept them hid all these years. I've been putting on a real facade."

"I have been trying to get things together. Making sure I keep Gordon happy. I have something to tell you. Diane this is hard for me to say, but I must, I was molested every weekend until the age of eighteen by my uncles. They came by the house every weekend. It was my Uncle John, Uncle Jim, and Uncle Richard. Uncle Richard was the main one. I have nightmares to this day about those weekends. It was easy for him to do it in our big house."

"Oh my God. Oh no, my friend. You must have been traumatized. You're a walking miracle," Diane said. "What did your mother say? Your father? I'm glad you're finally letting it out. At least you're finally talking about it."

"They don't know. My mother thinks her brothers are angels. I wouldn't dare tell my father. He would kill them. I believe they wouldn't have done it if my father had been at home all those years. I'm glad he stopped traveling. Maybe one day I'll tell them."

"It might be good to tell them. I'm glad your daddy stopped traveling."

"All of you thought I was a virgin until I was eighteen. But I lost my virginity at ten years old. I thought I did something to cause this. I thought I was ugly. All my relationships with other men have failed."

" I'm so glad you realize you're beautiful. Your hair is so adorable. Your brunette hair is so soft and flowing. You have always been an eye-catcher."

"That's why it took me so long to get married. Gordon is an angel. I don't want to mess up my marriage."

I'm glad you realize you weren't at fault. It's important to forgive your uncles. I met your uncles and I've been around them several times throughout the years. I would have beaten those men up if I knew they were molesting you."

"Diane, you've always been so supportive of me. I feel better now that I have finally opened. Thanks for listening."

"I'll be right here if you need someone to talk to."

"Thanks again Diane. You're such a great listener. Let's change the subject, tell me what's happening with you."

They ended up talking and laughing for at least an hour. Great conversation. That's what friends are for.

Fifty-Two

Big Things for Rachel

~~~~~~~~~~~~~~~~~~~~

<u>Ruth and Rachel in Cedar Lake</u>

Ruth's family was eating and just having fun. There's a knock on the door. "Come in," Ruth said.

The door opened. "Oh my! It's Rachel. Come on in. We're so glad to see you," said Ruth's father. "Give me a hug. It has been a long time."

"I didn't know you were coming home too. It's so good to see you."Ruth said.

"Same here. I wanted to tell the neighborhood, my family, and all my friends I'm going over to Europe for five years to study and speak on the books I have written." explained Rachel, smiling.

"Congratulations!" Everyone said in unison.

"Thanks everyone! I appreciate that." Rachel responded with tears in her eyes.

"It's bittersweet," said Ruth's mom. "We understand the tears. Have a seat. Visit with us for a minute. Would you like some dessert?"

"Sure! I can sit for a few minutes and relax. How's everyone doing?" Rachel asked.

"My husband and I are doing fine. We're getting older, but we have no complaints." Mrs. Perry said.

" I'll be getting married within the next year. My fiance is going to Europe also. I'm glad I waited. It took a while."

"You deserve everything God has blessed you with." explained Ruth.

"Thank you, my friend. I hope we can still be friends."

"We will!"

Rachel laughed very loud. "We were serious about that pact. Our times together have dwindled, please know that you're considered one of my lifetime friends."

"Maybe that was a stupid pact we made in the fourth grade. I wonder if everyone still writes in their diary. I do."

"I do too. I wonder if our seasons are winding down."

"Everything has changed in so many ways all these years."

"Yes, life keeps us busy. We've done good considering!"

"We have!"

"I drove to Pittsburgh to see Diane and Fred, we had dinner together at their house on Friday night, it was a going away dinner. I stayed for the weekend. Diane insisted I stay for the weekend. She said it didn't make sense to drive four hours on a Friday afternoon and leave the next morning. We had breakfast, shopped, laughed, and watched movies." Rachel said as she made herself more comfortable.

"Diane is a great host."

"She's the best. Three weekends before my Pittsburgh weekend I went to New York and hung with Patricia. We had a ball in Times Square, we saw a Broadway play, shopped till we dropped. You know with Patricia there's nonstop laughing. Our friend is a character."

"And we love that character." Ruth said.

"I was going to ride on a train to see you next weekend, but here you are. I get to see you and your parents, all at once."

"And on that note, stay for dinner, prop your feet up, and lets spend some time together. Who knows when we'll see each other again."

"I have no problem with that."

Rachel ended up staying at Ruth's parents house for almost five hours.

Fifty-Three

It's So Hard to Say Good-bye

Diane wrote:

What an awesome time we had in New Orleans during that Super Bowl Weekend when Fred and the team won the championship. We had plenty of great times in Cedar Lake. Florida was an awesome time with my girls. Houston was very enjoyable except for that one incident before we left. Jamaica was very nice, celebrating Sally and Thomas's wedding. Glad the four musketeers of that weekend healed of their minor injuries. Thank God they were minor. I love the way our friends showed love towards Marion while she was alive and now we have the foundation. The foundation will always be a part of our lives. Visiting Ellen in California was always a great time.We made it through the challenges Kenneth and Ellen had. God healed Ellen of cancer. We were very patient with Tanya and her secrets. We never met the Boss. We still loved Tanya through it all. Sally and her family, we thank God for healing those relationships. Patricia and Gordon found true love. I'm truly happy and grateful Patricia found love. It was a little rough for my friend in her younger years. Rachel is the last one to get married and she tied the not in Paris. Thank God all of my friends found true love.

My friends and I are close but not as close as we were. That's part of life.

We have been through some changes. Seasons do change. We've tried to keep in touch as we've gotten older. We're still friends but we don't get to talk or see each other that much.

I'll cherish the time my friends and I have shared. We have so many beautiful memories. I know we'll always love and pray for each other. We'll be able to say we had great times together and we're glad we met over thirty years ago.

Still friends forever.

www.ingramcontent.com/pod-product-compliance
Lightning Source LLC
Chambersburg PA
CBHW032205030726
47494CB00020B/621